WILDER ANIMALS
BOOK FIVE OF UNDERDOGS

Geonn Cannon

Supposed Crimes LLC • Matthews, North Carolina

Published in the United States.

ISBN: 978-1-952150-43-2

www.supposedcrimes.com

This book is typeset in Goudy Old Style.

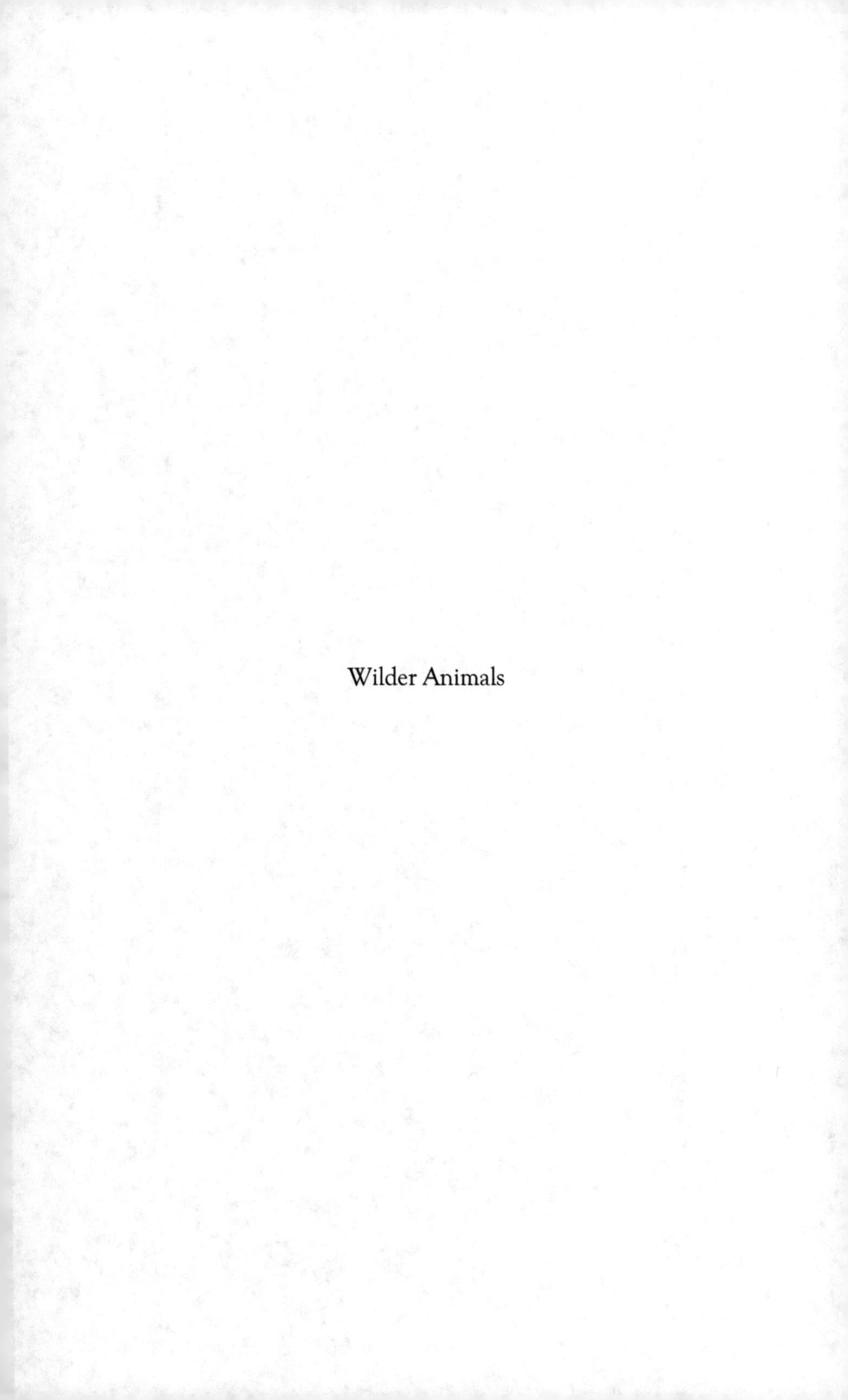

Wilder Animals

PROLOGUE

ANOTHER SEIZURE gripped Ari's body, her arms tightening against her chest as her entire body went rigid in Dale's lap. Dale stroked her partner's hair and turned away to watch the streets of Madrona speeding past out the window.

"Hold on, puppy," she said. "We're almost there..."

Ari's doctor, Aaron Frost, glanced over his shoulder when they approached the next intersection. He met Dale's eye but didn't offer any reassurances before he faced forward again. Gwendolyn Willow's home was still two blocks away. Frost took the corner so fast that Dale was thrown against the car door. She wanted him to hurry, wanted him to drive over lawns or crash through fences if it got them to Gwen's faster. Ari suddenly seized again, her hands rising in claws as her entire body went rigid. Dale wished she had put the seatbelt between Ari's teeth, but it was too late now. She couldn't tell if Ari was conscious or not; her face was coated with sweat, her lips pulled back over her teeth.

Dale had never felt so useless. Years earlier, when she saved what she thought was a stray dog and ended up with a naked woman in her bed, she dedicated herself to learning everything she could about *canidae*. Known in literature and pop culture as werewolves, they were technically an entirely separate species. Not entirely human and not completely wolf, they were a blend of the two born with a gene that gave them the ability to transform at will. Their bite could transfer that ability, as could a blood transfusion, but humans past the age of puberty couldn't survive the ensuing transformation. Their bodies just couldn't cope with the strain. Eventually the urge to change became too much to refuse and their skeletal framework twisted itself into a pretzel trying to do something it was never meant to do.

Ariadne Willow, Dale's partner and girlfriend, was born without the gene. When she was a baby, her mother found someone willing to perform a risky procedure that would give the newborn the *canidae* gene and allow her to transform into a wolf. The procedure worked, to a degree. Ari could transform, but it was a far more painful process than it should've been. Every change left her with aches and pains that had once been manageable with massages, but in the past few months it had progressed to a degree that Ari's doctor was warning them of paralysis and permanent disability.

They were both aware of the danger, but they were equally knowledgeable of how dangerous the potential cure might be. Ari didn't want to get the bite until it was absolutely necessary, just in case there were side effects they hadn't thought of. Dale was willing to let Ari set the schedule since she was the one taking the risks, but she knew they were working on a very tight deadline.

Now it seemed as if their time had run out. That morning, Ari was hurting too badly to get out of bed. Dale managed to loosen some of the tension with a massage and helping her get into a hot shower, but Ari still needed her walking stick. The stick terrified Dale, because Ari only used it when she could no longer pretend the pain was crippling her. At lunchtime she turned down any food due to cramping in her stomach. She tried to laugh it off ("The last thing I need is to start my period today of all days.") but Dale could see the pain was real.

She got up to take a pain pill and her legs gave out under her. Dale ran to her, the phone in her hand already dialing Dr. Frost. Within two minutes of his arrival, he had carried Ari out of the apartment to make a mad dash for Ari's mother. "I should have insisted we do this a month ago," he said as he pulled out of the driveway. "Hopefully we're not too late."

Dale was the one who came up with the plan in the first place. A *canidae* bite was only fatal to humans because their bodies didn't know how to survive the change. Ari's body could do it, but the wolf part of her DNA wasn't strong enough to do it properly. Dale suggested a bite from Ari's mother could "infect" her, finishing the process that began when she was an infant. If it worked, Ari would be able to transform with only the normal amount of pain. If it failed...

She looked down at Ari and stroked the hair out of her face. She was drenched with sweat, her eyes closed but fluttering too much that Dale couldn't tell if she was conscious or if she'd passed out. She kept talking just in case she could hear her.

"What if she's not home?" Dale asked.

"We have to pray she is," Frost said.

He laid on the horn as he pulled into Gwen Willow's driveway, barely bothering to come to a complete stop before he was out of the car and opening the back door. He was an older man, with the white hair of a grandpa and the wiry frame of a scarecrow, but somewhere he found the strength to gather Ariadne in his arms. He had just picked her up when Gwen appeared, drawn by the commotion.

"What's...?" She looked at Ari and began moving toward the house. "Inside. Kitchen table."

Dale followed Gwen and Frost into the house and closed

the door behind her. She ran into the kitchen and, at Gwen's instruction to "just sweep that shit off," knocked the centerpiece and dishes off the table to the floor. Frost placed Ariadne on the table. Her hands and the heels of her feet knocked against the wood as another seizure washed over her.

"She waited too long," Gwen said angrily, pulling off her clothes. She knew about the plan and had been bugging Ari to follow through on it. She understood Dale's reasoning and believed there was no reason to worry, but she also respected Ari's fear. Now she was angry. At Dale, at Ari, at herself, her anger didn't seem to have a target. She was suddenly nude, but Dale was too focused on Ari's pain to care.

"Where... where does she need to be bitten?" Dale said.

Gwen was suddenly the wolf, her transformation so seamless that Dale never saw any hint of a transition. She leapt onto the table and clamped her jaws down on Ari's left arm. Dale screamed and clapped a hand over her mouth as blood welled around the wound and dripped down Ari's forearm. She knew what had to happen, but her brain couldn't process that with the violence of the act. Ari screamed when she was bitten, but her thrashing stopped and her eyes opened to look down at her wounded arm.

Frost put a hand on Dale's shoulder to keep her from moving toward the table. She was grateful to him for that.

After what felt like minutes, Gwen jumped to the floor. Thirty seconds later she rose as a human, slightly out of breath and sweating. Ari's blood was still smeared across Gwen's bottom lip and the right side of her chin. She pulled on the shirt she'd been wearing and stepped to one side as Frost moved in to tend to Ari. He wrapped her arm with gauze but didn't apply antibiotics, grimacing as he skipped that vital step. This was the rare occasion when they wanted the bite to transmit something. They could only hope that nothing else had been hitching a ride in Gwen's mouth. Animal mouths were notoriously dirty.

"You're not an animal, though," Dale whispered.

Gwen looked at her. "Sorry?"

"Nothing. Sorry. Just..." She shook her head and hugged herself. "What happens now?"

"Now we let her rest."

Frost was already injecting Ari with a sedative. She had calmed considerably after the bite, and the drug made her slump against the table as if someone was letting the air out of her.

"You're both welcome to stay here until she wakes up, of course." Gwen put a hand on Dale's cheek and forced her to look away from Ari. "Do you drink?"

"What?" She blinked and shook her head. "Uh, sometimes. A beer every now and then..."

"You're going to have a drink and lie down. There's nothing you can do for her now, and you look like you're in shock. You need to rest, too."

Frost said, "That's a very good idea, Miss Frye."

Dale nodded. "Okay."

"I'll take you to the kitchen. Dr. Frost..."

"I'll make sure Ariadne is comfortable."

"Through this door, at the end of the hall. There's a guest room."

She put an arm around Dale's shoulders and led her to the kitchen. Dale looked back and saw Dr. Frost checking Ari's vitals. He looked concerned but unconcerned, so she allowed her own worry and fear to dissipate as she let herself be steered away. The panic was past and her mind could clear, could focus on what would come next.

Dale didn't intend to nap. But the loss of adrenaline and the alcohol combined to knock her out. She only meant to put her head down on the couch, since Gwen had such lovely and huge throw pillows, but the next thing she knew, it was dusk. She sat up quickly before she was fully awake or aware. Gwen was standing at the window looking out over the backyard. She turned at Dale's violent waking and then looked back outside.

"She's not awake yet. Dr. Frost wanted to let her sleep."

"Oh." It was cold in the house. "Does he know how she's doing?"

Gwen shook her head. "Not yet. When she does wake up, will you tell her I'm sorry?"

Dale frowned. "For what?"

"For hurting her. Again."

"This is what Ariadne wanted, Miss Willow. Yes, she was scared, but she knew it was the best chance she had at getting better."

Gwen sniffled and Dale realized she was crying. She got up and went to her.

"I'm glad she has you. Watching out for her, keeping her safe."

Dale said, "I'm glad she has you back in her life. She needs both of us, Miss Willow. I know it took a lot for Ari to trust you again, but she got there. She forgives you for what happened when she was a baby. And while she might not agree with what you did, she doesn't disagree with the choice itself. Ari loves her wolf. She loves being *canidae*. That... you gave her that. You made sure she wasn't a hunter. Ari was born to be the wolf. You just made sure she fulfilled her purpose."

Gwen looked at her. "Thank you, Miss Frye."

"I wish you'd call me Dale."

"Would it be out of line to ask you to call me 'mom' in return? I know you and Ariadne aren't married, but you certainly seem devoted to one another. I wouldn't... I wouldn't mind if you wanted to."

Dale said, "I'd be honored."

Frost knocked on the door frame. "Miss Willow, Miss Frye? Ariadne is awake. She's asking for Miss Frye."

Dale touched Gwen's shoulder and followed Frost out of the room. "How is she doing?"

"Groggy, but doing well. A *canidae* bite doesn't manifest itself this early. Rarely if ever are there signs before the first transformation urges kick in. I'll keep an eye on the situation, of course, but we may not know until the next time she tries to become the wolf." He put his hand up. "I'll tell her, but I'll also tell you. I don't want her transforming for at least three weeks. Preferably, she'll stay in human form for at least a month. Humans who get bitten start to feel the urge around that time, so it implies that's how long it takes for the 'virus', for lack of a better term, to spread through her system."

"Okay. Well. After today, I don't think she'll be in any rush to transform." They reached the guest room. "Will the bite leave a scar?"

"No, that shouldn't be an issue."

She thanked him and waited until he was gone before she knocked on the door. She went in and found Ari propped up by pillows, eyes closed, her hands folded on her stomach. The overhead light was off but a lamp on the bedside table was casting a soft golden shine onto Ari's face. Dale approached quietly and sat on the edge of the bed. Ari opened her eyes when Dale touched her hand. Her lips twisted into a weary smile.

"Hey." Ari's voice was weak, and her eyes immediately began drifting shut again.

"Hi."

"I guess I waited too long. Sorry."

"You were scared. I get that." She reached out and touched Ari's cheek. "I was scared, too. How do you feel?"

Ari took a deep breath. "Well, Dr. Frost has me on a lot of drugs. So I feel great." Her gaze drifted toward the ceiling. "It's a weird cocktail. Keeps me safe from. You know. Normal... stuff. But lets the wolf thing do its thing. Thing." She made a face and closed her eyes. "I remember being in the car with you. You were holding me. I liked that."

Dale smiled. "I liked it, too."

"Hey."

"Hm?"

"I was less scared with you."

Dale bent down and kissed Ari's lips. "Get some sleep, puppy."

Ari chuckled. "You call me puppy."

"Yeah, I do." She brushed her cheek against Ari's.

"I love that. I'd hate it from anyone else. You know? But I would be sad if you stopped." She pursed her lips. "Kiss puppy."

"Wow, you are on a lot of drugs." She pecked Ari's lips. "I'm going to let you sleep."

"I can sleep with you here."

"Are you sure?"

"Mm-hmm. Even better."

Dale toed off her shoes and stretched out next to Ari on the bed. Ari rolled to face her, and Dale rested her hand on Ari's hip. They'd done enough research in the months since Dale came up with the plan, they knew the risks and they knew the real threat was that the bite would do nothing. Ari had been bitten by other *canidae* in the past without any effect. But the fact it was her mother's bite could make all the difference. And even if it didn't help, the odds were extremely slim that Ari would actually die.

Still, even a fraction of a chance was more than Dale wanted to entertain. She put her face against Ari's shoulder and fell asleep quickly to the sound of her breathing.

They stayed overnight at Gwen's house, and she drove them home in the morning. Neka Teller, the young woman they rented their basement apartment from, came out to meet them in the backyard. She was a tall, athletic Native American, currently dressed in her pajamas. She was still holding the spoon from her breakfast when she came outside and, at a loss for what to do with it, stuck it into the pocket of her pajamas.

"Everything okay? I caught a glimpse of you guys leaving

yesterday. Looked kind of like an emergency." She looked Ari up and down with concern. "Was that you who got carried out?"

Ari nodded. She was still weak, still heavily sedated from whatever Frost pumped into her, but she made an effort to look as normal as possible even if the mere thought of speaking exhausted her. "Everything's better now. I was just... I was having an episode. It's all sorted out now."

"Are you sure? If you have medical bills or whatever I can be a little lenient on the rent."

"Thank you. But that's not necessary. Sorry if we worried you."

Neka said, "Sure, sure. As long as you're okay. You guys are the best tenants I could have asked for. Just let me know if you need anything."

Dale thanked her again. Neka lent a hand getting Ari down the stairs to their apartment and told them to let her know if they needed anything else. Ari thanked her again but, once they were alone, protested that she wasn't an invalid.

"I feel completely fine," she said as she was guided to the couch. "I appreciate all the help, but it's really not necessary."

"I know. But you went through a really traumatic experience yesterday. Forgive me for being concerned. You're going to be pampered whether you want to or not. Understood?"

Ari groused a little, but then said, "Thank you. For everything."

Dale kissed one of her eyebrows and smoothed down her hair. "Lie down and relax. Do you want the TV? The laptop?"

"I'll take a drink. Something not... uh, just something cold... I don't care."

"One drink, coming up." She went into the kitchen. She got some ice from the freezer, put it in a glass, and cracked open a carton of juice. "How do you feel? I mean, overall?"

The couch groaned as Ari eased herself into a more

comfortable condition. "Sore from everything yesterday. How bad were the seizures?"

Dale looked down into the glass. She wondered if she should lie, pad the truth a little so Ari wouldn't feel guilty. But then they had always been honest with one another in the past.

"They were bad, Ari."

"I'm sorry."

"Don't be." She closed the fridge and brought Ari her drink. "None of it was your fault."

Ari said, "If I'd just let Mom bite me a month ago, it wouldn't have gotten so bad."

Dale shrugged. "Bygones. The important thing is we got you to your mother's in time."

"Right. Well, in a month we'll know if worked. The fact that my seizures stopped doesn't mean anything."

"Dr. Frost gave you a sedative before we got in the car, but it didn't affect you. After the bite, you settled down immediately." She took Ari's hand. "I have faith."

"If you do, then I do."

Dale was willing to close the agency for the rest of the month, but Ari insisted she could still do the work. She spent the first day post-bite recovering at home, but the next morning she was up and dressed before Dale. She looked healthy, normal, and only after ensuring she wasn't putting on a show of wellness did Dale agree to drive her to the office. There were a few surveillance cases that didn't require more than staring at a video feed, while Dale covered the heavy lifting of background checks and following digital trails for other cases. Ari used credit card receipts to find a woman who had gone missing. Her disappearance was a choice, as it turned out, and Ari reported that fact to her concerned soon-to-be ex-boyfriend.

There was the case of the stolen laptop, the workman's comp fraud, and surveillance on a small office where someone was suspected of stealing credit card numbers from clients. Ari and Dale worked cases from the safety of their office, solving cases by digging around in the electronic garbage people left behind without realizing how much they had accumulated. Dale kept an eye on Ari's condition, monitoring her health without acting like a mother hen, but she seemed to be back to normal.

The troubles started in the third week. Ari woke up in the night with more cramps, but insisted they were different from the ones that preceded the seizures. At Dale's insistence she called Dr. Frost to describe the symptoms. He told her they were just the wolf trying to get comfortable. He warned her not to attempt transforming until she was absolutely sure she was ready. Ari wasn't there yet.

She wouldn't get to that point until the twenty-fifth day. Her bandage had come off days earlier, but she was complaining that her healed wound was itchy and driving her crazy. She was queasy and feverish at breakfast, and a freezing shower didn't help lower her temperature. She called Dale into the bathroom and huddled with her next to the bathtub.

"It has to be now," Ari said. "If it works, then... it works... but if not." She swallowed hard and closed her eyes. "I want you to know that you're the best and most amazing thing in my life."

Dale smiled. "You kind of say that all the time."

"I don't care. I'll keep saying it until you get sick of hearing it. And if this is the last thing I ever get to say, I want it to be that. I love you, Dale Elizabeth Frye."

"I love you, too." Dale kissed her and then spoke against her lips. "Let the wolf out, Ariadne. Hold onto me, if you need to."

Ari wrapped an arm around Dale's neck and hunched forward. Dale looked at the curve of Ari's back, the water from her shower still glistening on the skin as it began to ripple. She hated to watch the actual moment of transformation, but this seemed important. She felt like she had to witness this. Ari jerked and twitched in her arms and then her shoulders spread out and snapped upward so suddenly that Dale yelped. Ari started to fall to one side, but Dale caught her and held on.

"It's okay, puppy. I'm here..."

The rest of the transformation happened with a sort of gruesome elegance. Ari's body broke from the inside, her skin hardened in places and erupted in a pelt the same mahogany brown as her hair. When she lifted her head, her face had lengthened into a snout. The skin around her eyes was black, and her teeth had been replaced with fangs. She locked eyes with Dale and, with a final violent jerk of her body, she fell onto the tile.

When Dale moved to kneel beside her, only the wolf remained. Her sides rose and fell with rapid breaths. Her eyes were open and staring in confusion, but she lifted her head when Dale touched her cheek. She locked onto Dale and blinked, and Dale could see her partner within.

"Puppy?" Dale whispered.

Ari gave a pained whimper before scrambling up onto her feet. She shook her fur, which had retained the water from Ari's skin. She hadn't realized how worried she was until the moment was past, and she laughed through her tears as she wrapped her arms around the wolf's neck. She also hadn't realized how much she had missed her girlfriend's lupine counterpart. She pressed a kiss to the top of Ari's head between the ears and looked into her eyes again.

"Well, I guess you won't have to decide what to wear to work today."

Ari huffed.

Dale had hooked a leash onto Ari's collar before they left the house, ignoring the look of betrayal Ari tried to fix on her. "If you want to be a wolf in the city, you have to obey the leash laws. That is unless you want to spend another night in the pound." The walk to the office was without incident, although a few people did stop to ask if they could pet Ari and inquire as to what kind of breed she was. "We're not exactly sure," Dale said. "She looks kind of like she's got a bit of wolf in her, doesn't she?"

Dr. Frost was already waiting at the office when they arrived. He gave Ari a complete physical and, while he didn't want to be too optimistic too quickly, but his body language said enough for Dale. He wasn't anxious or concerned, and he actually smiled when he finished looking Ari over. He told them to take it slowly for a few days. No unnecessary transformations. No quick back-and-forth from wolf to human. He actually commended Ari for staying in wolf form and told her to wait a few hours before going back.

Before he left, Dale said, "Broad strokes, Doctor. We all know something could still go wrong, but... she transformed. She went from human to wolf. That by itself is encouraging, right? Humans can't do that at all. I mean, if I got bitten, I would have died just trying that."

"It's absolutely encouraging, yes," Frost said. "But we won't know if the bite actually cured anything until Ari goes back to human form. The wolf never experienced the crippling pain Ari had when she was bipedal. Right now her fist is clenched. That doesn't mean she can open it again. But I'm confident." He looked at the watch on the inside of his wrist. "I'll be back around two o'clock. I'll observe her transformation in case there are any complications."

Dale nodded. "Thank you, Dr. Frost."

"Of course. Ariadne is a very interesting case." He looked at Dale. "As are you, Miss Frye. I don't want to call myself a bigot, but I've never really been trustful of non-wolves. I didn't think there could be any who understood our unique existence. But you've proven me wrong time and again. Ari is very lucky to have you in her life."

Ari barked softly and bumped her head against Dale's hip. Dale reached down to pet her head.

"I always thought the woman I settled down with would have to be special. I just didn't know how special she would end up being."

Dale passed the time by transcribing Ari's notes from a past case, while Ari paced and wandered around the waiting area. Occasionally she went to the window behind Dale's chair to look out at the street, but she quickly got bored with that. Finally, she sat down behind the desk and rested her head on Dale's thigh. Dale reached down to scratch her neck.

"Only an hour to go," she said.

Ari huffed, whined, and went into her office with her head and tail hung low.

She climbed onto the couch and rested her head on her forepaws, watching the large clock on her wall as if staring could make it go faster. Her transformation to the wolf had been so easy this time, like putting on her favorite sweater on the first day of winter. But Frost and Dale were right. The pain never happened when she became the wolf; it only manifested after she went back to human form. There was every chance that her next change would be the one that crippled her. In an hour - actually fifty-six minutes - she could be in greater pain than she'd ever experienced. But all she could do was wait.

Finally, Dr. Frost arrived. He checked Ari's vitals and reported there were no warning signs. "If you're ready," he said, "you can go ahead and try transforming back."

Ari looked at Dale, who gave her a nod. She closed her eyes and dropped her head. For her entire life, she'd experienced the change as a violent process. She braced herself by planting her forepaws on the ground and hunching her back. Her body hitched and trembled, and her paws turned into hands. She watched as her fingers uncurled and her palm flattened on her office carpet. Dale rushed forward and covered her with a blanket as the transformation completed.

When she lifted her head, lips parted to gulp air as she grabbed the blanket to close it around herself, she did an evaluation of her pain.

"Well?" Dale asked.

Ari swallowed hard. "It's, uh... it hurts. It still hurts. But not as bad. Nowhere near as bad."

Frost said, "On a scale from one to ten?"

"I don't know," Ari said. "Like going to the gym for the first time after skipping it for three months. Manageable, though. If before was a ten on the scale, this is... this is a one. Hell, this is a point-three." She laughed and leaned against Dale, who bent down to kiss her forehead and her hair. "You saved me, baby."

Frost smiled. "Well, let's not get ahead of ourselves. I still want to examine you and make sure this wasn't just a fluke."

Dale kissed Ari again. Ari was willing to go through with the examination, and tests, and anything Dr. Frost needed to do. She could tell the cure had worked. Something was different inside of her. It felt as if the wolf had finally found a comfortable spot inside her brain to curl up and rest when she didn't need it, and going from one to the other felt more natural than it ever had before.

"You saved me," she whispered again, this time pressing her face against Dale's throat and rocking with her.

A week after the change, Ariadne was still reveling in the fact she could transform without excruciating pain. And only now did she understand just how debilitating that pain had been. There was still pain involved with the process. Transforming from human to wolf and back again required her skeleton to be bent, broken, and rearranged so drastically that there was no way it could be pain-free. But now the knots and twinges could be soothed by having Dale give her a massage.

She knew a big part of her euphoria was the fact she had let go of her stress. For the past few years she'd feared turning Dale into a full-time caregiver. Now it seemed like that wasn't going to be an issue. She'd gone out three times that week, with only Dr. Frost's warning not to overdo it keeping her from running every night. The wolf seemed completely revitalized.

Ari could feel its joy as it leapt over fallen trees, as she burst through a pile of dead leaves. She had Sheryl Crow's "Steve McQueen" playing in her head when she exploded out of some underbrush and scared the shit out of a raccoon.

Tonight she was running on Marsh Island, a fish-shaped wedge of land on the northern edge of the arboretum. From the northern shore, she could see the lights at Husky Stadium light up for a football game. She paused there to catch her breath and listened to the shouts and screams, the war drums of the marching band, and she threw her head back to add her howl to the symphony.

Soon she would have to start for home. It would have been over three miles back home if she could stick to the main roads, but that wasn't an option for a wolf in the city. She would have to move through backyards and stay out of sight as much as possible. By the time she finally got back to their apartment, she might have traveled a total of six or seven miles. Then again, she could always find a stash and call Dale to come pick her up. It wasn't late enough for her to be in bed yet.

Then again, the football game meant there might be fewer people in the street. And she was still making up for a whole month without transforming. The wolf needed to stretch her legs. With a yelp of happiness, Ari put her head down and started south.

In the end it was another hour before she arrived at Neka's house. She hunched in the underbrush across the street to watch the windows that looked into the living room. Neka was there with her boyfriend, and Ari waited until both of them were away from the window before breaking cover. The backyard was unfenced so she had no trouble reaching the stairs. She transformed when she reached the last step, reveling in the fact she only hurt as much as anyone who had just gotten back from a twenty-mile jog.

She stepped inside, achy and dripping sweat. "Hey, Dale. I practically ran a marathon tonight..." She froze when she saw her mother sitting on the couch. She and her mother had never been self-conscious about being naked in front of each other, given their nature as *canidae*. Still, her presence was so unexpected and it had been so long since they went for a run together, that Ari stepped toward the closet and pulled a coat off the hook.

"Sorry. I didn't know you were here."

"Dale asked me to come. She's in the bedroom."

Dale appeared at that moment and smiled apologetically. "Oh. Hey, Ari."

"Hey." She looked between them. "What's... going on? Is this an intervention?"

Gwen smiled. "No. Why, are you involved with something we should be intervening on?"

"No." She looked at Dale. "So... what's up? Just felt like a family dinner?"

"Not exactly." She looked down at Gwen, who nodded for her to go ahead. "I've been thinking a lot this week about you and the wolf. The new thing you have going on. This is the first time you've really been a full-fledged *canidae*. You can change without hurting, which is huge. It means that you're different than you used to be. You're a different kind of wolf. You need to learn how to handle it. And since your original lessons with your mother were cut short, I thought it would be good if you had a chance to remedy that."

Gwen said, "Dale made a very good point when she called me, Ariadne. You may think you know how to be the wolf, but I think there's still a lot for you to learn."

"And you also need a chance to get to know your mother," Dale said. "Make up for lost time. She can take you somewhere out in the woods where you can really stretch your legs. You can bond, and she can help you learn to deal with the wolf stuff outside of a big busy city. You won't have to stay hidden in bushes or run from park to park."

Ari said, "The woods?"

Gwen said, "I know someone who will lend us a cabin as long as we need it."

"I can't just leave. The agency..."

"We can take some time off. There are cases I can work without you. Due diligence and background checks. I can do enough work like that to keep the lights on. We have some savings. I mean, as long as you eventually come back, I think we could handle a bit of a hiatus."

Ari glanced at her mother and moved closer to Dale. She lowered her voice. "And... us? Everything is okay with us, right?"

"Everything is perfect with us," Dale assured her. "But Dr. Frost and Gwen both asked me to keep an eye out for any unusual behavior. You're acting cooped up. You pace around the apartment and the office both. You go out running as often as possible, but you never seen satisfied. You're..." She glanced toward Gwen and leaned in to whisper in Ari's ear. "The rough stuff..."

Ari tensed, eyes wide with fear. "I asked~"

"It was fine! It really was. But you have to admit, it's rare with us to go so crazy. I think your wolf needs a little room to stretch its legs before it settles into domesticity. It needs to stretch the limits, and you can't do that in Seattle. I'm going to really hate being apart from you, but it's necessary."

Gwen said, "Dale is making very good points, Ari. I think it could be hugely beneficial to you at this stage in your..."

"Recovery," Ari said. "We're calling it recovery."

"Right."

Dale said, "Tonight is the perfect example. Gwen has been here for almost two hours waiting for you to get home so we could have this talk. I'm just worried that if you don't do this, one night the wolf is just going to start running and won't stop until it gets to Vancouver."

Ari took Dale's hands. "I want you to come with me."

"I have to stay and cover the agency, babe. We can't afford to completely shut down." She cupped Ari's cheek. "Besides, it needs to be you and your mom. Willow wolves only."

Ari grinned. "Willow wolves?"

Dale shrugged. "You need this. Your mom needs it. I get you every other day of the year. I can cope with a few weeks."

"Okay," Ari said. "I have to admit, it sounds amazing. And I could always take a break and come down to see you if I get too homesick."

"Exactly."

Ari nodded. "Okay. Let's do it." She looked at Gwen. "When do we leave?"

"We should go in the morning."

"Then I guess I should pack." She touched Dale's cheek. "And I promise, I won't be away from you longer than necessary. Three weeks. Four at the outside."

Dale said, "Absolutely. Come on, I'll help you pack."

They made love twice that night and fell asleep in each other's arms. Ari woke at dawn, kissed Dale goodbye, and headed out. Dale woke up just enough to tell her to be safe and stay in touch. Gwen said there was a ranger station near the cabin where they could check their voicemail every other day or so. Dale promised to leave as many messages as possible. Ari bent over the bed and smoothed down the tangles in Dale's hair, kissed her eyelids, and whispered for her to go back to sleep.

"I'll be back before you know it."

"Bye, puppy."

Ari waved goodbye and shrugged into her backpack. Dale heard the door close, but she was asleep before she could hear Gwen starting the car.

She wouldn't see Ariadne again for over three months.

CHAPTER ONE

ARI HAD been gone for three months.

There were a few phone calls at the beginning, before Ari let it slip how far she had to travel just to get a signal, and Dale told her it was okay to miss a few. After that the calls stopped completely. Dale was still leaving voicemail messages to let Ari know what was happening at home, with the office, and just in general. She told herself every day when there wasn't a message left in return that Ari was busy. She was getting to know her mother. She was re-learning how to be a wolf. She was probably constantly exhausted.

So Dale went to the office alone. She did paperwork in an empty room, playing her iPod at full volume to make it feel less lonely. She had Thai for dinner, because Ari didn't like it, and she went home to watch TV. She restricted herself to only watching shows she knew Ari didn't want to watch so she wouldn't get too far ahead. She checked her voicemail before bed and as soon as she woke up, and again a few hundred times per day, but there was never anything new.

Toward the end of the third month, her messages became

a bit more frequent and urgent. Not because she was getting incredibly anxious and angry, although she was, but because one of Ari's cases was going to trial after six months of legal wrangling. The lawyers needed Ari to testify about her investigation. The lawyers had agreed that Dale could give the testimony if Ari wasn't back in time, and the deadline was currently less than an hour away.

She was dressed for court, sitting on the edge of the bed she'd slept alone in for the past ninety-two days, giving it one final shot as she put on her shoes. When the phone beeped, Dale tried to keep her voice neutral.

"Hey, Ariadne. It's me. Again. I don't want you to worry about the Nelson Cook case. The judge decided I was involved enough with the investigation to testify. Everything is fine." She finished slipping on one of her flats and sat up straighter. "It's taken care of. I don't want you to think anything's gone wrong. It would've been nice to see you. Or hear from you." She scratched the bridge of her nose with her thumbnail. "I don't want to think anything bad happened to you. But I'm starting to think that's the only explanation. You're scaring me. You're making me mad, puppy, so just... I don't know, pick up the goddamn phone, okay? You nearly died. You were having a seizure in my arms, and now I haven't heard from you in months, and my mind keeps... I keep thinking there's been a relapse, or you're lying in some creek paralyzed."

She stopped and pinched the bridge of her nose. She was breathing hard, her anger threatening to explode out of her like a teakettle. She took a deep breath. When she spoke again, her voice was more measured. "I'm sorry. I'm not mad. I'm just frustrated. I love you. I miss you. Everything is taken care of. You can take all the time you need, but I'm missing you like crazy. I just need to hear your voice, wolf girl. Give me a call. Please."

She hung up and left the apartment, taking care to make sure Neka's car was gone before heading out. Neka was great, the best landlady Dale had ever had, but she was convinced Ari had broken up with her. Dale denied it, of course, but she couldn't explain exactly why Ari and her mother had hightailed it out into the mountains for some wolf-pup bonding. So she got the sympathetic looks, the pity invites to dinner, the offers to talk. She appreciated and resented it in equal measure. She wasn't single, she wasn't dumped, she was just... alone.

Their hearing was scheduled for eight am, and she arrived at the Municipal Courthouse just before seven. The metal detectors refused to cooperate so she had to be patted down by an overzealous security guard who then pointed her to the elevators. She went rode up to the eleventh floor going over the information from the case she'd put onto her phone. Nelson Cook was accused of stealing equipment from his heating-and-air job to start a new company. Ari got into the shack where Cook was keeping everything and compared the serial numbers to the items missing from the former employer.

It seemed easy enough. She didn't have to bring up the fact Ari had been a wolf when she did the snooping. The elevator arrived and she slipped her phone into her pocket as she entered the courtroom. It was a small, cozy space with wood paneling and the typical setup of two tables facing the judge's bench. There were a handful of people seated in the gallery, and one of them twisted around as the door swung shut behind Dale.

It was Ari.

Dale was so startled that she said, "Puppy!" out loud before clapping a hand over her mouth. The judge, lawyers, and the defendant of the case currently being heard turned to look at her.

"I'm sorry," Dale said. "I'm so sorry."

She retreated back into the hallway. Ari followed, slipping through the door just before it closed. Dale pressed back against the wall and Ari pinned her there, cupped her face, and sighed with what sounded like relief as she leaned in for a kiss. Dale melted against her, slipping her hands under Ari's blazer and clinging to the back of her shirt. Any lingering anger Dale had about Ari's absence was shattered by the kiss. It was worth the long absence just to be in her arms again. And she felt different. She was thinner, though Dale didn't know how that was possible, but she felt stronger.

They broke the kiss and Ari moved her face to Dale's hair. "The second you opened that door, I smelled you. It was like waking up. God, I've missed how you smell."

Dale kissed Ari's cheek and reluctantly pushed her back. "How long have you been back?"

Ari looked at the clock above the elevators. "Eighteen minutes. Literally. We went down this morning to check my messages, and we got all of yours about testifying here today. So Mom drove me down here as fast as she could. I got the suit from her place and came here."

"You just happened to check the messages today? That was lucky."

Ari averted her gaze. "Not... exactly."

The anger threatened to come back. "You've been getting all my messages. You just haven't been responding to them."

"Dale, I'm sorry. I was..."

"No, I don't care." She kissed the corners of Ari's mouth. She could be angry later, after she'd gotten used to Ari being in front of her.

Ari smoothed her hand over the back of Dale's head. "Dale, I'm so sorry. I let you down. I was letting down the agency."

"No. You weren't. I talked to the judge and he was going to let me testify. It's fine. It would've been fine."

"I wasn't just talking about today," Ari said. "It could've been bad. I'm sorry I wasn't leaving you more messages in return, but things..."

"You can tell me all about it later." She hesitated. "If... if you're here later. I don't know if you're going to go back up. If you are, it's fine, but-"

Ari shushed her. "I'm staying."

Dale breathed out in relief. "Good. It would've been fine if you were leaving, but... good. Can I ask, though...? You have suits at home. And it would've been less out of the way for you to stop by there instead of going to your mother's house."

"Right," Ari said. "But you would have been there. If I'd walked in and seen you, I wouldn't have wanted to leave."

"Aw, you big sweetheart." She kissed Ari again, and Ari cupped the back of her head, holding the kiss until Dale began to chuckle. She swatted Ari's shoulder and pulled away. "If you're not careful, we'll be back here fighting a public indecency charge."

Ari grinned and took Dale's hand to lead her back into the courtroom. The judge glared at them when they entered, but Ari offered an apologetic wave as she took her seat. The defense attorney was turned to look at them over her shoulder. She was blonde and beautiful, wearing an ice-blue suit that matched her eyes. Her hair was pulled back in a severe bun and her posture was rigidly perfect. The overall impression was intimidation, and she found herself uncomfortable after a few seconds under the woman's gaze. Oddly, though, it didn't seem antagonistic or angry about Dale's earlier interruption.

Dale looked away from the lawyer and focused on her own hand. She hadn't even felt Ari taking her hand, but now their fingers were linked. She squeezed, Ari squeezed back, and Dale bit her lip to keep from smiling too broadly.

When she looked up again, the blonde lawyer had turned back around.

"Please state your name and explain your connection to the case."

Ariadne did, then spelled it. "I'm a private investigator. I was hired by Nguyen Brothers Heating and Cooling to determine if the defendant stole equipment from them before resigning."

The prosecutor was Fred Beech, an old acquaintance. Ari had worked with him dozens of times and they knew how to work together without too much prepping or rehearsal. Still, she could tell he was irritated about not having her available for a quick run-through of the case. He stood behind his table, leaning forward to read the file before asking his next question. Ari took the time to look past him at Dale, watching from the gallery. Dale was wearing her forest-green "court costume," with its conservative skirt that ended just past the knee. She was wearing white stockings, and Ari couldn't get them out of her mind. How they would feel against her skin, how easy they would peel away if~

"Explain how you went about this case, Miss Willow."

She blinked and focused on the task at hand. Ari went through the case beat by beat, hiding the fact that she'd done a bit of the investigating on four legs. She hated this part of testifying. Technically it wasn't perjury, since she had performed the actions and seen the evidence exactly as she described. The only fact she was omitting was cosmetic. No one needed to know if other investigators were wearing a red shirt or a blue shirt when they found evidence. It was equally inconsequential if she was a wolf when she followed Cook home, and when she watched his house to make sure he was gone before she went into the backyard. They certainly didn't need to know she had been naked when she got into the shed and made a note of the serial numbers on the equipment she found there.

"I compared it to the list Jeremy Nguyen gave me and there were nine matches," she concluded. "I passed the information along to Mr. Nguyen and he alerted the police. And here we are."

Beech smiled. "Thank you for your help, Miss Willow. Nothing further."

The judge gestured to the defense, an icy blonde woman

Ari had never seen before. She stood up, smoothed down her skirt, and stepped around the edge of the table. It was an unprecedented move, at least in real life. Ari had only seen lawyers do the dramatic pace and strut on television. She approached the witness box and smiled. Ari was happy to get a closer look; the woman was absolutely gorgeous. Her blouse was open at the throat to reveal a hint of pink skin, and she smelled earthy and rich. She had one hand behind her back, but the other was bent at the elbow as if in anticipation of gesturing. Her fingers were long, slender, finely manicured, deft, probably dexterous, probably could do all sorts of things in all the right places...

Ari forced her mind off that avenue quick. Three months of not getting laid had gotten her into a dangerous neighborhood.

"Hello, Miss Willow. We've never met before. I'm Cecily Parrish. I work for a firm called Gilles Girard and Moreau. I don't know if you've heard of us."

"Can't say I have."

"We've heard of you. Bitches Investigations, isn't it?" She offered another smile, but this one was smug and condescending. "Kind of an immature name, don't you think?"

Ari said, "There are people out there who think women don't or shouldn't do this kind of work. There are clients who have second thoughts about hiring us if they find out a woman is going to be investigating. Our name is a way of taking it back from anyone who might use it against us in a pejorative manner. Sometimes you need a bitch to get the job done. I'm sure you know what I'm talking about, Miss Parrish."

"How do you mean?"

"Oh, I'm positive you've been called a bitch by your colleagues from time to time." She looked at the judge. "I'm sure you have, too, your honor. Maybe not to our faces. But it's the price of admission if you want to be a woman in the workplace. So I put 'bitch' on my door. I'm proud of it. Being called a bitch means you're doing something."

Cecily nodded slowly. "How did you gain access to Mr. Cook's property?"

The question came without preamble or segue, so Ari was momentarily thrown. She had her answer ready, however, and answered without hesitation. "I waited until the house was empty and went in through the side fence."

"This was on Monday the thirteenth, correct?"

Ari nodded. "That's right."

Cecily walked back to her table and opened a file. She produced a handful of photographs and a tape in an evidence bag. "Mr. Cook's neighbor has a security camera on their back deck. It's positioned so that it captures a portion of Mr. Cook's property. It isn't a lot, but it's enough for us to see that the gate on the side fence never opened on that date." She handed the evidence to the judge. "Exhibits A through F for the defense. The fence latch and the door to the shed were also dusted for fingerprints. Would you be surprised to know that yours never showed up?"

Ari tried to keep her face neutral. "I would."

"Your prints are, of course, on record with the city of Seattle, per your private investigator license. How do you explain their absence?"

"I don't know."

Cecily arched an eyebrow. "That's it? You just... don't know?"

Ari shrugged. "I'm not going to speculate. I don't know what's on the tape. All I know is what I've told you. I accessed the property, I let myself into the shed~"

"How?"

"Excuse me?"

"The door was padlocked. The padlock was unbroken. So unless you had a key, how did you get inside the shed to check the serial numbers?"

I found a gap on the side next to the fence and squirmed under it.

But would that gap have been wide enough for a human woman to get through? She was thin, but the wolf was smaller around the torso. It was more flexible. She didn't think it would be plausible, but she also couldn't think of anything else that would appease the lawyer currently staring daggers at her.

"And you're positive," Ari said, "that the padlock was on the door when I made my visit."

Cecily smiled. "You're asking me?"

"To be honest, I don't recall having any difficulty getting into the shed. I didn't have to break or pick a lock. I touched things, so my fingerprints should have shown up. Everything you're telling me has me stumped, Miss Parrish."

"It has us stumped, too," Cecily said. "I think Mr. Nguyen gave you a list of serial numbers, then planted the items in Mr. Cook's shed."

Ari said, "That would be an impressive feat given that the lock was untouched. And I assume Mr. Nguyen wasn't spotted on the neighbor's camera planting anything. Maybe it's just a crappy camera."

Cecily shrugged. "I suppose that could be the case. But the fact remains that you can't explain how you avoided being seen."

"I can't," Ari admitted. "But I can swear that I did get in. He had a calendar on one wall from 2011. It was turned to May. I guess he liked the bikini for that month. I saw an old, rusted lawnmower in one corner next to a shiny new one. I know what I saw. There could be dozens of reasons I didn't show up on the neighbor's tape."

"And yet, you can't give us one that we'd consider plausible." She started back to her table. "Nothing further."

The judge said, "You can step down, Miss Willow."

Ari hated the dismissal. There was no chance to continue the argument, no possibility of coming out on top. The debate was over and she was sure any analysis of the back-and-forth would label her as the loser. She avoided looking at Cecily

Parrish as she passed the table and returned to the seat next to Dale. She shook her head, disappointed at her performance, but Dale took her hand in both of hers. It was a small gesture, but it went a long way to calming Ari's irritation. It had been far too long since she had felt Dale's touch or smelled Dale's scent, and it was like falling off the wagon with an extraordinarily healthy drug.

CHAPTER TWO

THE JUDGE eventually decided there was enough evidence to determine Nelson Cook had indeed robbed his former employer. Ari relaxed when the verdict was read and leaned over to suggest to Dale that they slip out before the rush. They were alone in the elevator riding down, and Dale took the opportunity to size up the changes in her partner. The most obvious was her hair. For as long as Dale had known her, Ari's hair had been long and straight. Now it was cut just above the shoulder and had a bit of a curl to the end. It was enormously attractive and served a dual purpose of making her look older and more mature.

She reached out and slid her fingers down the lapels of Ari's borrowed blazer, then teased the knot of her tie. "You're looking fine, puppy."

Ari smiled and put her hands on Dale's hips. "Three months away will make anyone look better. Like you. Before I left, you were just an angel. Now you're a goddess."

Dale pulled Ari's tie and kissed her lips. The elevator doors opened and they stepped away from each other, finding each other's hand as they walked out of the building. Ari had been dropped off by her mother with the intention of taking an Uber home. Dale slipped her arm around Ari's elbow and led her to where she had parked.

"Uber for Ariadne?"

Ari smiled. "Are you Dale?"

"I am. I hope I can expect a five-star rating from you."

"You'll have to earn that, Dale. What kind of perks do you have?"

Dale said, "Candy?"

"Ooh. Sold. Take me to the office. I want to update the paperwork as soon as possible so that whole ordeal won't linger in my mind."

They got in the car and Ari took a moment to run her hands over the dashboard and seat. "I've missed this car. I can't wait to see the apartment."

"Speaking of which, I had to take on a couple of roommates to cover your half of the rent. But it's okay, they're all non-violent offenders. And Harry's rabbit is practically housetrained."

Ari smirked at her and stopped her from starting the car. "Wait. Before you do that, there's something I want you to do." She reached into the pocket of her slacks and pulled out her collar. "We agreed I shouldn't wear this in court, for appearance's sake, but this is the first time you've seen me in three months. I hate that I wasn't wearing it."

"I didn't even notice."

"I did." She held it out. "Put it back on me?"

Dale smiled and took the collar. Ari lifted her hair and leaned forward so Dale could put it on her. It was a symbol of commitment without the faux-tradition of wedding rings and proposals. Neither of them believed in that kind of ceremony, so they'd come up with something specific for their relationship. Ari wore the collar, and Dale wore a bracelet made of Ari's hair twined with hair from the wolf. The leather of Ari's collar had a mark where it had been fastened, so Dale was able to easily reaffix it in the same place.

"Too tight?"

"It's perfect." She kissed Dale's wrist just above the bracelet. "I wore it every day when I was up at the cabin."

Dale smiled. "Let's go home."

Ari nodded and fastened her seatbelt.

"You look good," Dale said once they were on the road. "The hair, I mean. It's a good look."

"Oh." She reached up and touched it. "Yeah, it was a bit shorter, but it's grown out. I cut it myself the first day we were up at the cabin."

Dale said, "What was that like?"

"It..." Ari sighed and looked out the window. "It was good. It was what I needed. I was able to bond with Mom, which was fantastic. The wolf was euphoric. All that space to run around. No need to hide. Most of what Mom wanted to teach me was stuff I already knew or that you and I figured out together, but it was still really nice. Getting to know her. Getting comfortable with her again, after everything we went through. We had a lot of really great talks. We talked about you."

"Oh?"

Ari was quiet for a moment before she continued. "She loves you, Dale. She really does. She thinks you keep me in line."

Dale chuckled. "So you guys just hung out? Ran around a lot?"

"I was also getting to know the wolf. It was like reconnecting with Mom, you know? All these years, part of me saw the wolf as a source of pain. Every time I let her out, I knew I would be paying for it in a sore back or arms or legs. I'm finally seeing her as an extending of me."

Dale nodded. "So..."

"My transformations still don't hurt."

"Good." Dale felt the tension seeping out of her. She'd been waiting for that bombshell, afraid to ask. But Ari had moved well at the courthouse, so it wasn't a surprise that the cure was holding. She was surprised that the confirmation brought tears to her eyes. Ari leaned over and pecked her cheek. She chuckled self-consciously and said, "Sorry. I've just been worried."

Ari reached over and used her thumb to brush the tear from Dale's cheek. "I should've called more. Or, you know, at all. I kept getting your messages and every time I thought about leaving one in return, I couldn't think of anything to say. There was just so much to tell you that I didn't know where to start. So I just didn't say anything."

"I understand."

Ari said, "You should be pissed off."

Dale chuckled. "Wait until check your phone. There's a new message on there from this morning you probably haven't heard. I was frustrated about the lack of communication and this whole court thing. It's not that I minded testifying in your place. It was just the whole situation." Ari nodded. "So I kind of went off on you."

"Deservedly so. I look forward to it. I kind of like when you get all riled up."

Dale growled and snapped her teeth.

Ari laughed. "Stop it, you'll get me all turned on."

"Oh, really?"

Ari looked at her. Dale took her eyes off the road long enough to meet Ari's gaze. Neither of them had to say anything; Dale simply pulled into the next gas station parking lot and turned them around. The office and paperwork could wait. They had more pressing things to take care of. Ari had been gone for three months. Dale was surprised they were both still wearing pants.

As soon as she headed for home, her body began to react to the knowledge she was about to get laid. She'd gone three months without sex before, but not since she started dating Ari. She was suddenly breathless, eager, all too aware of the woman she loved sitting right next to her. Ari seemed just as eager. She was rubbing her hands against her thighs, shifting in her seat, eyes on the road as if she thought looking at Dale would tip her too far over the edge.

She pulled into the driveway they shared with Neka. "Bags?"

"Mom's house."

"Good."

They got out of the car and hurried toward the side yard. They were almost there when the front door opened and Neka came out.

"Ariadne!" She jogged over to them. "You're back!"

"Yeah," Ari said. "Just this morning."

Neka said, "I'm so glad. Dale kept insisting you two weren't broken up, but you just vanished one day. You two are so great together."

"Yeah," Ari said again.

Dale said, "We were just, ah..."

Neka's eyes widened. "You just got back this morning. After... three months. Oh, shit." She began retreating. "I'm sorry. You two, uh... I'll... I was just heading out, so you don't worry about... oh. Oh, shit. Sorry. Go on. We'll catch up later."

Ari said, "Thanks, Neka. It was nice seeing you again. Bye." She grabbed Dale's hand and led her around the corner as a red-faced Neka returned to the house. Dale fumbled with the keys and pushed the door open, stepping inside a moment before Ari wrapped her up in another kiss and pressed her against the wall. Now that they weren't in public they were free to be as passionate as they wanted, and Dale clung to Ari like she was in danger of falling.

"Neka knows we're having sex now," Dale said against Ari's mouth.

"Good. I want all of Seattle to know." She ran her tongue

along Dale's bottom lip. "I wanted that lawyer bitch to ask me under oath about my plans for the day so I could tell her exactly what I was going to do to you."

Dale whimpered. Ari started to take off her blazer but Dale stopped her. "Leave it on. Wait... is it your mother's?"

"No, it's mine."

"Good. Leave it on. Take my clothes off and leave yours on."

Ari smiled and kissed her again. Dale's suit jacket was draped over the back of the chair, her flats left behind next to the door. Her blouse fell once Ari was able to get her wrists free of the cuffs. Dale put a hand against the wall next to the bedroom door as Ari unzipped her skirt and let it fall. She kicked it away and Ari sank down into a crouch, running her hands over Dale's stomach and thighs. She spread her fingers over the soft material of Dale's stockings and closed her eyes before pressing her face against the crotch of Dale's underwear. She breathed deeply. Her hand curled into claws as a sigh escaped her lips.

"There you are," Ari whispered.

"Hi," Dale said.

Ari stood up and led Dale into the bedroom. When she turned on the lights she intended to ignore anything that wasn't Dale, but something on the bed caught her eye. Her pillow had been pulled to Dale's side of the bed, and one of her T-shirts was pulled over the slipcover.

"Aw, baby."

Dale said, "What? It smelled like you."

Ari turned and wrapped her arms around Dale's waist. "I had one of your shirts with me, too."

"The purple Laurelhurst one? God, I've been looking for that..."

Ari picked her up and carried her to the bed. "Whoa, puppy...! That's new."

"I'm feeling all butch from my time in the woods." She

dropped Dale onto the bed and knelt next to her. Dale scooted forward as Ari peppered her upper thighs and stomach with kisses. Dale reconsidered the "fully-dressed" idea and reached down to take off Ari's blazer, tossing it aside. Dress shirt and tie was sexy enough for the time being. She lifted her hips so Ari could pull down her stockings and underwear, then took off her own bra. She laid back and closed her eyes as Ari kissed the inside of one thigh, then the other. They were both breathing hard, eager to get right to the main event, but Ari was teasing her in the best and worst ways. She reached down and stroked Ari's head.

"Sorry..."

"No. Go slow."

Ari nipped at Dale's skin. "I've just missed you so much. Your taste and your smell. God, Dale, you smell fantastic." She turned her head and a cry of pleasure nearly choked her trying to get out. She opened her eyes and looked up at the ceiling, the same ceiling she'd stared at so many nights over the past three months. She moved her hands to the mattress, worried she would pull hair or leave marks in the skin if she kept gripping Ari's head. The time apart hadn't diminished Ari's skills or her knowledge of what made Dale tick. Her lips and tongue set the stage before she wet two fingers and went to work for real. One finger inside and the other teaming up with the tip of her tongue on Dale's clit.

"Ariadne," she whispered, closing her eyes and focusing on the sensations. Ari reached up with her free hand and touched Dale's left breast, her palm flat against the skin so she could feel her heartbeat. Dale covered Ari's hand with her own and grunted as she moved her hips against Ari's tongue. She looked down and forced her eyes open, and she saw Ari looking up at her framed by her thighs, lit from behind by the sunlight coming in through the window. It was almost religious, and Dale fell back to the mattress as she climaxed, teeth bared and a red haze drifting down her face to her upper chest.

Ari continued touching her until Dale began to twice and jerk away from her, the sensitive muscles taking it upon themselves to escape the stimulus. Ari slid up Dale's body and kissed her breasts, her collarbones, her throat. Dale hooked one leg around Ari's hip and rolled them both onto their sides.

"Why are you still dressed?" Dale asked.

"You said..."

"Take off your clothes."

Ari grinned and started with her pants. Her shoes hit the floor hollowly, and they were followed by the soft rustle of her pants. As she unbuttoned her blouse, Dale moved to position herself between Ari's legs. Ari clutched Dale's back and looked into her eyes as Dale began grinding against her. The curve of Dale's hip pressed against Ari's center and she knew just how far to go before sliding back down. Her leg and arm muscles were getting a hell of a workout, but it was worth it to see the look of desperation in Ari's eyes.

Ari whispered her name and Dale kissed her. There was a moment before Ari's orgasm when Dale froze, when they were tangled around each other and their bodies were both buzzing with sexual energy. Dale pressed her lips to the corners of Ari's mouth and moved again, slowly dragging her hip against Ari's sex. Ari's eyes closed, her head rolled back, and she dragged her nails up Dale's back on either side of her spine. Her entire body twitched, a terrible reminder of the seizure four months earlier.

Dale kissed her until Ari became responsive and began kissing her back. Dale allowed herself to be rolled, aware that Ari was still wearing her shirt and tie when she felt the silk of the latter tickling her breasts. Ari sat up, one hand on the mattress on either side of Dale's head, and Dale reached up to hold the hair out of her face.

"Now I'm better," Ari said. "The bite, the getaway with Mom, all of that was just part of the cure. But now... now I'm good."

Dale sat up and kissed Ari. "Welcome back, puppy. Don't

go anywhere." She wrapped the tie around her hand. "I've got a leash now. I'll just pull you back."

Ari smiled. "I'm not going anywhere, Dale."

They snuggled for a bit, neither of them feeling tired but also unwilling to let go of each other. After a few minutes Dale kissed Ari's forehead.

"Hey... this might be weird after what we just did..."

Ari looked up at her.

"I missed the wolf, too. Do you think... as long as we're cuddling... since it won't hurt..."

Ari smiled and kissed Dale's lips before sitting up. She positioned herself on her hands and knees and Dale watched as Ari's body went through its transformation. It looked beautiful now. The bones still broke, the skin rippled in a way she felt should turn her stomach, and it was horrifying to see Ari's face twist and bend to form a snout, but something had shifted in her mind. Now it wasn't nauseating because she knew Ari wasn't in pain. She knew whatever aches came with this transformation could be easily soothed with a massage.

The wolf was crouched on the bed next to her. Dale rolled onto her back and Ari stretched out next to her, head on her shoulder and paws stretched across her chest. The wolf was warm, and Dale dug her fingers into the soft, warm fur. She knew eventually they would have to get up, get dressed, and go into the office. But their bedroom had gone far too long without Ariadne Willow in it. They had a lot of lost time to make up for.

Chapter Three

Ari quickly got back into the swing of being in the city. Dale had put a pin in a few cases while Ari was away, and she spent her first week back contacting the clients to see if they still required her services. Some passed, others had moved on to other agencies, but a handful were still interested. Dale had managed well with background checks and scouring public access databases for a crumb of information. So much of private investigation involved sitting at a desk and knowing which server to search, but there were still jobs that required actual legwork. Ari found a stolen guitar after checking with three pawn shops and returned it to the rightful owner. She took pictures of a man playing a game of hockey which would cost him his disability checks.

On her first Friday back in the city, she surprised Dale by taking her out on a date. It wasn't anything fancy or expensive, just hot dogs and soda at an outdoor restaurant, but it was exactly what Dale needed. They held hands on the walk home and Dale felt their long hiatus fading. Every day without Ari had been a trial, and she'd grown to hate going to bed alone, but that was all in the past. Ari seemed lighter, more at ease, and comfortable in her skin.

As for the sex... Dale had never been a prude, but she blushed when she thought about some of their shenanigans. In the office, in the car, once on the dining room table, which had been more of a hassle than anything. The table really wasn't designed for that kind of activity, but they'd certainly given it their best shot.

And then there was the wolf. Ari had always been amazing as the wolf. Fast and powerful. She never suffered the transformation pain when she was in wolf form. But now it was as if she'd been supercharged. Ari's physical issues had been dealt with, so the wolf didn't have to concern herself with playing it safe. They were a true partnership now, not one entity allowing the other to take control. The wolf had become a true extension of who Ari was.

In the time they'd been working together, even before they were sleeping together, Dale had gotten used to late-night calls to come pick Ari up. She knew what the streets of Seattle looked like in the middle of the night almost as well as she knew them during the day. She knew how to get into the various parks and public areas of the city after hours. She knew where the all-night diners could be found. Ari acted as if it was an imposition, an unacceptable hassle to put Dale through, but Dale loved it. Even though it affected her sleep schedule and there were times when she had been grumpy about dragging herself out of a warm bed to drive off to Seward Park, she loved that Ari could count on her for the rescue. It made her feel like a knight in shining armor, riding off to save her woman.

One night she was woken up by Ari slipping back into their bedroom after a run. She was naked, out of breath, and sweaty. When she passed the bed, Dale smelled grass clippings. The shower turned on and ran for a minute or so, then Ari came back smelling clean. Her skin shined briefly before she turned off the bathroom light and crawled under the covers. Dale rolled over and touched Ari's hip.

"Did you go for a run?"

"Yeah. Just to the lighthouse and back."

Dale said, "What lighthouse? Alki Point?"

"Mm-hmm." Ari was already settled in, cheek against the pillow.

Dale sat up. "Ariadne, that's over eight miles away. And then another eight miles back. Are you okay? Are you hurt?"

"I'm just tired."

"You should've called me to come pick you up when you realized how far you'd gone."

Ari shook her head. "The wolf wanted the run. I wasn't tired, so I just let her go. I didn't need you."

The words hurt more than Ari could have known, more than Dale expected. She thought about waking Ari up to address how upset she was, but Ari had already drifted off. She didn't want to make an issue out of it when Ari obviously hadn't meant it the way it sounded. She bent down and kissed the corner of Ari's mouth, lay back down, and tried to fall back to sleep. Just before she drifted off, Ari shifted across the mattress and spooned her from behind. Dale smiled and stroked Ari's wrist, soothed enough to shut off her mind.

More nights like that followed, where Dale only knew Ari had gone for a run when she came back in. Ari never again said the dreaded "I didn't need you," and Dale decided to just let it drop. If Ari was able to go for runs without disturbing her, she might as well consider it a good thing. She was sleeping well, even if she did occasionally wake up at three o'clock feeling as if she needed to be somewhere. She'd been trained too well.

She wasn't going to complain. Ari was pain-free for the first time in her adult life. Dale wasn't about to look for the cloud on that silver lining and simply appreciate her girlfriend's new situation.

Ari was asleep on her stomach, one arm stretched out across Dale's stomach, when her phone startled her awake. Dale began to stir, but Ari whispered for her to lay back down. She had no idea how many hours of sleep she'd cost Dale over the course of their relationship, but it was far too many. Now that she didn't need to be picked up after the wolf went running, she was trying to let Dale sleep until morning as often as possible. Just the sight of Dale passed out, cheek flat against the pillow and bottom lip poofed out, made her feel guilty about all the times she called her for a ride at three in the morning.

She made sure Dale was settled, retrieved her still-ringing phone, and padded barefoot into the living room. "This is Ariadne Willow."

"Wow, professional even in the middle of the night. You're a class act, Willow."

She fought the urge to groan. "Wilcox? What the hell do you want?"

"And the professionalism is gone, just like that," he said.

Ari sat on the arm of the couch and blinked blearily out the window. Clark Wilcox was another private investigator, but Ari was ashamed to consider him a colleague. He cut corners, bribed witnesses, believed entrapment was the same thing as establishing evidence, and was generally inept at anything that required any actual investigation. He also thought women had no place being private investigators because they were too weak, delicate, and emotional. They'd crossed paths a handful of times over the years, and every encounter left Ari feeling in need of a shower and a change of profession.

"What do you want?"

"Sorry to interrupt your beauty sleep. I'm not even sure why I called you."

"I'm more curious about how you had my personal number."

"I'm a private investigator. I can get information when I want it."

"That's illegal."

He sighed. "Sure, sure." She heard the sound as he took a drink from a bottle. "Look, Willow, I'm drunk, but this isn't a booty call. I know you're hooking up with that hot little piece from your office." Ari's eye twitched. "It's funny, right? 'Cause if I hooked up with *my* secretary, you'd call it sexual harassment and a hostile work environment. But since you're a *lady*, I guess you get a pass perving on your employee."

"I'm hanging up now, Wilcox."

"No, no, wait. Hold on." He coughed. "Look, I didn't call just to be an asshole. Look, I've made some mistakes. I've gotten myself into a, a situation, I guess. I don't know." He took another drink. "I've been trying to fix things and I keep asking myself what you would do if you were in my place. So I guess I finally drank enough to make it seem like a good idea to call you and tell you this. I think you're a good private eye. Probably doesn't mean much coming from someone like me, but there you go."

Ari let go of her irritation enough to feel concerned. "Wilcox, is everything okay?"

"Everything's hunky-dory, Willow. I'm probably not going to remember making this call in the morning, and you're probably never going to admit I ever complimented you. Hell, I'll probably deny it even if I do remember. So hey. Just take it at face value, all right? You're a good private dick." He chuckled. "Get it? Cause you keep your dick in the nightstand."

She rolled her eyes. "Sober up, Wilcox. And then never call me at this number again."

"Hey, Willow."

She bit back a sigh. "Yeah?"

"What are you wearing?"

She hung up without saying goodbye. When she went back into the bedroom, Dale had rolled over onto her side of the bed. Ari slipped under the blankets and took the opportunity to cuddle. Dale murmured and adjusted her head on Ari's chest. Ari smiled and kissed the part in Dale's hair, putting thoughts of Clark Wilcox out of her mind.

The next morning, Ari was working from the couch in her office. Dale was behind her desk, and the door between them was open so they could see each other. There were no active cases to deal with, and Dale was busy transcribing some of Ari's notes so they would be legible ("Seriously, did you write this as the wolf? Hold the pen between your paws or in your mouth?") Ari had tried to institute a game of catch, but since Dale was busy typing, it ended up just being Ari throwing a ball at Dale's head. She apologized and Dale instituted a moratorium on throwing balls in the office. She was about to bring up lunch when there was a knock on the door.

Ari prepared herself for a client until Dale smiled and said, "Hey, Diana."

Diana Macallan was a detective with the Seattle PD and one of the few people who knew Ari was *canidae*. She was also an ex-girlfriend, but the relationship hadn't lasted long enough to make things awkward. Ari came out of the office and waved.

"Hey, Diana. I was just about to take Dale out for an early lunch. Want to come?"

"Thanks, but I'm here on business."

Ari said, "Everything okay?"

Diana said, "I don't know. Let's talk in your office." She looked at Dale. "No offense, Miss Frye."

"None taken."

Dale looked at Ari, who nodded to her that everything was okay as she escorted Diana into her office and shut the door.

"So are you looking to hire me or arrest me?"

"Hopefully neither," Diana said. "When was the last time you spoke to Clark Wilcox?"

Since Diana was ignoring the chair in front of the desk, Ari decided to remain standing as well. She crossed her arms and leaned against the front edge of the desk.

"Last night. Well, technically this morning. He called me in the middle of the night."

"Did you answer?"

Ari nodded. "I probably wouldn't have if I'd checked the Caller ID. But like I said, it was the middle of the night."

"What did he want to talk about?"

"He was drunk. I think he just needed a human person to listen."

"Is that a regular occurrence?"

"No. I didn't even know he had my number. Look, I know he's a shady asshole, but if he's involved with something you're investigating, I can assure you I'm not involved. I wish he'd told me something that could help you out."

Diana said, "We're not currently investigating him for anything. He killed himself."

Ari flinched and stood up, dropping her arms. "When?"

"This morning. His secretary showed up for work at nine o'clock and found him. Medical examiner put the time of death at around six hours earlier. I took a peek at his phone and saw that was around the time he called you. I think he pulled the trigger not long after hanging up with you."

"That's... unbelievable. You're sure he killed himself?"

Diana shrugged. "The medical examiner will confirm, but it looked like a pretty clear case of a self-inflicted gunshot wound. He put the gun in his mouth and pulled the trigger. The scene looked right to me. Did he say anything that might have led you to believe he was suicidal?"

Ari shook her head, trying to remember the conversation. "He was just talking. I guess now that I'm thinking about it, he seemed more introspective than I would have expected from him. He said I was a good private investigator. Considering the fact he was loud and proud about the fact he thought women didn't belong in the job, I found that odd. But I thought it was just the beer talking. Who else did he call?"

Diana said, "We're running the last few numbers now. I

just happened to recognize your number when I saw it and hoped I could eliminate you before anything official happened."

"I appreciate that." She tried to recall how she had ended the conversation, but she could only remember she'd been rude. Of course she had been rude. She'd never be anything but rude to Wilcox, especially with him drunk-dialing her in the middle of the night. "I can't believe I'm the last person he wanted to talk to."

"You're sure there was nothing in the conversation that might have indicated what he was planning to do?"

"As positive as I can be," Ari said. "Oh, God. The last thing he said before I hung up on him was asking me what I was wearing."

Diana made a face. "That doesn't sound like a man on the cusp of killing himself."

Ari said, "At least you're working the case. That means I can help you out."

"That's not what it means at all. Right now you're technically a suspect."

Ari rolled her eyes.

"A suspect I can pretty much rule out," Diana admitted, "but nonetheless. I can't exactly invite you to the crime scene to look around."

"Come on..."

Diana said, "No, Ariadne." She lowered her voice. "And I don't want to see any paw prints in the mud outside his office window, got me?"

Ari said, "Dale knows what I am."

"I know. I just feel ridiculous saying 'werewolf' out loud."

"Let me dig around. Do you really think the sort of people Wilcox dealt with are going to talk to a detective? As soon as they see that badge, they're going to shut you out. I can at least pretend I'm as shady as he was. Maybe I can get somewhere you wouldn't."

Diana sighed and tapped her hand against her thigh. "This is why we didn't work out as a couple, Ariadne."

"Because I'm super persuasive and I can talk you into doing anything I want?"

"Because you're stubborn. But you do have a point, as irritating as that might be. Do you know Wilcox's secretary?"

Ari shook her head. "We never really met. I might have seen her once or twice."

"You've been to Wilcox's office?"

"Like I said, once or twice. We've crossed paths before. We were rivals, but we never actually went after each other."

Diana thought for a moment. "I didn't tell anyone I was coming here to question you. So officially, you don't know about Wilcox's suicide yet. Maybe you can get in touch with the secretary, maybe she'll be willing to talk to using his call as a pretense. If you're just trying to figure out what he was up to, she might talk to you. But I'm leaving it up to her." She aimed a finger at Ari. "But that will be *it*. And his office is a crime scene. I don't want you getting spotted there and becoming an official person of interest."

Ari said, "I'll be good. I promise."

"Where have I heard that before?" She moved to the door and then looked back. "You've been out of town for a while. Everything okay there?"

"Did you just *Columbo* me? 'Just one more question, ma'am'?"

"Sometimes it works."

Ari laughed. "I was out of town with my mother. Wolf things."

"Well, whatever it was, you look good. I like the shorter hair." She opened the door. "I really don't think you had anything to do with his death. It looks like a suicide. And in my experience, no one in real life ever bothers to stage that sort of thing. If someone wants to kill another person, they just pull the trigger and walk away."

Ari said, "Right."

"I'm telling you to be careful. If there is something to find, it drove one man to suicide. I don't want you to get in too deep. This is my case. You can come to me for help if you need it."

"I understand."

Diana said goodbye to Dale on her way out. Dale got up and went to Ari, touching her arm. "Hey. What was that about? Who committed suicide?"

"Wilcox," Ari said. "Last night, after he called me."

Dale's eyes widened. "I can't believe it."

"Neither can I," Ari said. "So I'm going to see if I can figure out why."

CHAPTER FOUR

WILCOX HAD an office between the train tracks and the Alaskan Way Viaduct. Ariadne hated going anywhere near that part of town due to the tunneling project that seemed to have been going on since the turn of the century. Traffic wasn't as bad as she expected and, in less than half an hour, she found herself parking in front of a strip mall across the street from Wilcox's office that housed an army/navy surplus store and a Greek restaurant.

The front window announced the business as "PROFESSIONAL AND SECURITIES CONSULTANT." She watched in her side mirror as a forensic technician ducked under the crime-scene tape on the doorway. There was no way she would get into the actual office, but she could see the private parking area behind the building. Wilcox's car was parked there, along with a lime-green VW bug that she recognized from past visits. There was a chance someone had driven Wilcox's secretary home, but Ari took the chance she was still nearby.

She didn't spot the girl in Starbucks or the Greek

restaurant. There was a Latin restaurant on the corner and there, seated at a table by the window, was the secretary she recognized from her handful of brief visits to Wilcox's office. Ari unfortunately only knew the girl by her last name, Knight, due the placard on her desk. She was a college-age sorority type, with long black hair that reminded Ari of Morticia Addams. A book bag on the table was the same lime-green as the car parked behind Wilcox's office.

The restaurant was otherwise empty, despite the fact it was lunchtime. Knight looked up when Ari came in and tilted her head to the side with vague recognition. Ari approached her table with what she hoped was a reassuring smile.

"Miss Knight? I'm Ariadne Willow."

"Oh, right. From Bitches." She smiled weakly. Her eyes were red, but she wasn't currently crying. "You always seemed really cool. You can call me Tiffany."

"Thanks. May I?" She gestured at the seat across from Knight, who nodded. "I was just coming by because Wilcox called me last night, but all those cop cars... what's going on?"

Tiffany looked like she was on the verge of breaking down again. "Clark killed himself."

Ari feigned shock. "What? That's terrible. He didn't seem like the type. Are the police sure?"

"They seemed pretty sure. I kept telling them, you know, Clark had enemies."

"He had enemies?"

Tiffany shot her a disbelieving look. "You dealt with him, so you must know he had enemies. Heck, you were one of them. He deals with criminals who could turn on him at any moment, and good people just don't like him because he's a jerk. Yes, he has enemies. And one of them could have made this look like a suicide."

Ari used Diana's logic. "That really doesn't happen a lot in real life."

"I guess not."

"Wilcox didn't show any signs of this? He wasn't depressed or stressed?"

Tiffany rolled her eyes. "Clark was never stressed. Go with the flow." She opened her book bag and took out a small packet of Kleenex. She dabbed her eyes with it as a plane buzzed the neighborhood. It was landing at Boeing Field, judging by the angles, and Ari waited until the sound had diminished before she spoke again.

"So there was nothing specific that might have led him to... to this?"

"Nothing that I know of." She sniffled and focused on Ari. "You said he called you last night? That's so weird. He hated you. No offense."

Ari smiled and shook her head. "None taken. Our relationship was mutually antagonistic. That's the main reason I came down here today. It was just so out of character for him that I figured something must be up."

"He called me last night, too. I didn't answer. If you're a young woman and you work for a guy like Clark Wilcox, you learn not to answer your phone after a certain hour."

"Were there problems in that area?"

Tiffany shrugged. "Not problems-problems. He would flirt a little bit. I told him there wasn't a chance in hell, he would mention my ass looked great in a certain pair of slacks, stuff like that. Sexual harassment. You know."

"Sounds like a problem-problem to me."

"I just did the math in my head. How much he was paying me versus how much I disliked working there, divided by how much I'd get paid elsewhere and have to go through the same shit. I'm pretty. You have to factor in a little bit of harassment no matter what job you have."

Ari said, "That's grim."

"That's life. You know what it's like, though."

"Actually I don't. My only real boss was a woman, and now I'm my own boss."

"Sounds nice." She looked out the window again, so Ari did the same. The police had moved on, but the CSU truck was still parked in front of the building. Tiffany suddenly laughed. "I can't believe I'm crying. He was a jerk. He was an asshole."

Ari said, "But you knew him, and he's dead. So that deserves a few tears."

"He's not the sort of guy you waste tears on, you know?" She dabbed with the Kleenex again.

"Right." She folded her arms on the table and leaned forward. "I want to find out what happened to Clark. Neither of us think he would've done this. No one kills their favorite person."

Tiffany laughed and looked down at her hands. "Right."

"The police aren't going to let me anywhere near his office or files, but they'll let you in. Let me dig around a little and find out the whole story. In exchange, I can hire you on a temporary basis. Long enough for you to find another job."

"That would be a huge help," Tiffany said. "Maybe that was part of why I was crying. I know I'm not going to find another job that easy that paid that well."

Ari said, "Easy?"

Tiffany nodded. "I basically just answered the phone and passed along messages to Clark. He didn't want me actually dealing with the clients or anything like that. A lot of it was just sitting at a desk looking pretty." She cringed. "That's terrible, isn't it? God, I sound like such a whore."

Ari gestured at the bag. "What are you studying?"

"Pharmacology."

"I'm sure working for Clark helped with the expenses."

Tiffany laughed. "Oh, yeah."

"Wilcox wanted someone to sit around and look pretty, and you got money for school and time to study. I wouldn't beat myself up about it."

"Thanks, Ariadne. You know, I really did like whenever you butted heads with Clark. I'm sure it was hell for you, but it was nice seeing him go up against someone smarter than him."

Ari smiled.

Tiffany unzipped her bag and pulled out her laptop. "It's going to be a while before the police are done in there, but I can link up to his files from here. We can at least see what he was working on during the past few weeks."

"That won't get us in trouble?" Ari asked, twisting to look out the window. She didn't want the cops to be looking at Clark's computer when it was suddenly accessed remotely.

"No, it shouldn't. I'll be in the cloud. As for the client's privacy... huh. Well, I guess that could be potentially criminal." She chewed her lip and tapped her fingers against the tabletop. "Private eyes do consultations with each other, right?"

Ari shrugged. "Sure, sometimes."

"Well, there we go. Clark is... isn't going to be finishing these cases. I'm technically the only member of the firm left, so I'm authorizing you to look at these files to see if you can close them. I'm sure the clients would understand that."

"I'm not sure that would hold up in court, but it works for me."

Tiffany said, "Me too." The computer booted up and Tiffany's fingers flew across the keyboard. Now that she had a task to occupy her mind, she could forget about her tears. After a few minutes she said, "Okay, I can send you the files. Email?" Ari gave her the address. "You don't actually have to work the cases. I'll contact the clients and let them know what happened, issue refunds, that sort of thing. And I'll refer them to you. Just to make it all official."

Ari said, "Okay. I appreciate it."

"I figure I would be doing this anyway. Cancelling contracts and recommending other firms. I wouldn't recommend any of the other guys Clark hangs out with. They're all like him. They call me sweetheart and try to look down my shirt when they come into the office. You never tried that."

"So I get the business just because I was a decent human

being?"

"There are worse ways to get a job."

"True. Thank you for this. You really didn't have to help me."

Tiffany said, "No, I'm glad you came along. I was sitting here not knowing what to do next. You gave me a purpose. I'll get in touch with you when I've spoken to his clients."

Ari took out a card and wrote her personal cell number on the back before handing it over. "For the recommendations. And in case you need to talk."

"Thank you. That's very kind. And you're not hiring permanently, right?"

"Sorry."

Tiffany shrugged. "I had to ask." She wiped her eyes one more time, then began packing away her things.

"You said you don't know anything about his current cases. How was he spending the past few days? Was he out of the office a lot?"

She pursed her lips as she thought. "I don't think any more than usual. He was in and out a lot. He made a lot of phone calls, but that wasn't strange. He did a lot of his work over the phone or online. Are you officially on this case?"

"I don't think there's a case to be on. No one has hired me. But I do want answers."

"So do I." She unzipped a small side pocket on her bag and took out a keyring. "This is for Clark's apartment. He gave it to me in case I ever needed to drop off his mail or water his plants. I think it was really in case I ever decided to drop by wearing a trenchcoat with nothing underneath it." She pushed the keys across the table. "You can't get into the office right now, but you could probably get in his apartment without too much trouble."

"Thank you." Ari took the keys. "I'll get these back to you."

"I don't need them anymore." Tiffany's eyes started welling up again. "I should go. I can call the clients from home. Thank you, Ariadne."

Ari nodded. "I'll walk you out." When they were on the sidewalk, Ari said, "You might want to think about staying with a friend for the next few days. If something was going on with Wilcox, someone might come looking for him. If he's not around, they might take revenge on whoever is available."

"Yikes."

"I don't want to scare you, but I also don't want you to be caught off-guard."

Tiffany scanned the area as if she expected the anonymous bad guys to be lurking in the shadows. "I appreciate it."

Another plane passed overhead as they arrived at the lime-green VW, and Tiffany craned her head back to watch it. "Clark hated those planes. He always said they screwed up his thought process, but if I suggested wearing headphones, he would just bitch about not being able to hear himself think at all. And if it wasn't the planes, it was the viaduct project screwing up traffic. I think he just liked having something to complain about." Her face was pinched as if she was trying not to start crying again. "He wasn't a good man, Ariadne. He was a misogynistic jerk. But he could be sweet. I wouldn't have stayed here as long as I did if there weren't a few good days."

Ari said, "I understand."

"No one deserves to die that way, even if he did pull the trigger himself. A lot of people would've just said good riddance to bad rubbish, you know? I'm glad you're trying to find out why this happened, despite your history with him."

"A tragedy is a tragedy, no matter who it happens to." She held out her hand. "I wish I'd gotten to know you better."

Tiffany said, "I wish I'd met you before you hired a secretary."

Ari watched her drive away, waving one last time before the bug went around the corner. The parking lot was situated so she could see the forensics van in front of the building as well as the alley that ran behind it. The CSU officers were on the sidewalk putting away their toys, and from the looks of things, the office had been locked up tight.

The alley was a one-lane pockmarked street between buildings, every available space taken up by employee parking and dumpsters. The plain white brick walls were colored by a variety of spraypainted tags. Some of them had been covered by plain gray squares of primer, but the majority looked as fresh as the day they were painted. The name of Wilcox's agency - or firm, as Tiffany called it - was written on one of the plain metal doors. Ari stepped onto the stone half-circle that formed a step, tried the knob, and pushed it open.

"Technically not breaking and entering," she muttered, looking over her shoulder to make sure no one had entered the alley. She was still alone, so she stepped inside.

The door led into a cramped kitchenette across the hall from an even smaller bathroom. Ari paused by the mini-fridge and listened to the voices of the forensics team at the front of the building. They were talking about the Seahawks, some reality show that had aired the night before, and she heard the back doors of their van slam shut. One of them rattled the front door to make sure it was locked. She waited until the sound of engines faded before she stepped out into the hall.

She'd been in the offices a few times before, but coming in through the back made everything look odd and slightly different than she expected. She went past the main office and went forward to the waiting area. The front desk smelled of Tiffany's perfume and an air freshener that had apparently been sprayed liberally through the entire space.

Ari focused hard on natural smells, knowing that she would have better results if she actually became the wolf, but there was no way she was going to strip down and transform in a crime scene. The front room seemed clean, so she went back to Wilcox's office. She braced herself before going in, preparing herself for the various odors of death, and then opened the door.

The room was a testament to manliness. A football signed by Russell Wilson was in a place of pride directly across from the door. Every piece of furniture was chrome and leather, and the desk was a shiny black slab that reminded her of the monolith from *2001*. Wilcox's chair was twisted to one side, as if he had just stepped out for a moment and would be back in a few minutes. Underneath the prominent stench in the room, she picked up the usual elements of body odor, cigar smoke, and of course an assortment of alcohols.

And then there was the blood.

The wall behind the desk was splattered in a wide delta, thick and bright at head level and thinning near the ceiling. It dotted framed pictures of Wilcox with local celebrities and athletes, as well as his various documents and licenses. Mixed in with the smell of blood was cordite that got stronger when she moved closer to where Wilcox had died. There were other smells in that area, but Ari chose to ignore them.

Diana would obviously have searched for evidence that anyone else was present, but Ari had the benefit of a wolf's senses. She crouched next to Wilcox's desk and closed her eyes, breathing deeply.

Bodies, warm and fragrant, cologned and perfumed. She smelled the gun polish and oiled leather of their uniform belts. Cops all had a vague cigarette odor to them, even after the various stationhouses all went smokeless. Something about wearing a badge meant smoking or hanging around people who smoked. Diana's scent was mingled in with the rest of the cops, familiar like a note half-heard in a symphony. The police smells were all fresh and thick, so she pushed past them. She couldn't have explained how it worked to a non-wolf. The closest she could get was the bread and coffee aisle at the supermarket. There was a bombardment of different smells comingling until it was just a solid wall of indeterminate smells. A wolf could follow the thread of a smell down to the specific loaf, to a single slice, without fail.

Her nostrils flared as she smelled her way back through the morning. She agreed with Diana's timeline about when Wilcox's gun had gone off, based on how the odor had degraded. The smell of Wilcox's corpse diminished alongside the gunpowder, forming waves that Ari tracked all the way back to their origin. She opened her eyes and looked at the empty seat in front of her.

Wilcox had been alone in the office when he killed himself. She was ninety-five percent positive of it, though she could never have explained why in a court of law. But just because the wound had been self-inflicted didn't mean the case was closed. Someone had pushed Wilcox to this extreme, forced him into a corner where suicide was his only option. Wilcox was an asshole, to be sure, but he was the sort of person who could always find a way out. There was always an angle to manipulate.

Clark Wilcox had put the gun in his own mouth and he'd pulled the trigger, but Ari was going to find out who put him in that position to begin with.

Chapter Five

Fact: Clark Wilcox killed himself. Theory: Whoever he was in trouble with and-or running from didn't yet know that he was dead. They might come looking for him at some point, either at his office or his home. She didn't think she could stake out the office without eventually drawing attention to herself. And any 'bad guys' who came looking for him wouldn't even slow down once they saw the crime tape. She took a chance that the police hadn't gotten to Wilcox's apartment yet. She looked up the address using the internet on her phone after leaving the bloody office as she'd found it.

Glory, the woman who had trained her, had scoffed at the reach of technology. "I'm not saying it's bad, I'm just saying the amount of things you can do sitting on your ass typing is amazing. Private eyes are gonna be replaced by Ask Jeeves and Yahoo searches." She'd made sure that Ari knew how to find information in a library, how to dig up old records without relying on database searches, and all the old-school PI tricks. Ari chuckled as she remembered the outdated references, wondering what Glory would think of how far technology had come.

As much as Ari appreciated the hands-on approach, it was incredibly handy to find Wilcox's home address without first tracking down a payphone and thumbing through the Yellow Pages in the hopes he was listed. If she could achieve the same thing with just a few taps on the screen, then yay for technology as far as she was concerned.

Wilcox lived in a rundown condominium complex on a nearly-vertical street next to the I-5. Ari parked and hiked to the entrance, passing by used condoms and broken syringes that had been pushed into the gutters. Her thighs were burning when she finally reached the lobby. She couldn't imagine Wilcox getting a similar workout every time he came home. Either he parked at the top of the hill and walked down or there was a parking structure she'd overlooked.

She took the stairs, not trusting the urine-scented and seemingly long-neglected elevator with its doors propped open. A handwritten sign on the wall next to the elevator said, "This thing is like your sister: it goes down, and it goes down FAST!!! Use at your own risk!" Ari peeked inside and immediately retreated when she saw the state of the buttons. The stairs were as steep as the road, and again she wondered how someone as out of shape as Clark Wilcox could survive living in a place that was basically one big Stairmaster. She took the keys Tiffany had given her out of her pocket when she got to the fifth floor. She stopped at the head of the stairs and checked to make sure the hall was empty before she continued on.

The door was warped in its frame, but she managed to shoulder it open. By that point she'd started sweating a bit and was definitely out of breath. She wiped a hand over her face and shook her head once she was inside. She was starting to think Wilcox hadn't been lazy as much as just tired from walking home every night.

Once she caught her breath, she tried to figure out what

was odd about Wilcox's living room. At first glance it was just a typical living space. Couch, television, desk for the computer, armchair. She didn't realize what exactly was tripping her senses until she looked into the kitchen and saw the lime-green cabinets and third-hand fridge. The appliances looked like they had all been dragged up the stairs by their cords and then muscled into their current positions. The floor tile was had a faded and cracked pattern that would have looked tacky even in the eighties.

By comparison, the living room looked pristine. Everything new and shiny, everything top of the line. The armchair itself had to cost at least four hundred dollars. A flat-screen HD was hanging on the wall. Ari looked from the screen down to the stained carpeting and deduced that Wilcox had come into quite a bit of money in the recent past. He'd only taken the time to update his living area and hadn't yet gotten to the kitchen or his office.

"A man needs his sports," Ari muttered.

The new furniture also indicated his suicide hadn't been a long-term plan. Something had happened recently to make him desperate enough to do the unthinkable. She went down the hall, bracing herself for whatever den of iniquity Wilcox might call a bedroom. The door was open a crack and she pushed it open with her foot. The bed was a tangle of sheets and blankets, three pillows strewn against the headboard. She ignored the odors and kicked aside a pile of dirty clothes as she crossed the threshold. She really didn't expect him to have a diary or a journal, but there was always a chance he had some backup of his cases and notes.

She found an iPad on the top shelf of the closet and turned it on, carrying it with her as it booted up so she could search the rest of the room. When the screen came to life, she swept her finger across the screen and cursed when it prompted her for a security code. 1-2-3-4 and 0-0-0-0 were both failures. She didn't know Wilcox's birthday or any other important dates he might have chosen for the password. She turned it off again and hoped Dale would have better luck cracking it.

Ari had just started back out into the hall when she heard the front door being shoved open again. She immediately retreated back into the bedroom. She pushed the door shut to a crack and listened.

"Wilcox! You in here? You hiding from us, Clarky? That's not very nice."

If either of them had turned left when they came into the apartment, they would have seen her. Instead they continued forward to the living room just as she had. From the weight of their footsteps, she assumed there were two men.

"He's not here. No one's here."

"I told you, I saw her hanging around the office after the cops left and then five minutes later, she's walking into the building. She must've been right behind me on the road. Hell, she might have even followed me. What, you think she just happens to be a neighbor? She's snooping."

Ari backed away from the door. The goons wouldn't leave without a thorough search of the apartment, and the closet wasn't deep enough for her to hide. She shoved the iPad under the mattress and quickly shed her clothes. A part of her brain reminded her that she was undressing in Clark Wilcox's bedroom and asked her to consider that one of the signs of the apocalypse. There wasn't time to be disgusted. She kicked her clothes out of sight and shook out her arms. She fell forward onto her hands and knees and bit the inside of her cheek to keep from shouting when she transformed.

"Clark! We're not playing around, buddy. Just come on out and let's have a talk. You can get back to your little girlfriend when we're done."

Twenty seconds later, the bedroom door pushed open. Ari lifted her head off her forepaws and the man in the doorway recoiled.

"Holy shit. He's got a goddamn wolf in here."

Another man peered over his shoulder. "The hell? I never saw him with a damn dog."

The first man jabbed a stumpy finger at her. "What do you think that is? Some stray wandered in?"

"Look at this building. I'm saying it's possible they got wild dogs roaming the halls."

Ari growled low in her throat. The first man backed into the hallway and thumped the second man on the chest. "Clark obviously ain't here. Might as well get something for all the trouble of breaking in. Go look around in there, see what you can find."

Second said, "You're crazy. I'm not going in there with that thing."

First stared at her, one hand swinging by his belt. Ari didn't know if he had a gun stowed in the small of his back, and that not knowing was making her nervous. Transforming had seemed like her best chance to avoid detective, but now she was concerned that these were the type of people who would shoot a dog just for getting in their way. She stood up slowly and backed away from the men. When she reached the edge of the bed, she dropped down onto the floor and peered at them over the edge of the mattress.

First chuckled, relieved. "See? He's just a big chicken. Go on."

Second entered the room, but he stayed close to the wall and made sure he didn't turn his back on Ari until he had to. First left the doorway to continue searching elsewhere. Second put his hands on the closet shelf and stretched to look around. If he'd been five minutes earlier, he would have found the iPad. Ari climbed back onto the mattress in the hopes it would prevent him from looking underneath it. He turned at the sound of her moving, but relaxed when he saw she was just lying down.

"Lady isn't here!" First shouted from another room. "Told ya, you were just seeing things."

"Wearing the same freaking clothes, looking exactly the same..." Second muttered. He shook his head and went to open the nightstand. He dug through the items inside and wrinkled his nose at whatever he saw. "God, what some people..." He slammed the drawer shut and skirted the edge of the bed again. "There's nothing here, Tom. I'm telling you, the cops were there because ol' Clarky decided to hand it all over to them."

"That's idiotic. He wouldn't do that. Besides, they had crime scene tape up. Clark probably got his ass robbed last night, that's all it is. You better hope whoever ripped him off didn't find it."

First/Tom and Second appeared again in the hallway and moved toward the door.

Second looked back at Ari and hesitated. "Hey. Are we just going to leave him here all by himself? It's starting to look like Clark ain't coming back. It'd be cruel to just abandon the guy."

"Five seconds ago, you were terrified of him."

"I know, but... we could at least fill his dish. Did you see one in the kitchen?"

Ari couldn't let the men look for dog food that didn't exist. It might make them ask questions that didn't have answers, and she didn't want them confused. She stood up and barked as loudly as she could. Both men were startled so she barked again, baring her teeth at them before jumping onto the floor. Head down, ears back, eyes locked on the men, she started forward.

"Oh, shit." Second shoved Tom toward the door. "Okay. Okay, screw this asshole dog. Let's go. Let's go!"

They fled without bothering to lock the door behind them. Ari lay down on her belly and transformed back. Her joints twisted and popped into place, sending bursts of pain up and down her spine before settling at the ends of her extremities. The muscles that had been hurting after her long trek up the stairs and the steep street now howled in agony as they were twisted and contorted into a new shape. Ari bit back a scream and flopped onto her side, trembling through the final stages of the transformation. She looked down at her feet and flexed the toes, then stretched out so that she was lying flat on her stomach.

The pain faded until she was left with only a dull throb throughout her body. She pushed herself up, sitting with her legs folded underneath her, and flexed her hands. Her mother had told her that all *canidae* still felt pain when they transformed, but she never thought about what to expect. Her mother and Milo and every other wolf she'd known had acted like it was no big deal. When she transformed at the cabin and felt the pain, she'd panicked. She was positive the cure hadn't worked. Gwen reassured her, calmed her nerves, and determined the pain was at a normal level.

That was the moment she was grateful she wasn't with Dale. If she'd panicked, Dale would have panicked along with her. It was better to have the bumps and setbacks with someone who had been through them before. It saved Dale so much stress that Ari was able to justify the anguish of being away from her for so long.

She got to her feet and braced one hand against the wall, moving to lock the door before she went to the living room window. She pushed the curtain aside and looked down. There was a moment of vertigo as her brain tried to marry the angle with the fact she was standing on solid ground. Five floors below, she watched as Tom and the other man exited the building and walked across the street to a blue pickup. The angle was too steep and the apartment much too high for her to read the license plate, but she still craned her neck and gave it a shot.

The truck pulled away without revealing anything that would help her identify its passengers, so she left the window and went to retrieve her clothes. The thought of anything she owned spending time on the floor of Clark Wilcox's bedroom floor for any length of time was enough to make her want to burn them. But unless she wanted to change again, she had to wear something to get home.

After she was dressed again, she retrieved the iPad. She knew most people were incredibly lazy with passwords. Being a private investigator himself might have made Wilcox a bit smarter, but Ari doubted it. She went to the desk and looked for numbers on Post-Its or some other reminder. She wanted to search further, but she didn't want to be trapped by any other goons that came looking for Wilcox.

She locked the door as she left the apartment. The next door over opened and a woman stuck her head out. She looked at Ari with skepticism.

"You his girlfriend?"

"God. No."

"Good. You're too pretty." She twisted her neck. "He have a dog in there? I heard a dog barking."

"No dogs."

"Pets are against the rules," the woman said.

Ari nodded. "I'll keep that in mind if I ever move in."

She hurried downstairs, then went down the hill to her car. She stayed aware of her surroundings in case the goon who recognized her from Wilcox's office had someone waiting behind to watch for her. The street seemed empty so she tossed the iPad onto the passenger seat and drove back to the office.

Dale looked up as she came in. "Hey. How'd your morning go?"

"I'll tell you while you're getting into that." She handed Dale the iPad. "Wilcox put a passcode on it. I tried the usual, but~"

Dale held the tablet up flat in front of her face, turned it on, and tapped four numbers. The screen remained blank. She typed in four more, and the screen opened. She handed the iPad back to Ari.

"There you go. 7-5-2-1."

"How...?"

"The passcode keyboard pops up in the middle of the

screen, not in the usual spot. Wilcox left fingerprint smudges over those numbers. I went in numerical order, then reversed it. I just got lucky. It could have taken a lot longer to work all the combinations."

Ari said, "Redheaded genius."

Dale grinned. "So how was the rest of your day?"

Ari relayed what had happened with Tiffany and then her encounter with the goons. Dale waited until she'd heard the whole story before she spoke.

"You changed? How are you feeling?"

"I wouldn't say no to a massage. But otherwise I'm fine."

Dale said, "And you don't have any idea who these goons were?"

Ari shook her head. "One was named Tom. I'm good, but I'm not good enough to get anything out of that unless there's contact info on this." She held up the iPad. "Whoever they were, they didn't seem to know Wilcox was dead."

"If they keep lurking around, they're going to figure it out sooner rather than later."

"Yeah. Which means I should start digging through this." She tapped the iPad. "Thanks again for cracking the case, you hacker goddess."

Dale winked and gave her a thumbs-up as Ari took the tablet into her office.

CHAPTER SIX

ARI HAD a marijuana problem. It wasn't an addiction, but the opposite. When each transformation came with agonizing pain, Dr. Frost had suggested pot as an analgesic. It worked to a degree. It certainly lessened her pain levels, but it came at the cost of a foggy brain, drowsiness, and a permanent stink that was even worse due to her heightened senses. Now that the pain was at a manageable level, she could stop smoking it. The problem was that she and Dale had made sure she would always have enough available in case of any flare-ups. But now they had four glass jars of pot in their fridge and no intention to ever smoke it.

She had spent the entire afternoon at the office going through Wilcox's iPad, trying to figure out why the goons had wanted it so badly. The notes were filled with the various information related to every case: client's name, focus of the investigation, other names, addresses, schedules, etc. It was arranged by case number, and the majority of entries were written with shorthand. There was only so much she could do with information like "#208339 B Sm/w."

The real prize was in the Video app, but the problem there was far too much information. There were over six hundred videos of varying lengths that all featured the same plot: men and women, men and men, women and women, all of them engaged in various acts of... well, she'd be generous and call it 'romance.' Wilcox had an amazing ability to get in close to the action. Ari had seen porn that had been shot less professionally. Every video had a clear shot of the participants' faces, but each one was labeled to correspond with the cryptic notes. Ari wasn't about to watch every video and hope for a clue to jump out at her, so she put the iPad aside for the time being.

On the way home, she and Dale stopped for groceries. Ari was putting away the mayo when she spotted the jars of marijuana and decided the time had come to get rid of them. She took one jar and went to the stairs that led up to the laundry room between their basement apartment and the rest of Neka's house. When Ari first started using the treatment, they'd checked with Neka to make sure it was okay for her to smoke in the yard. Neka had agreed as long as they sometimes shared their stash.

Neka opened the door and smiled. "Hey. Gotta admit, it's still kind of strange getting visitors in the laundry room. Not that you're a visitor really..."

"I get it," Ari said with a smile. "I was just wondering if you wanted our pot."

"Is this some kind of reverse trick-or-treat?"

Ari chuckled. "Maybe so. The medical condition I was using it for is... passed... so I don't need it anymore. I never really liked the smell."

Neka took the jar. "Thank you. Yeah, if you're just going to throw it out anyway, we'll take it off your hands."

"We?"

"Oh, yeah. I started dating someone while you were away. Dale actually helped introduce us. He worked at the copy place with her."

Ari tilted her head. "Copy place?"

"Mm-hmm. The one on Prospect. She worked there for about five or six weeks. She met Simon there and thought we'd hit it off, so she introduced us." She tucked her hair behind her ear. "Actually, I wanted to invite you to dinner with us some night this week. Whenever you're free."

"Yeah, that sounds great," Ari said.

"And I'll give you a discount on the rent for the pot."

Ari managed a smile. "I appreciate it, but you don't have to. It's a gift." She gestured back down the stairs. "I need to, uh..."

"Sure. We'll work out the details later."

Ari went back downstairs. Dale was in the kitchen putting away the Pop Tarts. Ari stopped in the doorway of the kitchen and stared at her. "You worked at a copy place?"

Dale turned. "Oh. Uh, yeah, just for a few weeks." She scratched her neck. "Which bag had the oranges?"

The bag was on the floor. Ari stooped to pick it up and handed it to her. "Why?"

"Because I'm going to put them away...?"

"No, why were you working at a copy place?"

Dale sighed. "Because I needed the money. I could only take one or two out of every five or six cases we were contacted about, and that wasn't going to keep the lights on very long. The store needed someone to organize their books. You know, like when you hired me in the first place."

"You could have called me. Mom could have loaned us a little cash."

"Yeah, I could've called," Dale muttered.

"What?"

Dale sighed. "I could've called, but that was about the time you stopped bothering to answer your messages. It was just a part-time job, Ari. I'd spend the morning at the agency, but there wasn't a whole hell of a lot to do there. Meanwhile I had the rent on this place, I had the rent on the office, I had bills, and you were suddenly incommunicado. So I took a job. Are you mad at me for that?"

"I'm... I'm curious why you didn't tell me."

"Because it wasn't a big deal."

Ari pushed her hands through her hair. "You told me to go, Dale."

"I did."

"Going out there with mom was important. For the wolf, for my relationship with Mom~"

"I know." The oranges were all put away, so Dale folded the reusable bags to store them next to the fridge.

"Will you stop putting away the groceries for five seconds and look at me?"

Dale sighed and flattened her hands on the bags. "I didn't tell you because I didn't want you to know I nearly cost you everything. Okay? We could've lost the office. We could've lost everything you built. I was ashamed, Ari. And then you weren't answering my calls, so I didn't know if you were alive or if you were hurting again and your mother was just trying to spare my feelings. You just vanished. So I was scared and angry and worried the whole time you were gone. And then you just show up again. And I was thrilled. I'm so thrilled you're back, Ariadne. Sometimes I wake up at night just to touch you to make sure you're really there. So I put all that aside because it didn't matter anymore." She stepped back from the table and brushed past Ari. "Can you finish putting things away?" She didn't wait for an answer, disappearing into their bedroom and shutting the door behind her.

Ari wasn't sure if following her was the right thing to do, but she couldn't just sit down and stare at the wall. She knocked softly before she opened the door. Dale had left the lights off and was lying down facing the wall. Ari walked to her side of the bed and sat down, looking away from Dale.

"I stopped checking the voicemail because it hurt too

much. I loved being up in the woods. I loved bonding with Mom. And the wolf... the wolf needed it so much. But every time we would trek down to the ranger station to check the voicemail, I wanted to come running back to Seattle as fast as I could. Mom had to drag me back out to the wilderness a couple of times. I stopped because I knew you wanted me to be up there. If I'd known..."

Dale sniffled. "I didn't know how hard it would be," she whispered.

Ari turned and stretched out on the bed. She spooned Dale and kissed her shoulder. "Neither did I. I'm sorry."

"I'm sorry, too."

"You don't have anything to be sorry for. You kept everything going. I don't care if you worked at some copy place. You did it for us. For the life *we* built. Thank you."

Dale reached back and stroked Ari's hip. "I really am glad your trip went so well. You've never told me about how things went with you and your mom."

"It went great. We talked a lot. She..." Ari chuckled. "This might be a story for a less emotional time."

"No, I want to hear. What?"

"She slept with Milo."

Dale twisted to look at her. "Milo *Duncan?* But your mom is straight. And Milo's... Milo's *our* age. And oh my god *when?*"

Ari shrugged and laughed. "When she went to England, after wolf manoth."

"I thought she was going to hook up with the pack leader. Um. Bug?"

"Ant."

"Right."

Ari shrugged. "Apparently it didn't work out. Mom went to say goodbye to Milo and apologize for, you know, all the manipulation and everything. Next thing she knew, Milo had seduced her."

"Wow." Dale had fully turned to face Ari. She angled her

head to press her lips against the leather of Ari's collar. "I'm not mad at you anymore. You know that, right?"

"I know." She smelled Dale's hair. "But I still need to make it up to you."

"Okay." She sighed and settled against Ari's body. "We should go back out. Turn off the lights, finish with the groceries."

Ari said, "Mm-hmm."

"It's too early to go to bed."

Her voice fading, Ari agreed with a muttered, "Yeah."

Dale sighed again and closed her eyes.

In the morning, Ari waited until she was in the office to check her email. She'd received a message from Tiffany giving her the okay to start digging into Wilcox's client files, so she cracked open the file and began reading. He worked a lot of overnight security jobs, standing guard outside office parks and strip malls that were concerned about break-ins. There were seven of those in the past six months, some of them overlapping. Ari couldn't make the time tables work in her head and finally determined he had either hired someone to do the watching for him or had just skipped surveillance altogether. It would only be an issue if one of the businesses got robbed on a night he wasn't there, and he might've been willing to take the risk.

Dale came in with coffee and breakfast sandwiches while she was comparing the case files to the notes in the iPad, hoping for something that could crack the code. "Finding anything interesting?"

"I'm trying to decide if Wilcox was shady or dirty."

"Could be fifty percent of both to make up one entirely nasty whole."

Ari said, "Looking possible."

Dale dropped down onto the couch instead of going to her desk so they could ostensibly be having breakfast together. They had started the morning by making love to officially end the fight they'd had the night before. She was grateful Dale had been able to get out her anger; it gave Ari an idea of how far she had to go in order to truly make up for her absence. But first she had a pile of clients to go through. Wilcox had helpfully kept two files for every case. One included everything he'd managed to dig up on the case, while the other consisted of what she at first thought were diary entries. They contained his thoughts on the clients and various hassles he'd gone through in pursuit of the truth.

"Oh, God," Ari muttered when she realized what she was reading.

Dale looked up from her sausage biscuit. "What?"

"Wilcox was writing his memoirs."

"You're kidding me."

Ari cleared her throat and read from the file she had open. "'The rain came through the night before and scrubbed the whole city clean, but it didn't get into the cracks. Not the cracks way deep down, where the real scummy things lurked. I was in one of those cracks, still drunk from the night before so I wouldn't have a hangover for this job. Big mistake. But I could power through. It's what they paid me the big bucks to do.'"

Dale groaned. "I see it making a billion dollars as a summer blockbuster. They'd probably get Chris Pratt to play Wilcox."

Ari said, "And some twenty-year-old newcomer to play his love interest."

"And Charlize Theron to play the sexy rival private eye."

"Right," Ari laughed. "You just want Charlize Theron to be in everything after *Mad Max*."

"Hell yeah I do. Furiosa forever."

Ari scrolled through the pages. "From what I can tell, these are all based on real cases. I just have to dig through the noir nonsense to find the facts of the matter."

Dale said, "What are the facts of what you just read me?"

"He was on a stakeout and it was raining."

"And he was drunk. That rang true to me."

Ari snickered and skimmed the rest of the file. "It's helpful. He gave his impression of the client."

"So what are you looking for here? Someone who gaslighted Wilcox into pulling the trigger? Someone who was so pissed off that they manipulated him toward suicide?"

"I'm thinking about what he said when he called me. He said he had gotten himself into a situation and was trying to get out of it. I'm looking to see if there's anything like that in his files. A bribe or a con he was working, or maybe a partnership he entered into without thinking it through. I can dig through this lost masterpiece for anything that looks like that."

Dale had slid down onto her back, one leg bent with the other ankle resting on that knee. She stared at the ceiling and broke off a bit of her muffin. "Yeah." She tossed the muffin bit into her mouth. "If he was making deals with mobsters or something, he'd definitely put that down. Make himself look badass."

"Don't eat that way," Ari said. "You'll choke."

"I'll be fine."

"Dale. Please."

Dale rearranged herself so that she wasn't lying flat. "What are you going to do when you find them?"

"Whatever Wilcox got involved with, it had to be illegal. Right? My theory is that he had some criminal connections and it went bad. Remember how we first ran into him? He was working with that psychic. He would investigate the client and feed the psychic everything she needed to 'read from the spirits.' Wilcox probably had a lot of partners like that. One of them must have finally turned on him."

"So if you find out what it was, that means you'll be pissing off the same people who were threatening him."

Ari said, "I suppose."

Dale got up and went around to Ari's side of the desk. She bent down and cupped her face. "If I can't eat my breakfast lying down, then you can't be dismissive about this. Diana is involved in this. She's the one who brought you in. Maybe she did it in a roundabout way, but she's still part of it. Use her, puppy. I don't want to have to rescue you again."

"Maybe I like being the damsel in distress."

Dale's gaze didn't waver.

"I promise, Dale, I'll be safe."

"Good." She pecked Ari's nose and straightened. "I'm going to go get to work. See you for lunch?"

"I'll be here." She lowered her voice to a soft growl. "In my dark office with my feet up, cigar smoke curling around my head, thinkin' about killing another Jack Daniels... when she walked in with an offer I couldn't refuse."

"Do you want delivery or Mirch Masala?"

"I could do some Indian."

Dale blew her a kiss over her shoulder as she left. Ari looked around for something that could serve as a fedora and came up empty. She decided she was a pretty poor noir detective anyway and went back to reading Wilcox's notes. For all his shortcomings as a person, the man took beautiful notes. Ari was a little jealous of how easily she was able to arrange things into chronological order. She went back six months and slowly moved forward through the cases. Cheating husband, cheating wife, cheating wife, cheating husband. Ari really didn't tend to get many of those, and she was starting to think it was because Wilcox had the market cornered.

The phone rang in the outer office. She heard Dale answer, her voice a soothing murmur coming through the wall as she spoke to the person on the other end. After a moment, the intercom on Ari's phone lit up. She reached out and punched the button.

"Yes, Miss Frye?"

"Someone from Gilles Girard and Moreau is on line one."

Ari frowned at the wall as if Dale could see her through it. "The lawyers who tried to make me look like an idiot on the stand? Sure, I'll talk to them." She picked up the receiver and hit the button as it started to flash. "This is Ariadne Willow."

"Hello, Miss Willow. I'm not sure you remember me. Cecily Parrish."

Blonde ice queen who liked to play with security cameras. "You're the lady who thinks I'm a magician. Teleporting into sheds without leaving a trace."

A soft chuckle on the other end. "Magic doesn't exist, Miss Willow, and magicians are all just skillful liars. So in that respect, you're absolutely right. I do think you're a magician. I mean that with all due respect."

"Sure," Ari said. "It sounded like a compliment."

"I'd like to have a meeting with you sometime this week. Whenever is convenient for you. Wednesday would be preferable to me, unless you have a conflict."

Ari opened the calendar on her computer, but she knew it would be empty. Dale appeared in the doorway and lingered there. "I think I can find some time that afternoon."

"Shall we say two o'clock?"

"Sure." Ari typed in ICE QUEEN 2PM. "This isn't going to be about Nelson Cook's shed, is it? A true magician never reveals her secrets."

Another soft chuckle. Ari wondered if it was a recording Parrish kept on hand to mimic human emotions over the phone. "No, we're far too busy to dwell on past failures. We look to the future here, Miss Willow. I look forward to our meeting."

"Me too. See you then." She hung up.

"What was that about?"

"No idea. At first I thought she had figured out how I 'tricked' the security cameras, but she claimed it doesn't have anything to do with that."

Dale said, "You believe her?"

Ari shrugged. "I don't know why she would lie. She seemed like the sort of person who would be smug about it."

"True. And she was hot."

Ari hissed through her teeth. "So hot."

Dale chuckled and went back to her desk. Ari looked at the mark on her calendar and decided she didn't want to waste mental energy on trying to figure out what game Cecily Parrish was playing. She closed the page and went back to Wilcox's files.

CHAPTER SEVEN

ARI COULDN'T spend all her time staring at Wilcox's files trying to figure out his code. She was intrigued by the case, but it wasn't a paying job. The day after she got his iPad, she received an email hiring her to serve divorce papers. It took her most of the day to track down the husband and she waited until his friends had gone to the bar for another round to drop the bomb. No need to humiliate the guy, or at least that was how she felt until he splashed the dregs of his beer in her face.

Dale was furious when Ari told her what happened. "Since when is it shoot the messenger?"

"Since always," Ari said as she changed into a dry shirt. "The messenger is convenient, and you don't have to see them again. No consequences to throwing a drink in my face."

"That's because they don't know they could get their faces torn off if they're mean to you."

Ari said, "I'm not going to wolf out every time someone annoys me."

Dale said, "I wasn't talking about the wolf." She made

curled her fingers into talons and clawed at the air. Ari laughed and kissed her before they headed out to dinner.

She also accepted a custody case. A woman hired Ari to follow her husband to make sure he was being a responsible parent. Ari followed him for two days when the daughter wasn't present and determined he spent his time either at work or at home. On Monday he left work with a group of friends and spent a few hours at a bar attached to a bowling alley. He bowled a frame with one of his coworkers and arrived home just before ten o'clock. She was going to follow him again on the weekend when he had the daughter, but she was confident the case would have a happy ending.

On Wednesday she was following him to lunch when she received a text from Dale. "Appointment at GGM today at 2."

She smiled and sent a text back. "Thanks for the reminder. Lunch first?"

"You choose."

Ari slipped the phone into her pocket and continued watching the target. She wrote down that he seemed like someone who was just filling the hours, biding his time until the weekend. She hoped that theory held up when the daughter was actually in the picture. When he went back to work, Ari went to Potbelly and got two sandwiches to take back to the office. She got Dale the grilled chicken and cheddar and the Wreck Sandwich for herself. It was one of the days the wolf craved meat, so she gave it the most amount of meat one sandwich could provide: salami, roast beef, turkey, and ham.

Dale suggested stopping by the apartment to change into a more business-appropriate outfit, since the law offices were in a pretty upscale area downtown. Ari didn't know what to expect from her meeting with Cecily Parrish, but she didn't want to waste time changing clothes. Whatever awaited her would be met in comfortable clothes. Dale wished her luck and Ari headed out.

The address was actually in Belltown, and belonged to a

black-glass monolith surrounded on all sides by new construction. Ari was forced to park a block away and walk the remaining distance. A board in the building's lobby revealed Gilles Girard & Moreau was on the eighteenth floor. Ari had chosen to arrive at a slow time, so only one other person was waiting at the elevator bank. They stepped into the car together and the other woman pressed the button for forty. When she leaned back she let her eyes drift down Ari's outfit before snapping forward again with obvious distaste. Ari thought about letting it go, since she hadn't been dressing to impress anyone. But the way the woman held herself pissed her off.

"Nice suit," Ari said.

The woman said, "Thank you." She looked at Ari as if she wanted to return the compliment, but found nothing worth mentioning.

"No, I mean, it's really nice. Probably has an Italian label on it somewhere. What did something like that cost you? Four figures?" The woman didn't answer, but the corner of her mouth quirked. "Five? Wow." Ari whistled. "I don't have anything in my closet that cost that much. This shirt was three digits, but only if you count past the decimal."

The woman wet her lips to hide her smirk, shifting her weight.

"But what's the first thing you do when you get home? You toss all that shit on the bed and change into sweats. I know, I know, you need the outfit for work. So you pay highway robbery prices so you can look right at the job that pays you well enough to afford... the outfits you have to wear to get the job." She tilted her head to the side. "Seems like a vicious cycle."

The elevator doors opened and Ari stepped out, turning to face the woman. "The real difference between you and me?" She pinched the corners of her T-shirt to show off the logo. "I actually like this band."

The doors closed on the woman's sour expression. Ari turned and examined the waiting area she found herself in.

There was a large oak island directly in front of the elevators where three receptionists were speaking into headsets. GG&M was gilded on the wall behind them, and to either side of the backsplash were glass doors leading deeper into the building. Ari approached the desk and waited for the first woman to finish her call and direct her gaze on the new arrival.

"How may we help you?"

"Ariadne Willow. I have an appointment with Cecily Parrish."

"One moment please." She pressed a button and spoke softly into her headset. After a moment she focused on Ari again. "Someone will be with you in a moment."

The receptionist gestured at a three-sided square of padded seats in the corner. Ari sat next to a pile of magazines and chose one to thumb through. Her appointment was at two, and she'd arrived five minutes early. She made it through an issue of Time, not bothering to stop and read anything before moving on to some kind of car magazine. She knew jack-all about cars, but she had to reinforce her lesbian stereotype when she was in public. And the pictures were nice. The Economist was a last-ditch effort to fill some time, but even it wasn't long enough, apparently.

At a quarter past the hour, Ari looked through the glass to see if anyone was on their way to retrieve her. At twenty-five past, she had exhausted all the reading material that even halfway appealed to her and looked at her phone. No messages postponing the meeting. At two-thirty-one, Ari stood up and walked to the glass doors.

"Ma'am? You can't go in there unescorted."

"It's okay. I'm a detective. I'll find her."

She ignored the receptionist's further protests and continued on. To her left, along the exterior wall, was a row of identical offices. The center of the office space was taken up by a glass-walled conference room. A group of people in suits were huddled around a laptop at one end of the table and looked to be locked in a heated debate with whoever was on the screen. The walls were decorated with framed newspaper and magazine articles that mentioned the firm or its associates. There were also awards. She didn't know law offices got awards, but she supposed every profession had their own version of back-patting and gold stars.

Ari continued on, reading name placards until she reached the corner office and saw C. PARRISH - ASSOCIATE ATTORNEY. Ari knocked on the door even though the window next to the door revealed it was dark within. She went inside anyway.

The office was shaped vaguely like home plate, with the entrance at the wide end and Parrish's desk at the point. It was the polar opposite of Wilcox's office. Where he had gone for shabby and second-hand, Cecily had obviously spared no expense on her furnishings. Everything looked fresh off the showroom floor, shiny and untouched by every-day grime. The floor-to-ceiling windows flanked the desk like wings and let in the dismal gray light of the city. Ari walked to the south facing windows to see if Rainier was visible.

She had never been this high before, or if she had, there wasn't an opportunity to appreciate it like this. The city spread out toward the sea and the carpet of green hills, all sewn together under a fluffy gray quilt. She was grateful that, despite the weather, the mountain was indeed out. She knew that if the office faced the other direction she would probably have a view of the Space Needle. She preferred Rainier. Far below her, she could see the shape of the streets that made it look distressingly like a rat's maze, and a half dozen yellow cranes lurking over it all like vultures looking for their next meal.

Ari looked at the desk and saw three framed photographs next to the computer monitor: Parrish on a rock outcropping with Puget Sound behind her, a dog, and a third picture that Ari had to pick up and stare at before she determined it really was just a framed red square. No hidden image, no alternate hues that appeared when it was held in the light, just... red.

The office door opened and Cecily drifted in. "I was held up in court," she said, seemingly unperturbed by the fact Ari was snooping.

"Sure," Ari said, noticing the woman hadn't apologized. She walked around one end of the desk as Cecily came around the other. She'd left the lights off when she came in. Ari wondered if it had been a calculated move or if she just hadn't thought of it. The windows might have provided enough sunlight on a clear day, but with the clouds amassing overhead, it created a gloomy mood. Cecily took a seat and Ari did the same.

"Thank you for coming in, Miss Willow."

Ari nodded. "I was surprised you called, given our exchange in court."

Cecily shook her head. The light from the windows was enough to backlight her, casting shadows across the angles of her face. It also highlighted the low collar of her blouse. Her collarbone and cleavage almost seemed to be bronzed to draw the eye. Ari found her gaze drifting despite her best intentions.

"Water under the bridge," Cecily said, her voice low and throaty. "I don't harbor grudges. It's not as if the case was won or lost based on your testimony. Bygones."

"Good."

"I will admit I was intrigued by your involvement in the case. I was almost hoping you would explain how you pulled it off."

Ari said, "I thought our meeting wasn't going to be about that."

"It's not. You brought it up. And I suppose it is relevant in a tangential way. The security camera which you so masterfully avoided. Were you curious how we found it?"

"I assumed you have an in-house investigator."

Cecily nodded. "We did, until last week. Robert decided he wanted to move on to greener pastures in Chicago, leaving us shorthanded. I want to offer you the job."

Ari blinked in surprise. "Wow."

"You'd be paid a retainer, which we can negotiate, and you'd be given an office here in the building. You would work cases brought to you by the partners and associates."

"What about Bitches Investigations? What about Dale?"

Cecily said, "Your business would be moot at that point. You'd be working for us. As for Miss Frye, she could probably find other work at another office. We might even bring her onboard here. It would mean a steady paycheck for you. No more rinky-dink office--"

"Our office is fine, thanks."

"I'm sure you think so, Ariadne, but..." She gestured out the window.

Ari stood up. "Thanks for the offer, but I'm going to have to pass."

"Don't be so hasty."

"You're asking me to give up the agency I built from the ground up. The agency Dale sacrificed to keep afloat while I was away for a few weeks. Hell, you're asking me to cut loose the woman I love. I don't care how much the retainer is. I'm not going to sell my entire life just to come work in an office with a nice view."

"You would rather scrape by, hoping a client will walk through the door?"

"I'd rather remain my own boss."

Cecily stood up. "You would be your own boss. The only change would be your clientele. All of your clients would be here, all around you." She held her hands out to indicate the rest of the office. "The other lawyers. Me. In the course of bringing our cases to court, occasionally we need someone to gather evidence. It's much the same work you already do, only you'll be reporting your findings to us instead of some random Dan or Jan from Queen Anne."

"But without Dale."

"Again with Miss Frye. If we must find a place for her, I suppose she could work at the front desk."

Ari said, "That's not going to fly."

"Maybe you should ask her. It would relieve a great deal of stress. No more worrying about how you'd pay the bills or if you could afford rent that month. You could move out of that dreary basement where you're living now and buy a proper house."

Ari narrowed her eyes. "Just how much research have you done on us?"

"Plenty."

Ari chewed her lip and looked past Cecily to the window. If she took the offer, how long would it be before someone questioned her methods? Before someone realized she was doing impossible things in her investigations. This whole job offer could be a way to get Ari under a microscope to find out how she had gotten into the shed. Ari moved closer to the desk.

"If you think I'm the sort of person to manufacture evidence, why would you want me working here?"

"I don't think you manufactured anything."

"It's what you accused me of doing in court."

Cecily lifted one shoulder. "I was trying to win the case. I had unanswered questions. I didn't actually believe you were committing fraud or involved in a conspiracy with Mr. Nguyen. I just couldn't explain it. If I can't explain it, then the judge might question it as well. I only created reasonable doubt. That's all I have to do to win the case. Plant a seed of doubt and let the judge or jury do everything else. I really believe you're skilled at what you do. I looked into you after we found the security tape, just to confirm you weren't one of those shysters we so often run across. I don't mind taking down those jokers on the stand. I can tell you're something different. You actually care about your cases."

"I try to," Ari said.

Cecily gestured. "And that is why I offered you the job. We

have to hire someone to fill Robert's absence, and I would like it to be someone like you. I think I would really enjoy getting to know you."

Ari felt an uncomfortable prickle on the back of her neck. She stopped herself from reaching up to brush it away, but only just. The awkward silence hung in the air of the dark office and dragged out the seconds until Ari wanted to flee. Finally the tension was broken when Cecily broke eye contact.

"Feel free to take a few days to think about the offer. Talk it over with Miss Frye. I'll be here waiting for your response. But please be mindful of our situation. We do need someone as soon as possible and an expedient response would be appreciated."

"Right." Ari felt the meeting was over, but felt it would be anticlimactic to leave on that note. "What's up with the red picture?"

Cecily didn't look at it, instead resting her elbows on the desk and remaining locked on Ari. "How did you respond to it?"

"Confusion. Is it art?"

"No. It's not art." Her lips moved slightly, but not enough to call it a smile. "We'll be in touch, Miss Willow."

That was a better note to leave on. She turned, leaving the dark office for the fluorescent lighting of the main room. She felt like she had just crawled out of a deep cave and was once again standing on the surface. She took a deep breath, let it out, and started walking without looking back.

CHAPTER EIGHT

ARI SPENT the weekend watching a doting father spending time with his daughter. He picked her up after school on Friday and dropped her off Monday morning. Ari could tell he was trying to squeeze as much quality time into those two and a half days as possible. He took her to the aquarium and the library, they went on walks and stopped to watch an impromptu game of touch football. On Saturday, he skipped a Seahawks game to take her for ice cream. Considering the lanyards hanging from his rearview mirror and the cap he wore during the week, it was no small sacrifice. The girl was fed at a regular dinnertime, she had to turn off the TV at eight no matter how much she protested, and he always kissed her goodnight.

By Sunday night, Ari wanted to be adopted by him. She finished filling out her report for the wife and left to spend some quality time of her own with Dale. It was after business hours, so she knew Dale would already have headed home for the night. She still hadn't yet revealed Cecily Parrish's job offer. When Dale asked what the meeting was about, Ari had been honest. She said she wasn't ready to talk about it until she had some time to process, and Dale said she would be there when Ari needed a sounding board.

Taking the offer would be smart, in terms of business. It was a guaranteed paycheck and steady employment. But with all the work they'd done building the agency, and then everything Dale did to keep it alive while Ari was away, it seemed like giving up would be a slap in the face to her. Then again, Dale might appreciate the freedom to just be her girlfriend, not her employee and assistant. Sometimes she felt that Dale's entire life was built around making Ari's life easier, and she felt guilty about that. Taking the offer wouldn't be dumping Dale. It would be giving Dale the opportunity to do something different.

When Ari rounded the corner of the house, she saw Neka sitting on the back stoop with a joint. She waved off the smoke when she saw Ari and smiled apologetically.

"Sorry. You said you don't like the smell..."

"It's fine."

Neka said, "Do you and Dale have plans for Thanksgiving?"

Ari paused at the top of the stairs. "I don't think so. When is it?"

"This Thursday."

"Really? Wow." Ari pushed her hair back and shrugged. "I don't know. We usually just stay in and watch movies on Netflix or something."

Neka said, "Same here. I don't really celebrate. It's not a big Native American holiday, as you might imagine. But Simon's family is in Florida and he can't afford to fly out. So I thought I'd cook a nice dinner for him. I would really like it if you and Dale could be there, too."

"That's really nice of you. I'll mention it to Dale, see if she has anything planned. I'll let you know before Thursday."

"Okay. No rush. Either you'll show up or I'll leave some

leftovers at the bottom of the stairs."

Ari laughed. "That's win-win."

She said goodnight and continued downstairs. The living room was dark, but the bedroom light was on. "Dale? You here, sweetie?"

"I just got out of the shower."

Ari put down her things, plugging in the devices that needed to be charged. "You'll be happy to know that the case had a happy ending. The guy was actually earning his World's Greatest Dad mug. If he had one, which I assume he does." She laced her fingers together and stretched her arms over her head as she went into the bedroom. "Neka invited us to Thanksgiving dinner, if you want to go to... that."

Dale was wearing a knee-length skirt and a tennis shirt, her hair pulled back in an uncharacteristic ponytail. She sat on the edge of the bed and propped herself up in a way that thrust her chest out.

"Hey. You must be my roommate. This is a pretty cool dorm, huh?"

Ari was grinning through her confusion. "Uh. What?"

Dale held out one arm. "I'm Dale."

"Ariadne." She took Dale's hand and shook it.

"That's a cool name. So what is there to do around here for fun? I just came in from Pennsylvania. It's so strange being in the big city."

Ari laughed and sat on the bed next to her. "There's... there's some stuff to do." She reached up and brushed a stray hair from Dale's face. "But we could just stay in and get to know each other."

Dale's eyes widened. "Wow. I heard about this sort of thing happening in college, but I didn't think it would be this quick."

"What's going on?" Ari whispered.

Dale leaned in to whisper in Ari's ear. "I got Facebook friended by someone I slept with in college. It made me think about how fun those nights were." She nipped at Ari's ear. "Just two young people figuring things out together. I lost my virginity in a dorm room bed. And I was thinking it sucked that I never got to do that with you. And then I realized you never got to do that at all. So…" She kissed Ari's neck and leaned back. "So anyway," she said at her regular speaking volume. "I've never done this sort of thing before."

"That's okay." Ari moved her hand to Dale's leg and stroked her inner thigh. "If we're going to be roomies, we should get to know each other. Really… really well."

Dale smiled and pulled Ari to her as she fell back onto the mattress.

"You said something about Neka."

Ari opened her eyes. "While we were…?"

"No. Before that. When you came in."

They were lying in the middle of the mattress. Ari was naked, but Dale had taken the time to put her shirt back on. She had one leg hooked over Ari's hip and her cheek was against Ari's breast.

"Oh. She invited us to Thanksgiving dinner with her and Simon."

Dale said, "That's sweet of her. We're not going to your mother's?"

"I didn't think about it."

"After all the bonding you did with her up in the mountains?"

Ari said, "Yeah. I think we're all bonded out. Our relationship is better than it's ever been, but that's no reason to force a holiday on each other."

"She might not feel the same way."

"I'll call her and see what she's thinking before I give Neka an answer."

Dale nodded and kissed Ari's chest. "I'm tired. I think I'm going to fall asleep in a second. Do you need to get out from under me first? Are you going for a run?"

"Yeah, I think I will."

"Don't go until I'm asleep."

Ari nodded. They rearranged themselves, and Ari draped the blankets over Dale before stretching out next to her. Dale made a valiant effort to keep her eyes open, but soon she was drifting off.

"Will you call me?" Dale asked. "When you're ready to come home?"

Ari said, "If you want me to. But I hate waking you up."

"Otherwise I wake up alone," she said. "I mean. I still wake up alone. But then I get to come rescue you. And that makes it better."

"Oh. Okay." Ari kissed her between the eyebrows. "Go to sleep."

"If you insist, puppy..."

She stayed until she was sure Dale was unconscious, lightly dragging her fingers over the curve of her cheek and down across her bottom lip. Only when her eyes began moving behind the lashes did Ari finally ease out of bed and tiptoe out of the room. She stopped long enough to retrieve her robe, slipping it on as she went back out to the living room. Her phone had charged during their roleplay and she checked it for messages from Tiffany or any of her other clients. Nothing new, so she left the device on the table and went to the door.

The backyard looked empty. She opened the door a crack and listened; nothing but crickets chirping. She shed the robe and transformed, twisting her neck and shaking her arms like an athlete about to walk onto the field. She dropped to all fours and stretched her elongated spine, bared her teeth, and shouldered open the door. She sniffed the air and could tell that Neka had taken her pot inside at least half an hour ago. Confident she wouldn't be seen, Ari ascended the stairs and loped across the lawn with her head low.

She kept close to the lawns while she was still in the neighborhood. Most were shaded by trees or closed in by fences or decorate rock walls, so it would be easy for her to duck out of sight if she spotted any pedestrians or slow-moving cars. She normally waited until later to go out so she wouldn't have to deal with traffic, but the neighborhood was pretty slow. She had a sixth sense about what animal control's headlights looked like, so she took extra care to avoid those.

Ari ran without a destination in mind, turning west when she reached Yesler because that was where the wolf wanted to go. Her human mind slipped a little, losing details like street names and distances. The wolf had different landmarks to keep track of where she was. The apartment building that had been designed to look like a castle; the streetcar tracks; the barbeque place and the little coffee shack, both of which still smelled of their respective specialties even at this late hour.

When she reached the overpass she stopped on the pedestrian sidewalk to watch the cars streaming by underneath. Downtown sprung up to the north in all shining lights and gleaming towers. Ari listened to the hum of cars and remembered the last time she'd heard that sound. She turned around and backtracked until she found a street that took her north. She followed the curve of Eighth Avenue to Ninth, then went down James Street to Seventh Avenue. It didn't dawn on her that she was using the actual street names instead of landmarks until she was already running along the off-ramp. The wolf had retreated and given back control to her analytical mind.

Sorry, babe, she said to the wolf. *I'll give you a solid run another night, I promise.*

Her mother had taught her how to treat the wolf as a true partner. More than just equals, but another soul sharing her body. Letting the wolf run free was vital to the well-being of them both. Ari had been selfish considering herself a human woman who sometimes ran on four legs. She was a woman, yes, but she was also a wolf. That wolf had needs of its own, and it was up to Ari to see they were met.

She wended her way through the maze of streets next to the interstate until she finally found herself back outside Clark Wilcox's condo. The wolf had fewer problems with the angle of the street than she'd had on two legs, even though she had just run close to two miles. She tilted her head back and looked up at the windows. Over half of them were lit. After a few minutes of searching, she spotted the one that would look into Wilcox's apartment.

The light was on.

There were several possibilities. Wilcox could have been the type to have his lights on timers to dissuade criminals. In this neighborhood, that would be a smart security measure. Or, and this was the theory she found more likely, Tom and his anonymous friend from the other day had come back. If not them, someone else. Had they not heard about Wilcox's death? Maybe they knew and were taking the opportunity to tear apart his place looking for the iPad. Leaving the light on was a good indication they weren't worried about being caught.

Ari moved to the sidewalk and walked along the row of parked cars, looking for the blue truck she had seen earlier. She hoped it would be the same guys as before, but it seemed her luck wasn't holding out. None of the cars seemed familiar, and she hadn't gotten a good enough sniff of Tom and the other guy to identify him. So she sat and waited, she watched the apartment light, she paced, and finally her patience paid off.

The light switched off, and close to five minutes later a trio of men came out of the building. One of them was Tom, but Ari didn't recognize the other two. One of the new men was carrying a plastic garbage bag that looked heavy judging by how he was listing to that side. The man in the lead was carrying a shock stick. He tossed the weapon into the back of a white truck.

"Waste of time. Know what I had to go through to get that thing?"

"I told you, last time there was a fucking dog," Tom said.

"Huge thing. It looked like a wolf. Mikey saw it, too. Ask him when we get back, and he'll tell you there was a dog."

The men got into the truck with their bag of loot. A nearby streetlight illuminated the driver's side door as it swung open, and Ari saw a logo she didn't recognize over a name written in a font too small for her to read. The shock stick was vaguely terrifying. She was glad she hadn't decided to stake out the apartment. They may have brought it just as insurance, but she knew what happened when men like that had the chance to hurt an animal.

"Hey, mutt! Come over here! C'mere, mutt!"

It brought on the memory of one of the most terrifying moments of her life, surrounded by a group of teenagers who had a seemingly endless supply of rocks. She'd been distracted and hadn't heard them coming up behind her. Then she was cornered. Every time she tried to fight back, one of the other kids threw a rock and hit her in the shoulder or it glanced off her head. She was sure she was going to die there. And then...

"Get back, you goddamn creeps!"

She had come running down an incline, her coat flapping behind her as she swung a PVC pipe. She had dropped the bag of fast food she'd been carrying so she could wield the weapon with both hands. The kids saw her coming, saw the lack of fear in her expression, and chose to flee. She continued screaming insults at them, cursing them out as they retreated. She stood between them and Ari, shoulders heaving with her breath as she watched to make sure they weren't going to circle around and come after her. When they were finally gone, she dropped the pipe and turned to face Ari.

"You poor thing. Don't worry. I'm not going to hurt you."

She sacrificed the patty of her cheeseburger to gain Ari's trust, then tenderly examined the wounds on her head. Then she cupped Ari's face in her hands and they locked eyes.

That was the day Ariadne met Dale. The most terrifying moment of her life had morphed into the moment her entire life changed for the better.

When the memory faded she realized she was running down a street she couldn't identify. The wolf had taken advantage of her distraction to get underway again.

Okay, wolfie, she thought, *you're in control. Just get me to a park with a stash when you're ready to go home.*

The wolf put on an extra burst of speed and Ari left the animal side of her brain take over for a while.

CHAPTER NINE

LIKE A sleepwalker suddenly waking up, or a commuter who pulled into her driveway without remembering the drive home, Ariadne stumbled on the grassy incline and grabbed a tree to catch her fall. The wolf had started the transformation while still in motion. It forced her off all fours and onto two human legs, which affected her balance and made her look like she was falling horizontally. She balanced herself against the tree and swayed briefly to catch her breath and regain her bearings. She could see and smell Puget Sound, and judging by her position along its edge, she guessed she was on the south side of the Queen Anne greenbelt.

"Boy, when I let you off the leash, you really go crazy."

She pushed through the underbrush, aware that her legs and arms had already been scraped up getting this far into the wilderness. She had to go back up toward the road to get her bearings before she could plot a course for the stash Dale had left her. When had they left the bag in the greenbelt? It had to have been over eight months ago. When she knew what road she was on, she turned around and went back through the underbrush. The wolf was good at making sure it transformed somewhere close by the burial site, saving her the trouble of wandering around Seattle's parks in the nude.

Her feet slipped in mud and she stepped on more than a few twigs and stones, hissing every time the sharp end of a branch dragged across a thigh or snapped against her biceps. Dale had chosen a bush that was in the very edges of a nearby streetlight's reach, so as Ari approached it looked almost as if the bush itself was aglow from within. She crouched and reached under the leaves and branches, scooping away the compost that had accumulated over the hump of the duffel bag so she could pull it out.

"Sweetheart..."

Ari froze and looked over her shoulder. The man looked like he was seven feet tall. He was wearing so many jackets and shirts that his body looked like a boulder, his face obscured by a beard and the brim of his hat. He was holding up both hands with the fingers splayed, his weight on the heels of his feet so he was angled away from her.

"Sweetheart, are you okay? Did somethin' happen to you?"

It was a reasonable question to ask a naked woman in the middle of a city park. "I'm fine," Ari said. "I promise." She pulled the duffel bag out and showed it to him. "I'm just getting my clothes."

He sighed. "It's not smart. I know it sounds fun, but you can't be streaking. It's too dangerous." He looked toward the street. "Where are your friends?"

"They're on their way," Ari said, not willing to tell this apparently-harmless man she was alone. "I was the first one to get here. I won."

"You got lucky," the man said. "Don't let me catch you out here again, okay?"

Ari nodded. "I promise. Sorry."

He shook his head and continued on his way. Ari unzipped the duffel bag, ears perked for the sound of his return. She found a T-shirt, sweatpants, underwear, socks and shoes, and money for a payphone if she couldn't find any all-night places willing to let her use the phone. It hadn't been that long since the stashes were a necessity, but she couldn't help but feel nostalgic about the process. She started to put the stash back where she'd found it but reconsidered. She wanted to give the bag to the homeless man who'd tried to help her, but she thought it might do more harm than good. Giving him a duffel bag of clothes he could trade for things he really needed might be a nice idea in theory, but if anyone found a seven-foot homeless man with a bag full of women's clothing, they would jump to awful conclusions.

She put the bag into the bush and stood up. Going to the east would put her in a residential area, so she went south. She passed the encampments of homeless in pop-up tents and sleeping bags, and she waved to them as she moved through their territory. She'd been one of them a long time ago, running from her mother and the horrible thing that had been done to her as a baby. She'd lived in parks and under overpasses and pushed her way between a stand of trees to find her way blocked by a chain-link fence. She sighed, climbed over, and walked across the street to an all-night laundromat.

Inside was a man in a beaten-up wool jacket and a knit cap who looked like he'd be headed to the encampment when his clothes were done. Ari took the money from the stash and approached him cautiously. He tensed away from her, but she held up the bills.

"Hey. Sorry. Change for the phone?"

"Uh..." His eyes moved toward the change machine.

"I just need the fifty cents. You can keep the rest."

He hesitated but eventually nodded. She handed him the bills, took the coins, and went to the trio of phones at the far end of the store. She dialed Dale's number and slumped against the wall. Memories leaked their way back into her mind, fading in from the wolf as she listened to the phone ring. She saw flashes of light and heard loud, growling sounds of other animals and pedestrians as she raced by them in the dark. She remembered seeing the men leave Wilcox's apartment as the phone was answered mid-ring.

"Hi... puppy?"

"Hey. I need you."

Dale chuckled quietly. "Tell me where you are."

Ari looked out the window and tried to remember the name of the street. "Queen Anne, southeast of the greenbelt. By the train tracks. All-night laundromat..."

"I know it." Ari heard the mattress squeak and suddenly felt very homesick. It reminded her of just how much it had hurt to be away from Dale for three full months. Their home, their life, had been waiting for her, and it took everything she had not to go running. She closed her eyes and smiled at the fact she would be home with Dale very soon.

"Damn, that's going to take me a minute, puppy."

"Sorry. I let the wolf take over and I guess she wanted to stretch out a bit."

Dale said, "It's okay. I'll be there as soon as I can."

"I'll be waiting."

She hung up and went to wait in the chairs lining the front windows. The homeless man had just finished loading the dryer and shut the door with a slam. He looked at Ari, averted his gaze, keeping himself busy by folding the clothes that were already dry. After a moment he apparently decided the silence was too awkward to continue.

"You ain't got a load?"

"No, I just... I'm waiting for a ride."

He bobbed his head. "Just... any time I see a girl in sweats and a T-shirt in a laundromat, it's 'cause their good stuff is all dirty."

Ari smiled. "You have a point there." She looked outside, at the marquees and signs that were standing dark at this time of night. She thought back to the logo she'd seen on the side of the truck outside Wilcox's condo. "Hey, can I ask you a question?" He shrugged and motioned for her to go ahead. "I saw a logo tonight that I can't identify. Maybe you've seen it. It looks like..." She held up her hands and tried to frame it. "A hollow square with three sides, open on top, and the inside of the square is kind of poofy."

He frowned and stuck his lip out, shaking his head slowly. Then his eyes widened. "Oh wait. Could it have been..." He turned in profile and flexed, forming one side of the square with his forearm.

"Yes! That was it."

"The Flex," he said. "It's a gym over in Westlake. It's like, um, muscle laundering."

"Muscle laundering? What does that mean?"

"You know how when you launder money, you gotta have an explanation for where it came from? In case anyone gets suspicious? Well, if you're just shooting up steroids, people are gonna wonder why you never go to a gym. So you go to the gym and juice up. Then you... I don't know... punch a bag or do jumping jacks for a half hour, then you go home. Muscle laundering."

Ari laughed. "I like that. Sounds like the right sort of place, too."

"Happy I could help."

"When my ride gets here, I'll give you a little cash for the info."

He waved her off. "You already gave me enough."

"It's not charity. I'm a private investigator. We pay informants for information like that."

He looked suspicious, but he didn't protest further. Ari leaned back and watched the street until Dale's car appeared. She promised her new friend she'd be right back and hurried outside. Dale's hair was pinned back and she was wearing glasses instead of her contacts. When she rolled down the window, Ari saw that she had put on a sweater over a long T-shirt.

"Do you have twenty bucks?"

"Why?"

"Informant."

Dale opened the console.

"And some business cards."

Dale handed everything over. Ari went back inside and handed over the money and the cards. "Thanks for the help. If you ever want to earn a little extra, come on by. Even if it's just watching an apartment building for a few hours..."

He took the money and looked at one of the cards. "Bitches?!" He laughed. "Well, that's a hell of a name."

"The people we've gone up against would testify to its accuracy. I'm Ariadne."

"Brad."

She shook his hand. "It's good to meet you, Brad. I hope to hear from you soon. Feel free to pass those around to anyone you think might be interested."

He nodded and tucked the cards into a pocket of his coat. Ari went back outside and got into Dale's car.

"New friend?" Dale asked as she pulled out of the lot.

"New employee, maybe. The stash was hidden near one of the encampments they have up here. I ran into another homeless guy, and he warned me about running around town naked."

Dale said, "It's good advice for anybody, really."

Ari nodded and reached across the seat to squeeze Dale's thigh. "Thanks for coming to get me."

"Thanks for calling. I know you think it's a burden, and maybe it is. I don't know. I just know that I'm used to it. And I miss it when it doesn't happen. I got three months of full-night sleeps, and I prefer this without a doubt."

"Okay. I'll keep that in mind."

"Although... it's incredibly dangerous for you. Running around naked, getting seen by men. Yeah, these two were nice, but what if you'd met up with one of the bad ones?"

Ari wanted to defend the homeless, but she had to admit that for every down-on-his-luck good guy, there were also drug addicts and criminals looking for their next score or an easy victim.

"How about this? I won't call you every time I run just to keep myself safe. But maybe once a week, I'll make it a point to give you a call."

Dale said, "I can live with that."

"Since we're on this side of town anyway, can we make a quick stop? I want to find a gym in Westlake that might be connected to Clark Wilcox's death."

Ari looked up the gym's address on her phone as she explained to Dale what she had seen while in wolf form. It was slightly out of their way, north of the marina, but Dale said she didn't mind. She slowed when Ari pointed out the logo she'd seen on the side of the truck. Dale pulled over in a place Ari could see the front of the gym as well as the parking lot next to the building. The frosted glass block window next to the door was dark, but the truck she'd seen earlier was in the parking lot.

"Want to go take a look?" Dale asked.

Ari shook her head. "I don't know what I'd be walking into. I want to play it safe, scope it out in the daytime first. Okay. Let's go home."

Dale pulled away again. "What do you think you're going to find there?"

"The guys at Wilcox's place didn't strike me as the ones in charge. Brad told me this place was a muscle laundry operation." She explained the term and Dale laughed. "I think whoever Wilcox was in trouble with hired some people from this place to make Wilcox cooperate. If I can find out who they are, maybe I can get a name."

"Sounds like a plan." She sighed. "I still don't understand why you're going through all this trouble for Clark Wilcox. The guy was so scummy, Ariadne."

"Yeah, he was. And he was completely alone. I know that if anything happened to me, I'd have you to find out what happened. You and Diana and Mom. Milo would probably show up to lend a hand, if she could. Wilcox didn't have anyone like that."

Dale said, "No parents or siblings?"

"I was leaving that up to the real cops. Might be time to check in with Diana and see where they are with the case."

"Something to do tomorrow, then." Dale looked over and saw Ari's eyelids were getting heavy. "Go to sleep, puppy. I'll get you home."

Ari smiled drowsily. "You always do."

She closed her eyes on the sight of the Space Needle lit up, a shining beacon of the future built two decades before she was born and still shining out over the Sound.

Chapter Ten

Ari was a frequent enough guest at the station that the desk sergeant let her go up without making her wait for Diana to come down and get her. One of the detectives told her Diana was running around somewhere nearby and pointed her to the right desk. Ari took a seat next to the desk and twisted to look at the personal items clustered around the computer monitor. There was a small snow globe, a single bishop from a chess set, and a framed photograph of Diana with a blonde Ari assumed was Diana's wife, Lucy. They were standing on a rock with the Snoqualmie Falls behind them. Ari picked up the picture and examined Lucy.

Diana came up from behind her. "That's Lulu."

"Lulu?"

"Sorry. I slipped. You should never call her that."

Ari smiled and put the picture back. "She's gorgeous."

"Mm-hmm." Diana straightened the picture, trying to act professional but unable to keep the emotion from her face. "So what brings you all the way down here, Ari?"

"Clark Wilcox. I wanted to know where you were on his case."

Diana frowned and rested her elbows on the edge of the desk. "There is no Clark Wilcox case. Medical examiner confirmed it was suicide. Did someone hire you to prove otherwise?"

"No," Ari said. "But I knew him, Diana. The guy was not the sort of person to just end things that way. He would never admit defeat."

Diana pressed her lips together and sat up straighter. "When I was in college, I had a girlfriend. She was bright, sunny, always a smile for everyone she met. Everyone loved her. Straight-As. She had a job that paid fairly well. Good enough for a college student, anyway. Then one night she took a bunch of pills and never woke up. The only thing she left behind to explain why was a note on the back of a binder she always carried with her. 'The End.' Two words, Ari. That was all the explanation anyone got. You and I have jobs where we try to explain what's going on in people's heads, so we know how rare it is to actually get an answer."

Ari nodded absently, then sighed and shook her head. "There has to be an answer here. There's too much evidence that something was going on. Something led to this."

"What have you found?"

"Some guys broke into Wilcox's apartment on at least two occasions. They were looking for something. The second time, they left with a trash bag. I don't know who they are, but I have a lead. I'm going to check it out later. Were you able to get in touch with his family?"

Diana reached out and tapped on her keyboard. "I reached out, but I didn't find anything. Parents are long gone, only child. He had an ex-wife who sounded like she was going to turn it into a national holiday." She turned the monitor so Ari could see the file, but Ari didn't try to read it. "You were the last person who spoke to him. You said he was maudlin. Depressed.

Maybe the fact he didn't have anyone finally got to be too much. Maybe all the shitty things he did in his job got to be too much. I think it's great that you're going to all this trouble to find out why, but to be completely honest, I don't know why you're bothering."

Ari started to give a flippant answer, but when she spoke something else came out. "Because I nearly killed myself."

Diana stared at her. "When?"

"Earlier this year. Before the summer. You know all about my... pain issues." Diana nodded. "They were horrible. And I was looking at a whole lot of bad options. I was looking at paralysis in just a couple of years. And that would've made Dale my caregiver. I didn't want to do that to her. And the cure... the cure had a possibility of death, too. I was terrified of even trying it. So one night when I couldn't hold the wolf back any more, I transformed knowing that going back to human form would be hell. I knew I'd spend the morning in agony, and Dale would have to take care of me. So when I went out that night, I ran to Montlake Bridge and watched the cars go by. I kept telling myself if there was a truck big enough, going fast enough, I would just step into the road and let it happen."

Diana looked horrified. "Have you talked to Dale about this?"

"No. No, I pretty much pretended it never happened."

"Why did you... I mean, at what point did you walk away and decide to keep the pain?"

Ari shrugged and looked down at her hands. "I thought about Dale. Either way, I was going to cause her grief. If I hung in there, at least she could have a chance to say goodbye."

Diana said, "Maybe that's the only difference. Clark Wilcox didn't have someone like that to bring him back from the brink. He took out the gun and there was nothing to talk him out of pulling the trigger." She reached out and put her hand on Ari's wrist. "I think you took this case for the right reasons, but I also think it's time for you to stop."

"What about his secretary? Tiffany. She deserves to know."

"I agree. But that's not on you. That's on Wilcox for not knowing how much she cared. You don't have to beat yourself up trying to find answers that might not be there."

Ari said, "I can't just give up."

"Okay." Diana took her hand back. "In that case, just be careful. And tell Dale about what happened. She deserves to know what was going on."

"You're right." She took a deep breath and knocked her knuckles on the desk. "Okay. I'm going to do whatever I can do. Thanks for the therapy session."

"My pleasure." When Ari stood, Diana added, "Do you have Thanksgiving plans?"

Ari said, "Maybe. We got an invite. Why?"

"I thought if you and Dale were just staying in, you could come over. Lucy comes from a big family, so she likes to cook a ton of food even when it's just us. If you're there, it'll be two fewer slices of pecan pie in the fridge for me to eat over the weekend. Besides, it would be nice for you to meet Lucy. She's dying to meet you."

"Oh. Does she know about...?" Ari made a growling face.

"Not that. She knows we used to go out, she knows you're a private investigator, but the other thing... no. I didn't want her to think I was crazy. Also, it wasn't my secret to tell."

Ari said, "Okay. I'll talk about it with Dale."

"Let me know. We'll have enough food for an army whether you're there or not, so there isn't a deadline."

"Thanks. I'll let you know by Wednesday, just to be polite."

Diana smiled. "Wow, Ariadne Willow giving the courtesy call. Long way from the woman I kept picking up on public nudity charges."

Ari laughed. "I'm all grown up now. I'm better at hiding my indecency."

On the walk back to her car, she thought about the case and the possibility she was only in it for herself. She didn't care about Wilcox's memory. It would be nice to give Tiffany some closure, but was it worth the amount of time she was spending? She got to her car and sat behind the wheel for a long minute as she weighed the pros and cons.

If a "dog" had been hit on the Montlake Bridge, would it even be reported on? Would there have been a story for Dale to find even if she scoured every news broadcast? More likely Animal Control would get a call, they'd come out to remove the remains, and her body would be incinerated. She didn't think Animal Control would bother to bury roadkill. She flinched at using that word, at thinking of herself in such horrible terms, but she'd been one leap away from making it a reality. Dale would only have known that she went out for a run one night and never came back.

She would've hoped someone would have been there to unearth the truth for Dale. Even a heartbreaking answer was better than never knowing. In Wilcox's case, it was obvious he'd done himself in. But one day someone might come forward. An illegitimate child, a long-lost brother, someone who would care. By that time the trail would be cold. And she had to admit that she was curious about Mike and Tom and the other muscleheads who had cleaned out Wilcox's apartment. What were they up to? What was their interest?

Her motivation restored, she drove back to the gym. Now that it was official business hours, there were fewer places for her to park. She found a place at the far end of the lot, secluded enough for her to do a near-strip tease. She had dressed with a set of workout clothes under her normal street outfit just in case she decided to see what the inside of the gym looked like. Now in a tank top over a sports bra and leggings, she retrieved her bag from the backseat and headed for the entrance.

Part of her was worried about running into one of the men from Wilcox's apartment. At least one of them had seen her there and at the office, so he would know she was connected to him. She could have had Dale go instead, but she wasn't going to send Dale into a potentially volatile situation. She would just have to hope they either weren't there or didn't make the connection.

The building was drab cinderblock painted black, with only the sign to advertise it was open for business. Some gyms went with flash and flair to draw people in, while others had the distinct air of a boys' club. Directly inside the front door was a tall counter wallpapered with advertisements for boxing matches, exhibitions, weight-loss and muscle-building supplements, and all sorts of ephemera Ari didn't bother to catalogue. She was surprised to see a woman behind the counter, one sneakered foot up on the counter so she could prop up her clipboard against the thigh. She smiled as Ari entered and sat up straighter.

"Hey, good morning and healthy morning. I'm Patsy. Are you an old friend or starting on a new journey?" She tilted her head and ran her eyes down Ari's body. "Although from the looks of you, I'd say this isn't your first time in a gym."

Ari said, "Actually I don't get out to them much. I like to jog. In nature."

Patsy bobbed her head. "Cool, cool, I get it, that's cool. So are you looking for a new home?"

"Maybe. I thought I'd give it a shot."

Patsy slipped off her chair. "Well, great! Let me show you around. What's your name?"

"Ariadne."

"Oh, I like that name. Do you go by Aria?"

"Yeah." Sure, why not.

Patsy grinned and winked. "Like the little girl with the sword on that show. She's such a badass."

"Yeah," Ari said again, at a loss for any other response.

"Okay! Let's get to it, Aria."

Ari stepped around the counter and followed Patsy into the main room. Three boxing rings took up the majority of the space with more traditional exercise stations shoved back against the walls. Ari was surprised to see a handful of women using the machines. Patsy led her toward a recumbent bicycle and gestured for her to get on.

"More women here than I would have expected."

"Sure are!" Patsy said, resting her hand on the monitor that was mounted between the pedals. She winked and lowered her voice. "There are male members, if you're looking for a little eye candy. They tend to come in and use the speedbags or the boxing ring mostly. They get nice and sweaty, bouncing around all shirtless in the ring. It's like a free show." She wet her lips and chuckled throatily. "Sorry. I'm not usually this big of a horn dog..."

Ari smiled. "No problem. It's not really appealing to me, though, to be honest. I have a girlfriend."

"Oh! Okay." Patsy bobbed her head again and looked down at the pedals. "Why don't you get a feel for the machine? Just a quick little test run."

Ari began pedaling. "You wouldn't happen to know a guy named Clark Wilcox, do you? I heard he comes in here from time to time."

Patsy stuck out her bottom lip as she considered the question, eyes still on Ari's feet. "The name doesn't ring a bell. The muscle tone on your legs is outstanding. You said you just go jogging...? Where, in the parks? On the trails? How far?"

Ari said, "Oh, you know. Nowhere specific. Sometimes I lose my head and go for ten miles without thinking about it."

"Well, it's working for you. Wow." She reached down and touched Ari's calf. "Sorry to be handsy."

Ari said, "That's all right." Patsy's hand began to move up, grazing past her knee to her calf. "Uh. That isn't."

Patsy jerked her hand back. "Wow. That's really inappropriate. I'm sorry. I don't even like... uh." She reached up and scratched behind her ear. "I'm really sorry. That sort of stuff won't be an issue here, I promise. You can work out in peace."

Ari could tell Patsy was sincerely thrown by her behavior, so she didn't feel like pushing it. Still, she wished she had worn a hoodie or something to cover her tank top. She also didn't want Patsy to think she'd scared her away, so she gestured toward the speedbags. "Do you have many women who use the rings, or are those just for the guys?"

"We have some ladies who spar." Patsy's spiel was more subdued now, but she quickly found her rhythm again. "We even have some who have gone on to be MMA fighters."

"Very cool."

A door on the back wall opened and Ari turned toward the sound. As two men came out, Patsy followed her gaze. "Oh, our locker rooms are fully equipped. Shower, sauna, the works~"

She continued on, but Ari was watching the men. All the men she'd seen at Wilcox's building moved in a cluster toward the front entrance. None of them looked toward her; they all looked pissed off and tired.

Patsy noticed where her attention had wandered. "Oh. The Creep Cousins."

Ari said, "Say what?"

"Don't worry about them. They're here maybe half an hour every other day. They don't use the machines much. They just kind of hang around in the common areas and the locker rooms. I don't want you to get the wrong idea about this place. It's not... there aren't drugs all over the place."

Ari smiled reassuringly. "Patsy, you've been great. Really you have. The Creep Cousins and the wandering hand? I understand. I just have to go."

"Oh. Okay. Well, I hope you consider coming back sometime. Bring your girlfriend. I promise no more funny business."

"Okay."

Ari quickly freed herself from the girl and hurried outside. The Creep Cousins - at least she now had a great collective name for the group - were gathered around one of the trucks in the parking lot. Ari fished a baseball cap from her bag and pulled it on. She tugged the brim down over her face as she walked past them. At least one of the Cousins knew what her face looked like, and she didn't want to risk it.

"Hey!"

She kept walking.

"Honey, don't waste your money on this place. You are *done*. Ow!"

Ari kept her head down until she was back at her car. She pulled out of the spot, turned south out of the lot, and pulled to the side of the road. She could still see the entrance of the gym's parking lot and waited patiently until an unmarked van pulled out of the lot. There were a lot of uses for unmarked vans, but given that she could see one of the Cousins behind the wheel, she wasn't going to give this one the benefit of the doubt.

She waited until he was almost to the intersection before she pulled out and began to follow him.

CHAPTER ELEVEN

THE CREEP Cousins drove south through downtown. She got an uncomfortable feeling of someone walking over her grave as she followed them past the spot where she and Dale had been caught in a gunfight with a group of hunters earlier that year. Ari had been undercover to find the leaders of wolf manoth, so she and Dale had actually been on opposite sides of that altercation. The feeling of familiarity grew when the van slowed behind the Westin Hotel to let out two of its passengers. The men began to walk while the van continued forward.

Ari was forced to choose between who to follow, and she chose the men on foot on the assumption they would be easier to keep track of. She parked behind a maintenance truck and got out, jogging to catch up with them. They checked traffic and crossed the street toward McGraw Square. Ari followed, waving an apology to the driver she had just jumped out in front of, and kept her eyes locked on the men. In her periphery, she spotted the van again. It had driven around the corner and was now idling at the curb in front of Bartell Drugs. Ari noticed a

FOR LEASE sign on the third floor where Orarian had been located before she and Milo's pack had wiped it out, but she couldn't waste her focus on that.

The square was crowded with tourists, pedestrians, and patrons of the three food carts currently doing business on the south side, near the monorail tracks. The two Creeps on foot were using one of the carts as cover. The van was waiting ahead of them. Ari found a place between the two spots and saw a group of college-age women seated at a table. It took her a moment to recognize one of the women as Tiffany Knight, Wilcox's secretary. The walking Creeps started toward her.

"Ah, shit," Ari muttered.

She ran across the square on an intercept course. They were closer to Tiffany than she was, so she couldn't grab her first. She was almost on top of them before Creep Number One - whom she now recognized as Mike - saw her coming. He turned toward her and she threw herself at him. She grabbed him around the waist in the hopes her momentum would be enough to tackle him. He rocked on his heels but Ari might as well have tried to tackle the statue of John McGraw. She hit him and immediately dropped to the ground, landing flat on her back.

"Hey, this is the chick who was hanging around Wilcox's place," she heard one of them say.

Mike bent down to grab her, putting all of his weight on his right foot. Ari kicked out at that ankle and this time he did fall, collapsing to the side with a howl of pain. His companion reached down and grabbed Ari's jacket to haul her up. She drove her elbow into his gut to make him let go, then swung her fist up into his face. He grabbed his nose and she kicked Mike's arms out from under him as he tried to get up.

"Oh, stupid bitch!" he grunted as he fell flat again.

Ari fled, knowing she couldn't hold her own in a fight against them for long. Tiffany and her group of friends were already watching the altercation, and Tiffany stood up when she recognized who was involved.

"Ariadne?"

"Run! This way." She grabbed Tiffany's arm as she passed, guiding her in a direction that would avoid both the van and the pedestrian Creeps. If it was a movie, there would have been a streetcar passing that they could jump onboard and escape, but the tracks were empty. She heard the screech of tires and a blaring car horn as the van tried to join the chase. Tiffany stumbled but Ari managed to keep her upright as she looked for an escape route.

She was close to giving up when the air was filled with sirens. Ari turned and saw one of the girls Tiffany had been sitting with had her phone out, and two squad cars had responded to her call for help. Mike and Creep Number Two were running for the van, their kidnapping attempt aborted. When the police swarmed toward Ari, Tiffany waved them in the right direction, but the van was already around the corner and out of sight.

"She's helping me! They were trying to... to... oh, god, were they going to kidnap me?" She looked at Ari. "Was I seriously just almost kidnapped?"

Ari put a hand on her shoulder. "You're okay now. Has anyone been following you? Maybe watching your house?"

"I've been staying with a friend." The adrenaline was starting to wear off and Tiffany was shaking. "If you hadn't been here... holy shit. Thank you."

"I'm sorry they got so close."

One of the uniformed officers had reached them. "Does someone want to explain what's happening here?"

"I'm Ariadne Willow. I'm a private investigator. I had reason to believe the men in that van intended to kidnap Miss Knight."

Tiffany said, "She's been helping me since my boss killed himself."

The cop held up his hands to stop them. "Okay. Let's just

sit down and get your statements."

"I don't want to leave Ariadne," Tiffany said, grabbing onto Ari's shirt.

"It's okay. I think you'll be safer with him than with me."

Tiffany still seemed reluctant, but then she grabbed Ari's face and kissed her hard on the mouth. Ari recoiled, but Tiffany didn't seem to notice.

"Thank you," Tiffany said, letting the officer guide her away.

"Uh. Yeah." She frowned and waited until Tiffany's back was turned before she wiped her sleeve across her mouth. She'd never had problems attracting women, but it was starting to get ridiculous.

Another officer took Ari's statement, asking her to go all the way back to Clark Wilcox's suicide to explain her presence there. She told them the guys from the van could probably be found at the Flex. When they finished, Ari told him to check with Detective Macallan to back everything up and hoped Diana wouldn't be too irritated at being pulled in. When the police finally left, Tiffany sheepishly approached Ari.

"Hey. Sorry about the kiss earlier. Adrenaline... I guess?" She averted her eyes. "I was just really grateful you were there."

"It's fine. I'm glad I was there, too." She looked around, half-expecting the van to have reappeared. "As much as I want to assure you they won't try again, these guys are ballsy and stupid. It's a dangerous combo. The fact they knew you were here makes me think they have someone watching you. Have you noticed anything unusual?"

Tiffany said, "No, nothing. I've been staying with my friend, Lisa. It's been fine. It's been normal. Until today, I guess."

Ari said, "They cleaned out Wilcox's apartment last night. I'm guessing they didn't find what they were after and decided you were their best bet."

"What are they looking for?"

"I think it's an iPad. Did you ever see him with something like that?"

Tiffany shrugged. "Sure. It was where he kept his sensitive materials. Like if he found out someone's passwords or bank PIN or something during an investigation, he'd put it in there in case it 'came in handy.' But he took it with him everywhere. If it wasn't at the office, then it had to be at his apartment. If they trashed the place, then they found it."

Ari shook her head. "No, because I have it. Listen, if these guys try to come after you again, just tell them I have it. Send them after me."

"I couldn't..."

"You saw what I just did, right? I can handle myself. I'll know they're coming."

Tiffany reluctantly nodded. "But I don't think it'll be an issue. My parents offered to fly me down to Sacramento for Thanksgiving. I think I'm going to take them up on it."

"That would probably be a smart idea," Ari said.

Tiffany gave Ari a number where she could be reached, then hugged her and thanked her again. A police officer was enlisted to drive Tiffany home. Ari gave her card to the other officer and told him where he could find her if he had any more questions.

When Ari got back to the office, Dale immediately stood up and went to her. "Hey. Diana called. Are you okay?"

"I'm fine." She kissed Dale and accepted a hug before she went into the main office. "Diana already called? That's pretty fast."

"Your shirt."

Dale was pointing at her sleeve, so Ari twisted until she saw the rip. "Ah, damn it. So much for that shirt." She started undoing the buttons. "But the important thing is Tiffany is okay and the Creep Cousins are going to have to deal with the police."

"The who?" Dale chuckled.

"Oh, the Creep Cousins. It's the name this girl who works at the gym used for them. I figured it was apt, so..." She put the torn shirt aside in the hopes she could sew up the damage at some point. She kept a few shirts in the bottom drawer of her desk for emergencies. "Maybe this whole Clark Wilcox thing is finally almost over."

Dale said, "Hope so." She had moved to stand on the other side of the desk. "Seeing you shirtless in the office kind of takes me back."

Ari smiled. "Yeah? Back when you had to stop yourself from going below the waist?"

"I never had to stop myself. We were just friends. Come here." Ari came around the desk and let Dale do the buttons for her. "But if we're being entirely honest... yeah... a couple of times, I wondered what you would do if I just... slipped my hand between your legs." She looked up at Ari through her lashes. "Would you have liked that? If I just started fingering you?"

Ari said, "Well. Sure, I wouldn't have been against it..."

"Oh, really..." She moved her hand to the front of Ari's pants.

"Dale, it's the middle of the day..."

"I know." She leaned closer. "Fuck me, Ariadne."

Ari took a step back. "What the hell is in Seattle's water today? The woman from the gym tried to grope me, Tiffany kissed me for rescuing her, and now you."

"You don't like me coming onto you?"

"I love it, Dale. You know that."

Dale's lips spread into a feral grin. "Then bend me over the desk, wolfie."

Ari stepped out of Dale's embrace. "Cut it out, Dale. I'm not in the mood right now."

"Fine." Dale dropped her hands and turned on her heel.

"Wait, are you mad at me now?"

"Nope."

Dale slammed the door behind her as she went back to her

desk. Ari rolled her eyes and finished buttoning her shirt. That wasn't like Dale. In fact, the roleplay the night before hadn't been like Dale, either. Maybe she should just throw the shirt out if it was going to draw women to her like flies. She put the strange encounter out of her mind and picked up Wilcox's iPad. If she and Dale were going to be mad at each other, she could at least use the time to decrypt his notes.

She'd been working on it for ten minutes, hoping "Flex" might lead her somewhere, when her phone rang. She pushed down the flashing light. "Yeah, Dale?"

"Puppy... I'm not going to go in there... I just wanted to say I'm sorry."

Any lingering anger Ari had faded. "You don't have to be sorry, Dale. I'd be worried if you didn't occasionally get the urge."

"It's not just that." Dale sounded worried. Or scared. "As soon as you walked in, I wanted you. I needed to have you right there, Ari. I don't know where the urge came from, but it vanished pretty much the second the door was closed. Same thing last night. I spent all day just... *wanting* you. And, yeah, it's a great problem to have. But it's kind of freaking me out."

Ari said, "Are you saying that..." She frowned and stared at the phone. "What are you saying?"

"I'm saying that something weird is going on. Once my head cleared, I started thinking about the other women you said came onto you or touched you. Are you in heat?"

"That makes *me* hump everything in sight, not vice versa." She thought back over the day. "But Diana didn't do anything. She was perfectly behaved."

Dale said, "Something weird is going on, though. How long has it been going on?"

"Uh..."

"Yeah, yeah, you're an incredibly attractive specimen. I've been to bars with you, I know. But at this level? Come on."

"A couple of days. Hey, come to think of it, Diana did

invite me to Thanksgiving dinner."

"That's not unusual. You and Diana are friends. Neka invited you to Thanksgiving, too. Do you think she was attracted to you?"

Ari chewed her lip. "No. Not really."

Dale said, "Okay, hold on."

The phone was set down, and a second later Dale stepped into the office. She walked up to Ari's desk and rested her hands on the edge. Ari stared up at her. They stayed like that for a long moment, like Dale was trying to identify an unusual odor in the room. Finally she sagged in defeat and nodded.

"Oh, yeah. I want you bad."

"More than you did out there?" Ari asked, pointing at the door with her pinkie.

Dale nodded. "Yeah."

Ari hung up the phone. "Is it my shampoo? What the hell is going on?"

"I don't know. I'm always attracted to you, but not like this. Not like... just... gotta have you right now feeling. Not all the time, anyway."

"Maybe it's the fact I was gone the whole summer."

"Maybe. But that doesn't explain the other women. Which I kind of want to get into when this whole mystery is solved. Wilcox's secretary *kissed* you?"

Ari said, "Briefly, by surprise, and instantly thwarted." She thought for a second. "Cecily Parrish didn't seem particularly attracted to me. I was attracted to *her*."

"Hell, we both were." Dale shifted her weight from one foot to the other. "Call her. See if she wants to come down. We can have some fun with her."

"Dale," Ari snapped.

"Right." Dale pushed her hands through her hair. "God. I need to take a cold shower."

Ari pushed back her chair and put the iPad to sleep. "I'm going to go see what I can figure out from home. You... stay here and control yourself."

"I will." She stepped back to give Ari room. "Don't kiss me goodbye. Fuel on the fire."

"Is this going to be a serious problem?"

Dale shook her head. "No. I don't think so. Maybe I'm just regular-level horny, and then whatever is going on pushed it over the edge."

"Would it help if I just had sex with you?"

Dale exhaled shakily. "I-I don't know. Probably best not to risk it."

Ari nodded. "We'll figure this out. And if we don't, and the worst thing that happens if I have to have sex with you every morning~"

"You've *really* got to stop talking, Ariadne."

"Right." She moved toward the door. "Uh. Okay. I'll call you later."

Dale said, "Yeah. I'll keep trying to figure out the iPad's code from here. I love you."

"Love you, too."

Ari left and stood outside in the fresh air. She lifted her arms and sniffed underneath them, not finding anything objectionable or overly attractive about the result. She hadn't changed any of her bath supplies, so there was no reason women should start flinging themselves at her. And Dale was really a mystery. Their sex life had always been fantastic, so there was no need for a boost. Her trip to Cecily Parrish's offices seemed to be the tipping point. If there were answers to be found, that was where they'd be. She was almost to her car before her phone buzzed with a text from Dale.

"Fire's out. Something is definitely up."

"Never thought I'd be happy to hear you weren't hot for me."

Dale sent back a smiling emoji and Ari grinned as she put the phone back in her pocket. The police were currently working on Flex and the Creep Cousins. She had a feeling she could get Diana to tell her anything they found out, so she had a few hours where she could investigate her own private mystery. And that included figuring out how to walk into a lawyer's office and ask if she knew anything about the women who were suddenly throwing themselves at her feet left and right. Shouldn't be too awkward at all.

CHAPTER TWELVE

ARI STOPPED by the house and took a long, hot shower. She sniffed her soap and shampoo but didn't detect anything odd about either. She also didn't use either of them. She'd washed her hair that morning, and now she wanted nothing but hot water to hopefully sluice off whatever was causing such a wild reaction. They shared a laundry room with Neka, so she went up to sniff the detergent and fabric softener to see if there was maybe something amiss there. Nothing. It didn't make sense that something, some odor, was affecting everyone around her without the wolf smelling it. Her sense of smell was strong as ever so it wasn't as if that was on the blink.

Eventually she dressed and drove back to GG&M. She had no idea what she was going to say when she confronted Parrish, but she could pinpoint the sudden change in behavior to the time she spent in their offices. She rode the elevator up and stepped out to see a different receptionist in place behind the desk. Despite that, the girl smiled and greeted her by name.

"Good afternoon, Miss Willow. How can I help you

today?"

"I'm here to see Cecily Parrish."

She had anticipated another long wait, but the receptionist nodded. "Of course. She's in court at the moment, but you can wait in her office if you'd like. Do you know the way?"

"Yeah," Ari said, suspicious of the warm welcome. "I'll... just go on, then."

The receptionist nodded and went back to her work. Ari went through the doors and walked down the corridor. Maybe Parrish believed so strongly that Ari would take the offer that she'd already given her all-access to the building. That seemed incredibly sloppy for a law firm, but she would be stupid not to take advantage of it. She passed Parrish's office and continued around the corner. A few of the other offices were occupied by men and women in suits, some typing and some on phones. One woman seemed to be asleep, her head propped up on her fist.

The corner across from Parrish's office was open and had been turned into a break area. A man was sitting in one of the chairs provided, halfway through a blueberry muffin when he noticed Ari. His eyes drifted down her body, but this time she had to wonder if he was judging her clothes or if he was attracted to her.

"Hi. Do you need help finding something?"

Ari said, "Coffee. And I think I can figure it out from here." She walked to the carafe. "I'm Ariadne Willow. I'm a private investigator."

"Oh, right. Mrs. Parrish said she was talking with someone."

"Mrs. Parrish?" Ari repeated. "She's married?"

He chuckled under his breath. "Hard to believe, right? No offense to her, I just can't even imagine what that wedding was like. I think she must have negotiated 'love, honor, and obey' down to 'promise to occasionally listen to your opinion before I dismiss it out of hand.'" He stood up just enough to extend his hand to her. "I'm Denver Nelson. I'm a paralegal here."

She shook his hand and took a seat in one of the other orange plastic chairs. "So what is it like working here?"

"Amazing. They're really great here, and they're great about giving you opportunities to advance. Most of the lawyers are pretty chill."

Ari said, "And the partners? Gilles Girard and Moreau?"

"We never see them around. At least I never have. Most of the day-to-day stuff is done by Mrs. Parrish. That's why she's the one who gets to decide if you're hired or not."

"Okay." She sipped her coffee, which was surprisingly good. "Do you know if Gilles Girard is one person or two? There's no comma. I can't figure it out."

He grinned. "Two people. I think. But like I said, I've never seen them. So who knows?"

She nodded. "Can I ask you a strictly scientific question? I won't be offended if the answer is no. I'm just truly curious."

"And now I'm truly curious myself. Shoot."

"Are you attracted to me?"

He smiled and tilted his head slightly. "Sorry. No. I'm asexual."

Ari raised an eyebrow. "Wow. I've never met anyone who was asexual before."

"Oh, sure you have. They just didn't announce it."

"Okay. Doesn't really help my question, then." Although Patsy said she was straight, and Diana was definitely gay, so whatever was going on wasn't picky about orientation. Maybe Diana hadn't been affected for the same reason Dale had the worst case. Diana was committed to her wife so she was untouched, and Dale was committed to Ari so she was turned up to eleven.

Denver said, "Kind of a weird survey to go around asking people. 'Am I pretty,' check yes or no. You don't strike me as the vain sort."

"I'm not. It's just been a weird couple of days."

Denver had finished his muffin and threw the wrapper away. "Well, I'm going to go ahead and tell you it's a great place to work if you decide to come onboard. It would be nice to have someone who wasn't a stuffed-suit wandering around the halls." He offered his hand again. "It was nice to meet you, Ariadne Willow."

"You too, Denver Nelson."

When he left the break room, Ari watched him until he disappeared into the conference room. She got up and walked back to Parrish's office, hoping she would be less conspicuous waiting there. She opened the door and breathed deep, hoping there might be something in the air. Instead she just smelled the standard office environment and the stiff reek of chemical air fresheners. She moved closer to the desk and smelled stale coffee and perfume.

She thought about their first encounter with Parrish in the courtroom. She and Dale were both attracted to her despite her demeanor, attitude, and the fact she'd made Ari look stupid on the stand. Maybe her perfume had some sort of pheromones that had transferred just by spending time in her office. She couldn't detect anything particularly alien in the odors she was picking up. Maybe it was subliminal.

Or maybe she was just wasting her time. She was about to leave before she could be humiliated when she noticed the pictures on the desk. Last time she'd been in the office, there were three. Now there were two. She walked around to see the front of the pictures. Parrish on a rock outcropping was still there, as was the dog. The missing picture had been entirely and inexplicably red. It was also the only picture Parrish had asked her about.

Ari frowned at the space where the picture had been and tried to come up with a reason for it to have gone missing. She was still thinking when Cecily Parrish came into the office and stopped short.

"Miss Willow. Did we have an appointment?"

"No." She pointed at the desk. "Where did the red picture go?"

Parrish shrugged. "I like to keep my area fresh. It had been there long enough."

"But you weren't sick of the other ones yet?"

Parrish smiled and shifted slightly, adopting a more casual stance. Something about her demeanor pissed Ari off, but she still felt an undeniable pull toward the woman. She knew if Parrish told her to undress and get on the desk, she would have a hard time fighting the urge. She suddenly understood how Dale had felt, how Patsy and Tiffany had felt, and she had all the confirmation she needed that Parrish was involved somehow.

"If I wasn't clear last week, Miss Willow, we weren't offering you a position as interior decorator. Please get out from behind my desk."

Ari said, "What did you do to me?"

"Do...?"

"You did something."

"Miss Willow, I offered you a job. Nothing more, nothing less. I'm beginning to think it was a mistake to go that far. If you're suffering from some sort of paranoid delusions, the partners won't accept you as an employee anyway."

Ari said, "What is it? Perfume? Pheromones? Did it have something to do with the picture?"

Parrish was suddenly interested. All humor had faded from her face. "What are you talking about?"

"I'm talking about women. Straight women throwing themselves at me." She looked up at the ceiling to find the air vents. "Do you pump something in here to convince clients to settle?"

"You're experiencing unwanted advances?"

Ari rolled her eyes. "I'm not suing anyone for sexual harassment. I just want to know what you did to me and when it will wear off."

They had changed sides of the desk, with Parrish now backlit by the window. It made her look sinister as she took her seat.

"I did nothing to you, Miss Willow. I can assure you of that. It's been five days since our meeting." She reached up and brushed two fingers across her lips as her attention drifted toward the carpet. Parrish was acting as if she not only knew something, but she was surprised to hear it had worked. Or perhaps it was just unintended consequences of something else. Maybe what Ari was experiencing was accidental. "It shouldn't last much longer. I would be very surprised if it was still an issue tomorrow."

"What is it?"

Parrish turned her attention back to Ari. "What are you?"

Ari was completely thrown. "What?"

They stared each other down for a full minute without saying anything. It was Parrish who finally broke the standoff.

"If you want to take this further, I think we would both have to divulge information we're not ready to share with each other. You intrigue me, Miss Willow, so although you've now entered my office twice without permission, and overlooking your accusations that I've done something nefarious to you or to my clients, I'm keeping the job offer on the table. This week is Thanksgiving, so I would like an answer by next Monday."

Ari said, "We're not done."

"Oh, no. We are most definitely not done, Ariadne. But this conversation is finished. I look forward to continuing it at some point once we're both more comfortable with one another."

Ari didn't want to leave, but she also wasn't about to tell this woman she was *canidae*. She turned and walked out, but she looked back into the office as the door was swinging shut. Parrish looked shaken, completely confused, as she stood and went to the window. There were definite secrets that needed to be uncovered, but until Ari was ready to show her hand, she couldn't force Parrish to show hers. For the time being, she had to be content with the fact whatever had happened to her would wear off by morning. At least she wouldn't have to suffer through Thanksgiving with Neka coming on to her.

Ari called Dale and said she would work the rest of the day from home, just to be safe. When Dale arrived with dinner, Ari stood in the middle of the living room for inspection. Dale approached cautiously, biting her bottom lip as she stood in front of Ari and gauged her response. She leaned in and sniffed Ari's neck, and Ari laughed and kissed her shoulder. Dale lightly rested her hands on Ari's hips and sagged against her. She pressed her lips against Ari's collar.

"Well. I really want you. But I think it's just standard level."

"That low, huh?"

Dale leaned back and grinned. "What I mean to say is, I'd be fine with having dinner before you tore my clothes off and threw me on the bed."

Ari kissed Dale's cheeks, then her lips before taking the fast-food bags into the kitchen. She explained what had happened at Parrish's office as she served everything onto plates. Dale got their drinks and sat at the table.

"That's odd. So if you had told her you were a wolf..."

"I think she would have told me what she'd done. And I really do think whatever it was, she didn't intend for it to happen. She seemed completely thrown by what I was saying."

"I could maybe get into her work computer, see what she looked up after you left."

Ari shook her head. "I doubt she would look up anything incriminating on her work computer. Isn't it also... what's the word...? Illegal! That's the one."

"Only if we use it in court."

"You're such a wild child," Ari said.

Dale stuck her tongue out. "So we've met a mermaid, a gender-shifter, *felidae*... what else might be out there?"

"Vampires."

Dale glared at her.

Ari shrugged. "Is it so hard to believe? There are werewolves in the world, there are mermaids, so why not a vampire?"

"I guess not. I can get used to wolves because... well..." She gestured at Ari. "And I never even considered mermaids until I saw one transform right in front of me. I guess I won't buy vampires until one of them flashes their fangs at me. Fingers crossed it looks like Kate Beckinsale."

"Cheers to that idea."

After dinner they went to bed. Dale rolled over as soon as the lights were out, sliding her hand over Ari's stomach to tease the waistband of her underwear. Ari lifted her head and found Dale's lips in the dark, and they grappled for a bit under the blankets until Dale lifted up.

"Maybe I should hold back, just to prove to you that I'm not under the effects of whatever Parrish did to you."

"Could you hold back?"

"Sure. It would suck, but I could go to sleep right now if I had to."

Ari said, "And this morning at the office?"

"That was really touch and go."

"I think that's enough evidence." Ari cupped the back of Dale's head and pulled her down to continue their kiss. She would take Parrish at her word and hope that whatever effect she was having on the female population of Seattle would indeed fade by morning. The next day was Thanksgiving, so between Neka, Diana, and Lucy they were bound to have a good array of test subjects to determine if Ari's desirability had returned to normal levels. Until then, she was just fine with the attentions of one woman in particular.

Afterward, and after an all-too-brief shared shower, they changed into their pajamas; Ari into a thermal undershirt and shorts while Dale chose an oversized T-shirt that hung enticingly off one shoulder. Ari rested her head on Dale's chest and listened to the sound of her breathing. The room smelled of them both, of their lovemaking but also of Dale's perfume and lotions and various beauty products. Before going to the cabin, she'd taken those scents for granted. Her *canidae* senses were so heightened that she had to ignore a vast majority of what she heard or smelled. But three months away had been too long.

She gathered a handful of Dale's shirt and pressed her face against the material. Dale chuckled, brushed her hand down Ari's back, and kissed her hair. "I missed you, too."

Ari lifted her head. "There's something I have to tell you. I don't want you to panic or freak out. It's just something you should know."

"Okay..."

"When the pain was so bad, when I knew turning into the wolf would mean hours of agony afterward, I started thinking about what would happen if the bite didn't work. If I ended up paralyzed and you had to take care of me. I thought about ending it all. Not seriously, not in a... planning way. But the thought was there."

Dale guided Ari's head to the pillow and rolled onto her side so they could face each other. "I knew."

"You did?"

"I saw my mother when she got sick. When she thought that I was going to give up my chance to go to college just so I could take care of her, she had the same ideas. She figured she couldn't get in the way if she wasn't there, and I'd be free to do what I wanted. I could see some of the same things in your eyes. I was waiting for you to say something, but I understood why you didn't. I just knew that you weren't close to actually following through. And I understood the reasoning. You didn't want to be a burden. You didn't want my life to become all about taking care of you."

"Right."

"That's not your choice."

"I know."

Dale cupped Ari's cheek, extending her thumb to brush it over her bottom lip. "You're an amazing thing, Ariadne Willow. If my purpose on Earth is to make your life a little easier, I consider that an honor. You save everyone, puppy. You need someone to look out for you, too. I love you. And if that means my job turns from receptionist to caregiver, then I'll jump in with both feet. I know it doesn't mean much now that the bite worked and you're pain-free..."

"There's still going to be pain. Even if it isn't as bad."

"So my massages?"

Ari smiled. "Keep them up. They're worth your paycheck all by themselves."

Dale kissed her. "Whatever happens, puppy, I'm in it for the long run."

"Good. Me too... just for the record. No more pain, no more dark thoughts."

"Good." She kissed Ari again. "Now go to sleep."

Ari slid closer to Dale, who wrapped her in a tight embrace.

CHAPTER THIRTEEN

DALE HAD arranged their Thanksgiving schedule when Ari wasn't paying attention, making it the first thing she was thankful for on the holiday. Neka and Simon were having their meal at lunchtime, so Ari and Dale would eat with them before moving on to Diana and Lucy's for pie and drinks. Dale spent the morning cooking and when the dish was ready, rather than going through the laundry room, they actually went outside and walked around the house to arrive through the front door like normal people. Their knock was answered by a short, scruffy guy wearing a blazer over a V-neck shirt. His eyes were about as wide as the smile that threatened to break his face in half as he looked at Dale and then at Ari.

"This must be the infamous Ariadne Willow!" He stuck his hand out. "I was starting to think Dale and Neka had just made you up. A private eye seemed too cool to be true. But here you are! Sorry, I'm rambling. Hi! I'm Simon."

"Hi." She shook his hand and stepped inside.

"We're all set up in here. Why don't you come in and…

oh! You brought something. That's cool. Here, let me take it from you. I'll put it in the kitchen." He took the dish from Dale and brought it to his face to smell it. "Oh, wow, what is that?"

"Southern cornbread," Dale said. "It was my mother's recipe."

"Excellent! I'll put this in the kitchen. Neka's watching the game."

He disappeared and Dale guided Ari toward the living room. Ari leaned close. "Now *that* is a puppy."

Dale laughed. "He's excitable. I'll give you that. But you're the only puppy here."

Neka got up off the couch when she saw them. "Hey! Happy Thanksgiving!" She stepped around the table to give Dale a hug. "I'm going to tell you right now that I'm thankful to have you as tenants. I was afraid I'd get some convict or pervert or something, but you two have been amazing. Even if you do sometimes dog-sit for your friends."

Ari said, "Hopefully Tule is well-behaved when she stays here."

"Oh, she's great. She's great. Hardly notice her at all." She looked toward the kitchen. "What did you bring? I've been smelling that all morning, and it's driving me nuts."

"Just cornbread."

"It's not just cornbread," Ari said. "She's made it for me before. It's the most buttery, flaky thing you've ever tasted. I feel bad for your turkey. Its thunder is about to get stolen."

Neka laughed. "It wouldn't be tough, trust me. I'm not the best cook, but I try. I feel cooking is like dancing. Enthusiasm trumps skill every time."

They went into the kitchen where Simon was checking the turkey. "Almost done!"

Ari said, "I thought Neka was supposed to be cooking for you."

"That was the plan," he said with a chuckle. "But I think we established who has that skill in the relationship. But it's the thought that counts."

"What can I do to help?" Ari asked, unbuttoning her cuffs to roll up her sleeves.

The meal was served promptly at noon, and Dale's cornbread proved to be even better combined with Simon's gravy. The rest of the food was equally delicious, even the parts Neka claimed to have screwed up. They chatted about work - Neka was in school learning to build boats, which Ari found endlessly fascinating - and Ari gave them a few juicy tidbits about her life as a private investigator. She left out client details, and also any wolf-related activity, but still managed to have them hanging on every word.

Eventually it came time to say goodbye and move on to the next engagement. Ari apologized for the dine-and-dash, but Neka assured her that she and Simon would just spend the rest of the day watching Netflix or football games. Ari thanked her for the delicious meal, then went outside to wait while Dale retrieved the second dish of cornbread from their apartment. She called Diana to let her know they were en route, then headed out.

"Neka didn't seem to be overwhelmed with desire for you," Dale pointed out. "Neither did Simon."

"Yeah, but if the theory that Diana wasn't affected because of her commitment to Lucy..."

Dale shrugged. "True. But I still think we can relax a little bit."

"Let's hope."

At the car, Dale said, "You know, we could swing by your mother's place real easy. It's on the way to the Macallan household."

"Drop in unannounced on Thanksgiving? Rude."

"I'm sure you have an open invitation. I'm sure we both do."

Ari said, "I've kind of had my fill of her recently. Is that okay?"

Dale said, "As long as that's all it is. I'm worried something happened between you two."

"No, nothing happened. We're better than ever. We just..." She sighed and looked at Dale over the top of the car. "I spent three months with her wishing I was with you. Now that I'm with you, I don't want to share you with her. Does that make sense?"

"Yeah. But I want to see her at some point. I've never had a girlfriend's mother tell me to call her 'Mom' before."

Ari smiled in a way Dale found odd. "Yeah..."

"What?"

"Nothing. To Diana's!"

"To Diana's," Dale said, putting a pin in the conversation but not forgetting it.

Diana and Lucy lived in a picturesque townhouse in North Seattle. It was a gorgeous neighborhood that was closer to 'white-picket fence' than Ari had ever imagined for Diana. They found a place to park amid the fleet of cars and trucks lining both sides of the road and walked the rest of the way. Diana greeted them on the porch and escorted them inside, which was still rich with the smells of turkey and stuffing. The odor of the meal was threatened by the smell of baking pies. Through the living room, Ari could see into the kitchen. A redheaded woman wearing a black sweater was setting the places, her pulled-back hair falling over a pair of thick square-framed eyeglasses. Ari slowed at the sight of the woman, then recognized her from the photo.

"You must be Lucy. The pictures I saw were blonde."

Lucy grinned. "I go back and forth." She wiped her hands on a towel and came around the table with one hand extended. "It's so great to finally meet you, Ariadne. I've heard a lot about you."

"You too. You're an artist, right?"

"Artist, illustrator, kid who never stopped drawing on the walls." She chuckled. "And you're the private eye. The fact Di even gives you the time of day proves you're something special."

Ari said, "I hope so."

Lucy pointed at Dale. "You, I know less about. So let's get to know each other while our ladies prepare the pies. I want pecan."

Dale said, "Is there apple?"

"Apple for Dale," Ari said. "Got it."

Lucy guided Dale into the living room. Ari and Diana moved to the stove, and Diana lowered her voice. "Staying out of trouble today?"

"No kidnapping attempts yet."

"Good girl. A bunch of officers raided the Flex gym and picked up two of the Creep Cousins."

Ari smirked. "I'm glad that name is catching on."

"It's apt."

"Which two?"

"We matched two of the guys to the description you gave. Mike and Joel Murphy. They were the only ones we could put on-site for the attempted kidnapping. Lots of paper on both of them. Assault and battery, theft, property damage, general asshole behavior. They've also been picked up on drug-related charges. Sometimes they were picked up with accomplices, and I think that will help us tie together the rest of the Flex gang. Their rap sheets were eclectic enough that I figure there's only one of two explanations for it. One, either they just break the law with no rhyme or reason. Or..."

"They're hired out and do the dirty work of whoever is paying."

Diana nodded. "Whipped cream is in the fridge. We're letting them chill out over the holiday. Tomorrow I'm going to see what I can get out of them after they've had some time to sit and think. Hopefully whoever they were hired by isn't scary enough to risk going to jail for."

"Maybe we'll get lucky."

"Fingers crossed. And you need to be careful. We got the

Murphy brothers, but judging from their 'known associates' crossover, there are three others we weren't able to get. At least one of them probably saw you take down the goons, so they know what you look like. Keep your eyes open, okay?"

"Okay."

"Okay, with that out of the way, no more business talk."

"Deal."

They each took two plates and went to find their respective partners.

After having their pie, while they were watching football, Lucy picked up a pad and began doodling. When Ari and Dale decided it was time to leave, she tore off the top sheet and handed it to them. Ari was shocked to see a crude but incredibly detailed sketch of her and Dale. "It's just something I do with my hands to keep them busy. You don't have to keep it or anything."

"This is amazing. Thank you." She hugged Lucy and showed the picture to Dale. "We'll be back sometime before next Thanksgiving. Promise."

"You're more than welcome," Diana said.

They finished saying their goodbyes and started the walk to the car. Dale took Ari's hand. "Diana is so... grown-up."

Ari laughed. "Yeah. I get what you mean."

"Do you imagine something like this for us one day?"

"Absolutely. We could get one of these townhouses. Live like real adults instead of in a basement." She tightened her grip on Dale's hand and stepped in front of her. "The wolf loves you."

Dale raised her eyebrows. "Was that in question?"

"For me, a little bit. Yeah. When the subject of being bitten came up, my mother started talking about 'real' *canidae*. That meant no pain, changing like every other wolf in the world, but it also made me think about the fact that no *canidae* has ever had a real relationship with a human."

"Agatha and Johanna..."

"Yeah, two hundred years ago, there was one relationship forged during a war. You and I weren't forced together. We just... we just..." She brushed the hair out of Dale's face. "We just found each other. I thought maybe the wolf would fight that once she was at full strength. That was one reason I waited so long to go through with it. I was able to live with the pain if it meant I could still love you."

Dale smiled, her eyes wet. "And?"

"What do you mean 'and'?" Ari smiled and brushed Dale's cheek. "I love you as much, maybe more, than I ever did before. You're the woman who saved my life. And then saved it again, and again, and again. You know, it's almost a habit with you, now that I'm thinking about it."

"Purely selfish motivation," Dale said. "My life is better with you in it."

"Ditto. I'm thankful for you, Dale Elizabeth Frye. I'm glad those punks decided to start beating my ass. If they hadn't, you would have just kept walking and we'd never have met."

Dale hugged Ari tightly. "I kind of like this holiday confessional thing. I'm thankful for you, Ariadne Willow. I didn't know what I wanted to do or who I was going to be. I thought I would end up working in some office or behind a counter with a name tag on my chest like I did this summer. You gave me a career. You let me do something I love more than anything. I can never repay you for that."

Ari's smile wavered.

"What? Did I say something wrong?"

"No," Ari said. "Cecily Parrish offered me a job with her firm."

Dale blinked in surprise. "Wow. That's unexpected. Was that what she wanted to see you about last week?" Ari nodded. "What did you say?"

"I asked for time to think about it. I would still be a private investigator, I would just be in-house. I'd be on retainer with them. I would have a steady paycheck, an office, and it would probably be a lot less dangerous than some of the cases we've worked lately. No Wayne Francis Corbett or Katherine Gavin. No one throwing a drink in my face when I serve them with divorce papers."

Dale's voice was soft. "Doesn't sound like there's a lot of room for me or Bitches in that scenario."

"That's why I didn't say yes. It's why I'm not going to say yes. I can't just scuttle the agency and drop you."

"You can so." Dale took Ari's hands. "Your business, your decision. This is the next logical step in the evolution of the agency. If you decide to take it, I'll find something else to do. Maybe I could get a job at the police station or intern at Parrish's law firm. And if you want to keep things the way they are, I can get behind that, too. Make the decision that's right for you, and for us, and I'll go along with it. Even if Bitches goes away, you're stuck with me in your life."

Ari laughed. She kissed Dale's forehead and took her hand to continue the walk to the car. "I'm not sure it would be wise to work with Parrish if something in her office really did turn me into some kind of sex magnet."

"Maybe now that she knows you'll be affected, she can turn it off."

"Maybe." She took Dale's hand. "I have to give her an answer by Monday. We'll consider it together over the weekend. I don't even know how I would explain half the things I do without revealing the wolf's part in it. Maybe it would be better to just stay with you. Grow the agency, make something I can be proud of instead of just folding in with someone else."

Dale rested her head on Ari's shoulder. "I'll follow wherever you go, puppy."

Ari said, "That's all I need."

"Me too."

Stuffed from their meal and Dale's cornbread, they

decided to devote the rest of the day to recovery. Ari was reclining on the couch with Wilcox's iPad while Dale napped off the effects of the tryptophan. She did a search through the tablet for any mention of the Murphy brothers, but came up empty. She tried 'Creep Cousins' but that was a bust as well. She scrolled through the encoded notes hoping something would leap out at her now that he had an idea what some of the words might mean. Murphy, Michael, Mike, Joel, M&J... anything that might possibly connect and open the door to further information.

She was about to give up when she saw one entry listed as MM/F. Behind that was 500/00. She scrolled back to the search bar and entered /F and found multiple entries. MM/F, JM/F, KF/F, FP/F, and TC/F. They were all followed by amounts she felt comfortable assuming were monetary, prices between two hundred and a thousand dollars. After those marks, Wilcox had written some sort of code to indicate exactly what they had been paid for.

She sat up and found a pen and a scrap piece of paper. Working on the assumption that MM was Mike Murphy, she took the extra step to JM being his brother Joel. The slash-F was connecting them all to the Flex gym. The iPad handily kept track of when each note was made, so she made a list of the dates to crosscheck them with Wilcox's memoirs and his case files. If she knew which cases required payment for hired goons, then she might be one step closer to cracking the code.

He didn't know how long she had been working until Dale came shuffling out of the bedroom. She leaned against the entrance to the living room and held out her arm.

"Need my puppy."

Ari looked at the time. "Wow. I didn't realize it was so late." She turned off the iPad and set it aside. "I'm coming."

Dale came to join her on the couch as she organized everything so she could start again in the morning. "What is all of this?"

"This is the start of figuring out Wilcox's idiotic code. Once I know what all these annotations mean, maybe I can work backwards and figure out what he was into. Something in this iPad got him deep enough that suicide seemed like the only escape."

Dale kissed Ari's cheek. "Bring me some water when you come to bed."

"Okay. Go warm the bed up."

Dale nodded and went back down the hall. Ari examined the progress she had made, the rows of names, dates, and payments. Somewhere in that mess was the answer to Clark Wilcox's death. She was determined to find it and give the man some measure of peace, despite the hell he had given her in life. She knew he would never have done it for her if their roles were reversed, but that was why it was important that she give it her all. Clark Wilcox was not her role model, and she would do right by him no matter where the trail led her.

She sighed and got up, turning off the light before she went to get a cup of water for Dale.

CHAPTER FOURTEEN

ARI WAITED until Monday morning at the office to call Flex. She asked for Patsy and identified herself. "You might not remember me..."

"Oh, I remember you! Yeah. The, um. Weirdness."

"Right." Ari was hoping they could have ignored that. "I want to apologize again~"

"No, it wasn't you. Over Thanksgiving, I thought about it some more. I think it was more my fault than yours. A friend and I had a conversation. It was really good. I didn't think I'd get a chance to thank you. So thanks."

Ari smiled. It was always nice to help a woman discover her latent desires. "Sure. I hope it works out for you." She tapped her pad with the tip of her pen. "Listen, I'm actually calling for business reasons. And to confess. I wasn't really checking out the gym yesterday. I'm a private investigator. The case I'm working on led me to your gym and to the Creep Cousins."

Patsy snorted. "Why'd you have to go and ruin a good conversation?"

"Sorry. I know you probably can't divulge client names, but in the interest of cooperation, if I gave you some initials, maybe you could confirm full names."

"Hm. I could maybe be persuaded..."

Ari said, "Okay. I know Mike and Joel Murphy."

"Uh-huh."

"T.C., K.F., and F.P. Can you confirm those are Cousins?"

Patsy said, "We have several clients with those initials, ma'am. Tommy Carrow, Kevin Forrester, and Frank Pearl, for instance. I'm not sure how much help it would be, just having the initials."

Ari wrote the names down. "Yeah, probably a dead end."

"That's Forrester with two Rs, and Carrow is spelled C-A-R-R-O-W."

"Got it. They wouldn't happen to be at the gym now, would they?"

"No, it's still too early in the day. They usually come in after five o'clock."

"Thanks. You've been a big help."

Patsy said, "Sure. It might have been a breach of confidentiality to tell you Tommy and Kevin do something involved unloading down at the docks, and Frank works for a moving company called World Movers. Or maybe not, since that's not exactly privileged information. Either way, you never asked, so..."

Ari smiled and wrote the extra info down. "Damn. Maybe I'll find it some other way."

"I hope so, Ariadne. And hey, if you ever want to come down for the free trial membership, I'd be happy to show you around. Our saunas are, ah, real private."

"That's a sweet offer, but my girlfriend says I have to decline."

"Bring her. I can just watch."

Ari's cheeks flushed. "Wow. I woke a sleeping giant, huh?"

"You sure did." Patsy laughed. "Hope to talk to you soon.

Even if it is just case-related."

Ari hung up and looked up the number for World Movers. She dialed and settled into her Harriet the Harried Housewife persona.

"World Movers, we move your world. How can I help you today?"

Ari said, "Hello-o, yes, I'm sorry, I'm calling... one of your men was at my home this morning on a job? I think his name was Fred or Frank or something?"

The receptionist, guarded: "Uh-huh?"

Ari assumed she'd gotten more than a few complaints about him, judging from that reaction. She decided to take another angle. "He left behind a pair of gloves. They look brand-new, and they have F PEARL written right on the cuffs. I would hate for him to think they'd been lost! And I was about to head out on some errands, so if he was nearby on another job, I could return them without making him backtrack or miss any work."

"Oh!" The guardedness was gone now. "Well, isn't that sweet of you! Hold on, let me see." Ari could hear the sound of typing over the phone. "Kev is working alone today, and he's at Eighth Avenue, off Crockett. And listen, honey, because he sure as shooting won't say it, thank you so much. It's so kind of you."

Ari said, "Oh, just doing what I'd want someone to do for me, you know."

She hung up and grabbed her coat as she headed out. "Off to see one of the Creep Cousins."

"Take precautions," Dale said.

"Always." She blew Dale a kiss as she left the office.

Crockett was in Queen Anne, which meant Ari would most likely have to walk uphill at some point. She changed into a pair of comfortable shoes in the car and made the drive across town.

The houses were all built in the style that gave the neighborhood its name. They were all elevated, perched on higher tracts of land with stone or wooden steps leading down to the sloped sidewalk that popped and cracked with overgrown roots and weeds. The World Movers truck was blocking the traffic on Eighth Avenue, so Ari parked on the side street, took her precautions out of the trunk, and walked up toward it. As she drew near, she saw Frank Pearl carrying a large end table across the lawn, biceps bulging against the sleeves of his uniform shirt.

Ari waited for him to put it down in the back of the truck before she spoke. "Yo."

He turned, dabbing at the sweat on his brow. "You the lady who called Viv? I don't know what to tell ya, 'cause I've been here all day and I've got all my gloves."

"I'm not here about gloves. I want to talk to you about your friends."

"What friends?"

Ari stopped just out of his reach. He had the higher ground which she hoped meant it would be easier for her to evade him. If he swung, he would be throwing his weight downward. She could just sidestep and knock him down. Maybe he'd roll. That would be fun to watch.

"The Murphys? Mr. Carrow and Mr. Forrester? You guys hang out at the Flex, right?"

His expression hardened. "Cop?"

"Private investigator. Like your other friend, Clark Wilcox."

Pearl snorted and threw his head back. "Wilprick. Right. That dude wasn't a friend."

"He wrote an awful lot about you for you two not to be friends."

He looked at her again. "You read what he wrote? You have it?"

Ari said, "I wouldn't come any closer."

"Why? You got a gun?"

"Guns are a bluff. I pull a gun, at some point I have to pull the trigger to make it a worthwhile threat. That either brings cops, or I put a bullet in your head and that's the end of your usefulness. It also makes me a murderer. I'm not a murderer, Mr. Pearl. Are you?"

He narrowed his eyes. He looked toward the house as a diversion, then lunged at her. Ari backed up a step and swung her right arm out from behind her hip. The stun baton ratcheted out to its full sixteen inches and she pressed the button on its handle. Blue electricity arced across the tip as she jabbed it toward Pearl's midsection. His eyes widened and he aborted his attack, twisting to the side with his hands out to the side to avoid grazing the weapon accidentally. When he was back on his feet, he retreated a few steps with his arms still out to the side.

"Okay... okay, sorry."

"Right," Ari said. She had seen the shock stick the other Cousins had taken to Wilcox's apartment and hadn't been thrilled at the idea of ending up on the business end of it. Still, turnabout was fair play, and it was a lovely negotiating tool. "Can we have a conversation, or am I going to have to use this?"

"Easy! Put the cattle prod away!"

Ari said, "I think I'll leave it out until we're nice and friendly. Clark Wilcox. What's his connection to you and the other guys I named?"

Pearl said, "If you got his files, you already know."

"I was always a lazy reader. Summarize it for me."

"I'm not going to insinuate myself."

Ari tried hard not to laugh. "I'm not asking you to incriminate yourself. I just want the details. Maybe give them to me as a hypothetical. That way, no one has any proof you're selling out your buddies. It's just a story you're telling."

He considered that for a moment, or maybe trying to work out the meaning of 'hypothetical.' Either way, he eventually decided to talk.

"Let's say there's this group of guys. On weekends they do

bodybuilding competitions. You know, like Arnold used to do all the time."

"They still have those?" Ari asked.

Pearl said, "They have plenty, all right? All around Washington, some down in California, points in between. These guys do okay. I mean, they're not winning the whole thing, but they're getting recognized. Maybe a magazine cover or an interview. It's nice. And then one day, some prick of a private eye comes around. He gets pictures of these guys in the gym after it's closed, and pictures of their gear. Prick breaks into our lockers and takes the moral high ground? Right! Whatever." He exhaled sharply a few times, hands on his hips.

"So anyway... anyway, he goes... and he tells these guys he'll keep quiet if the price is right. He'll tell whoever hired him that there was no evidence of drug use and we can keep on performing. Then one month we're a little bit late. We showed up to pay him, and his office is covered with cops. We figured he was making good on his threat. We tried to find the videos so we could destroy them, but then we found out he was dead. All that evidence was out there in the world somewhere. So we started looking for it. That's all we were doing with the girl."

"Tiffany Knight?"

He nodded. "We weren't going to rough her up or anything. Tommy even got us all to pitch in so we could give her some money for the info. Four hundred and sixty-two dollars. We would've just driven her in a circle and then dropped her off with four Benjamins in her pocket. But because of that bitch getting in the way, Mikey and Joel are facing a kidnapping charge. If they talk, we're all screwed."

Ari said, "I'm sorry your failed kidnapping is causing you problems."

"Hey!" He took a step toward her.

"Hey." She lifted the baton

He backed off, hands in the air. "Do you know where his evidence is? If you handed it over, that would be it. You know, his secretary... we wouldn't have to ask her about it."

Ari said, "She doesn't know. And if any of you guys go after her, that bitch who stopped you at McGraw Square is going to become a real thorn in your side."

His eyes widened with recognition. "Hey..."

She waved the baton again. "Remember, I knocked down your two boys unarmed. You really want to feel what this thing is like? Even through your clothes, it packs a heck of a wallop."

"We don't want to hurt anybody. We just paid Wilcox every month. Sometimes we were a little late, but we paid. And we were going to pay that little... th-that receptionist of his. We don't even want to keep the damn computer. We just want our parts of it erased. We paid for it to be put aside. Just because Wilcox decided to eat a bullet, we got to suffer?"

Ari said, "Yeah, it's a real tragedy." She lowered the stun baton. "Okay, look. I have the videos he threatened you with. If you leave Tiffany alone, you don't have anything to worry about. But if I hear anything about you guys hassling her..."

"We'll back off. We promise. We just want to keep everything quiet."

"Okay. Then you have my word."

He exhaled with what she thought might be relief. "Look, we're just keeping up with the competition, you know? Everyone's juicing at least a little bit. And it's not like we don't put in the work, too. You can't do this kind of work~"

Ari held up her hands and patted the air. "You don't have to justify anything to me, pal. Just keep away from Tiffany. Nothing else has to happen with Wilcox's files."

He nodded and turned back toward the truck. Ari started to leave, but then a thought occurred to her. "Hey. When you tried to grab Tiffany, how did you know where to find her? You guys loaded up your Kidnapper Special van... but how did you know she was in McGraw Square. I assumed one of you was watching her, but you were all in the van. At least all the names I have."

Pearl shrugged. "What names do you have?"

"You, the Murphys, Forrester, and Carrow."

"You got us. But we're not the only ones who had a beef with Wilcox. You saw that damn computer. He's full up on enemies. One of them was watching the girl, and he knew we were watching, too. He figured we had a better chance of snatching her than he did, so he called us in."

"Okay. Care to enlighten me on this mysterious third party?"

He shook his head and turned his back to her. "I don't know his name. He called Mikey, did all the planning with him. But whoever he is, lady, he's dangerous. And he's seen you, after that little trick you pulled saving the girl. You might want to watch your back."

Ari feigned indifference. "Yeah, I'll do that. Thanks for the advice."

She waited until she was at the car, well out of sight from the moving van, before she took out her phone and dialed Dale's cell.

"Hey, puppy. Everything okay?"

"For now. Listen, I need you to get out of there."

Dale's voice lost its lightness. "What's going on?"

"Maybe nothing. But the Creep Cousins might not be the only ones we should be concerned about. Get Wilcox's iPad and go somewhere safe. Go..." She closed her eyes and wrinkled her nose, but she knew it was the only option. "Go to my mother's."

"Are you sure?"

"No one would think to look for you there. Go."

Ari could hear Dale going into the office to retrieve the tablet, so she got into the car.

Dale said, "How dangerous is it right now?"

"I don't know. The Creeps were only part of the threat. I think I've neutralized them... to a degree, anyway. We shouldn't have to worry about them. But there's someone else on that iPad that we don't know anything about. He set up a kidnapping to get the iPad once. If he knows we have it, he might do something else drastic. I would rather play it safe than sorry."

"Me too." There was a pause and Dale said, "Okay. Street looks clear. I'm heading over now."

"Okay. Be very careful. Watch for tails. Don't let anyone follow you."

"I'll be careful, puppy. Promise. Where will you be?"

"I'll be right behind you."

Dale said, "See you there."

Ari sighed and hung up. Sending Dale to her mother's was the only real option, but it meant that the truth about what was said at the cabin would come to light. She knew it would happen eventually, but now she felt like she was being forced into it. If she couldn't prevent it, she wanted to at least be there when Dale heard the story.

CHAPTER FIFTEEN

GWEN TRIED to disguise her shock at seeing who was on her doorstep, but she wasn't a very good actress. "Oh. Miss Frye. Dale. I-I didn't expect you..."

"It was a bit of a surprise to me, too. May I come in?"

"Yes, of course." She stepped aside and ushered Dale into the house. "Ariadne isn't with you?"

Dale said, "She's on her way. We're in the middle of a case, and Ari thought that I'd be safer here." Gwen closed the door and followed Dale into the living room. "I hope you don't mind."

"No, I don't mind." She stood in the doorway, rubbing her arm. "Um, please, have a seat. Make yourself comfortable."

Dale went to the couch. "I wanted to stop by on Thanksgiving, but Ari said it wasn't necessary. She said you two were pretty much sick of each other after the cabin."

"Right. Right." She joined Dale in the living room and sat across from her in a wingback chair. She crossed one leg over the other and smoothed down the material. "Has she mentioned much about what happened up in the woods?"

"Not really. She said it was a great experience and the two of you are closer than ever."

"Hum." Gwen looked away, the expression on her face guarded.

There was a knock on the door and Ari entered before Gwen could even start to get up. She looked between the two of them and lingered a moment on Dale's expression.

"You didn't tell her."

"Tell me what?"

Ari said, "Nothing. Never mind. Do you have the iPad?" Dale held it up. Ari went to the couch and sat next to Dale, taking the tablet and turning it on. As it booted up, she explained everything about the case to her mother and then filled in Dale on what she'd learned from Pearl. "So there's another player, one who is willing to use people like the Creep Cousins to do his dirty work. Whatever he's trying to hide is on this iPad."

She opened the notes folder and then went to the videos. She scrolled through until she found one that matched, and she clicked play. She recognized Tommy Carrow and Mike Murphy standing in an empty gym. The footage was shaky and often lost track of the principle characters, but it always managed to focus back on them eventually. They were talking but their voices were too low for the microphone to pick up individual words. Eventually Mike tapped Tommy on the arm and gestured with his chin. A third man entered, they chatted, and even though they were alone in a dark gym, they did their best to conceal what was changing hands.

"Steroids," Dale said.

Ari nodded. "This is what Wilcox was using the blackmail Murphy and the others." She closed the video and went back to the other options. "The guy giving them the drugs was too shadowed to see very well. He's going to be on one of these other videos. He did something that made him worthy of blackmail. Now I just have to dig through and find it."

"Maybe he's on one of the other Creep Cousin videos in better light. It could make it easier to figure out who is involved."

Ari nodded. "But until then, he knows we're involved. I don't want you to go back to the office until we know it's safe."

Gwen said, "She can stay here as long as necessary."

Ari looked at Gwen as if she'd forgotten she was in the room. "That~"

"That would be great," Dale interrupted. "I'd love to stay here. Maybe Neka and Simon should be warned, too. The last time someone was pissed at you and couldn't find you, they burned down the apartment."

"Right," Ari said. "I'll go call them right now."

She stood and left the room, pausing by her mother without saying anything before she continued on. Gwen watched her go and then sank back into her chair. Dale observed the women with concern, speaking only once she heard Ari on the phone in the other room.

"Can I ask what the hell is going on? Ari says you two are closer than ever after the getaway, but she's acting as skittish around you as ever. Worse, even. She's acting the way she did during wolf manoth."

Gwen sighed and nodded. "Yes. I suppose the whole story about what happened in the woods isn't as cut-and-dry as we were hoping to be. Ariadne and I are closer than we ever have been. For a while it was like her leaving never happened. We were truly a mother and pup." She smiled wistfully. "Then I had to go and ruin it all."

"How?"

Gwen sighed and rubbed the bridge of her nose. "I was stupid, Dale. I was very stupid. I let the wolf take over a bit too much and I spoke without thinking about the repercussions. With my bite, I basically made Ariadne a puppy again. The wolf she became was a newborn. We would roughhouse, fight, kill prey and then carry the bones around like trophies." Dale wrinkled her nose and Gwen chuckled. "It's not as disgusting as it sounds. It's all very circle of life."

"I know. And I know Ari sometimes makes fresh kills when she goes on a run. But that doesn't mean I want to picture her with some... animal in her mouth."

"I understand. And you have to understand what it's like for a *canidae* mother and pup. We transform in front of one another. We're frequently naked. In fact, most of our time spent in the woods, we didn't bother to wear clothes."

Dale said, "Oh. Okay. So what happened, did you... I mean, was there a boy wolf up there?"

"No," Gwen said, "nothing like that. I'm only telling you this so you understand how things were. Ari and I were stripped bare in front of each other. The line between us and the wolf was very, very thin even when we were in human form. You might not have recognized either of us if you happened upon the scene. And when you're in that element, sometimes things get said that you can't take back."

Gwen said, "Sitting by the stream post-run."

Ari tossed her phone onto the couch. "We were naked, sweaty, and sitting next to each other on the rocks. It was the best day we'd ever had together. I remember looking at her, and her eyes were still gold. Like the wolf's. That's why I'm not letting it get to me, Mom. Because I know it wasn't speaking for you. It was just being a stupid animal."

"Right," Gwen said softly.

"What did she say?" Dale asked.

"'You still smell like your human,'" Ari said. "'You reek of it. You're going to have to scrub long and hard to get that off if you want to be worthy of another wolf mounting you.'"

Dale said, "Oh."

"Yeah."

Gwen looked at Dale. "You have to understand..."

"I understand, Miss Willow."

Gwen said, "Dale… please. I asked…"

"I know what you asked." She shut off the iPad and held it to her chest. "I think we should go. We'll find somewhere else to hide out."

She hooked her arm around Ari's and let herself be led out of the house, not looking back. She was grateful she'd never called Gwen 'mom.' She would hate to have sullied the word with someone who would say something like that.

They drove back home in their separate vehicles to pack a bag, still undecided where they would run to. There was always Dale's family cabin, although the last time they'd gone there hadn't exactly been calming. Neka said she would stay with Simon for a few days, and Ari apologized for bringing potential danger into their lives. "Don't even worry about it," Neka assured her. "It's kind of exciting. Besides, part of me doesn't really believe anything bad will happen, so it's kind of like a game." She paused. "Don't insist on making me see the reality of the situation, okay?" Ari promised, and insisted on thinking of a way to make it up to her.

Dale was unusually silent while they packed. Ari kept looking over at her, hoping Dale would be prompted to say something, but finally Ari was the one forced to speak.

"I know you probably feel betrayed by what she said…"

"I don't," Dale said quietly. "I thought I was, back at the house, but driving over here, I realized she's not the problem. She's old-school. She can be expected to have those kinds of thoughts." She dropped a blouse into the suitcase and stared at it. "I thought about it while I was driving over here. Why you kept me away from her, why you wouldn't tell me what happened or what she said until you absolutely had to. If it was just because of what she said, you would've been upfront about it. Instead you made sure to prove the wolf loved me. You set out to prove that nothing had changed after you were bitten. You wanted me to be absolutely sure you were the same Ariadne that left."

"I am," Ari said softly.

"I know. But I also know how you react to things, Ari." She finally met Ari's gaze. "You're not mad at your mother for saying it. You're mad because a part of you believed it. That's what the whole 'the wolf loves you' thing was on Thanksgiving. And jumping me the moment we got back home. You were trying to prove to yourself that what she said didn't matter."

Ari said, "And I did."

Dale crossed the room and ran her hands through Ari's hair. "I don't care if you have doubts about us. I've had my own doubts. I'm a human dating outside her species. There have been times when I've wondered what the hell we're doing. But then I look at you, and I know. Do you know? When you look at me, do you know that you don't need another wolf?"

"Absolutely." Ari put her arms around Dale. "I don't want someone like Milo. I don't want someone I can run with and hunt with. I want someone who will be there to hold me when I get home. I want someone who can take care of me, and who I can protect in return." She looked around the apartment. "Not that I'm doing a very good job of that right now."

"You're doing fine."

Ari sighed. "We're running away again. Hiding."

Dale said, "That's the appropriate response when someone is hunting you."

"But is it the right response?" She sat on the edge of the bed. "If someone does come here looking for us, they'll see we're gone. And they... trash the place? Burn it to the ground like the hunters did with my apartment? How many homes are we going to lose because we're hiding? This is our first home together. When we leave, I want it to be because we're moving into the home you deserve, not because we were forced out." She looked at the suitcase and stood up. "We're not leaving."

"Ari..."

"If they come for us, at least we'll know who we're dealing

with. Neka is safe, and I'll keep you safe from whatever happens." She stood in front of Dale. "We're not running. Not this time."

Dale took Ari's hand, then nodded. She went to the suitcase and took out the clothes she had just packed. Ari breathed a sigh of relief and went to the small sliver of a window next to their bed. It looked out across the lawn at ankle height. Whoever was coming after Wilcox's blackmail folder might know her name and what she looked like, he might know the name of her business and where she lived, but she was absolutely certain he didn't know what the hell he was up against.

CHAPTER SIXTEEN

ARI GOT the whiteboard from the kitchen, erased the grocery list, and propped it up on the coffee table. She hooked up the iPad to their printer and went to work grabbing images from the videos Wilcox had made that were labeled with the Creep Cousins' initials, and printing out pictures of each one. She placed these on the boards and identified every video the men appeared in. Their dealer was unidentified, but she had a shadowy image of him taped to the top edge of the board as well.

"Wilcox was so lazy with the rest of his life," she said, "why does his blackmail scheme have to look like something out of *The Da Vinci Code?*"

"Screwing you one last time," Dale suggested.

Ari snorted and went back to arranging the information. She didn't want to change any of Wilcox's labels, in case there was a system she hadn't discovered yet, but she needed a way to keep track of everything. She copied the Cousins' videos into a new folder where she could arrange them as she pleased. She arranged them by name, and then by date. She watched each one and took screen grabs of the dealer in each one. Wilcox had used a small, cheap camera which was hidden somewhere near one corner of the Flex gym. People were often decapitated by the shot, or represented solely by a hand or shadow that made it into frame. Their voices echoed off the bare walls and weight machines so much that it was often difficult to make out what was being said, but there was enough to convince a ruling committee that they should be disqualified from a competition.

One of the videos had been made three days before Wilcox died. Ari clicked on it and put in her earbud. Someone moved in front of the camera as soon as the video began, a pair of legs crossing from left to right. The focus of the shot was on a corner of a boxing ring. The shadowy steroid dealer moved into frame followed by another muscular shadow.

"This stuff is guaranteed to 'pomp... you op'," one of the Murphy brothers said, mimicking the Dana Carvey character from the eighties.

"Just give me the cash. You're not as entertaining as you think you are."

The Murphy brother grunted. The dealer was looking down at his hands, counting off money Ari assumed. He looked up and waved a handful of folded bills.

"You're short."

"You know I'm good for it next time."

Dealer: "Short means there's not going to be a next time."

The other Murphy. "We had an emergency expense this week. It's fine."

Dealer: "That private eye? I thought you bully boys were going to take care of him."

"We are."

"By paying him?"

"It's keeping the videos from ever seeing the light of day."

The dealer sighed. "This is the last delivery until you're out of the crosshairs."

"You can't do that!" That from a voice Ari didn't recognize; she assumed Forrester or Carrow.

"You're putting me at risk here. The guy has pictures of you, then he has pictures of me."

Forrester again: "It's not pictures. It's video."

Murphy One: "How does that make it better?"

The dealer said, "Just everyone shut up. Deal with the private eye or this is the last you'll see of me. Understood?"

"Right," Murphy One said. "We'll handle it."

Ari sighed and took out the earbud. Dale, who had been reading in the armchair, looked up. "Problem?"

"No. Well. Maybe. I have to go talk to the guys I just sent to prison for attempted kidnapping."

Dale marked her place in the book. "Do you think they were involved?"

Ari said, "I actually don't. From what I've learned, they're all bark and no bite. I think Wilcox would have pegged them the same way. He would have fought back even if all five came after him at once. The stun baton made Pearl back off immediately when I waved it at him. I think the others would be the same way. But according to this, the Cousins might have been watching Wilcox the last few days of his life. They might have seen something that can help."

"Couldn't hurt to ask," Dale said.

Ari nodded. "I'll call Diana and see if she can set it up for tomorrow." She rubbed her eyes and pinched the bridge of her nose. "I've spent too long staring at the computer screen. I think I'm going to go out for a run."

"It's a little early. Do you think it's safe?"

Ari went to the window and peered out, gauging the light left in the sky. "Yeah, I might be risking the dogcatcher if I go out now."

Dale looked at her watch. "Well, it'll be full dark in about half an hour. What if I drove you out somewhere and dropped you off? The travel time would get you past sunset. Then you could run back and cover new ground."

"Sort of like a reverse of what we usually do." She smiled. "I like it. It'll give me a chance to see what the city's traffic is like before I let the wolf free. We could go all the way up to Woodland Park."

"Are you sure you could get back over the bridges?"

Ari said, "Yeah, after dark it won't be much of a problem."

Dale put down her book and sat up to put on her shoes. "We could do this more often, you know. I could dump you wherever you want and let the wolf find her way home. Since you don't necessarily need me to come pick you up every time. The wolf might like the chance to run toward a destination instead of just traveling in a circle."

"She does like to track. And I think we have the neighborhood pretty well-covered."

The lights in Neka's part of the house were dark when they left. Dale drove her north toward the bridge, then cut west along the shore of Lake Union to take Aurora into Fremont so Ari could see which route was busier and more likely to result in reports of a wolf wandering toward downtown. Her biggest fear was that some motorist would have a gun in their car and try to do the "heroic" thing. A wild animal loose in the city was a real threat, and the average citizen would have no way of knowing Ariadne from a threatening predator.

When they reached the park, Dale found a secluded area to park near the tennis courts. There were rolling hills and tall trees, spacious enough for a good sprint but with just enough coverage to keep out of sight if someone happened by. It was as good a place as any for the wolf to run around before heading home. The sun had indeed gone down, and now the shadows had grown to cover most of the area around the car. Soon the overhead security lights would snap on. She scanned for any homeless or joggers or cyclists who might wander past as Ari climbed into the backseat. When she was certain the coast was clear, she twisted and looked back as Ari began to undress.

"You sure you want to watch?"

"It doesn't hurt you anymore. Well, not as much. It's part of who you are. I want to witness it as much as I can. Unless you don't~"

Ari said, "No. It's fine with me." She took Dale's hand and squeezed. They both checked once more for witnesses as Ari pulled her feet up onto the seat. Dale wished she could turn on the overhead light, but she didn't want to draw undue attention to what was happening. Ari pulled her arms in tight against her chest and rolled her head back, looking like a magician trying to escape a straitjacket. She pointed her chin toward the roof and thrust her chest forward before collapsing back. Her legs straightened out and then bent again.

Dale forced herself not to blink. Ari's skin turned dark as her face twisted and shifted. She was witnessing a miracle, basically, her girlfriend transforming into another creature. It was an act that the majority of people would deem impossible, and yet. Ari opened her mouth wider than any human should've been able to and Dale saw a narrow set of wolf teeth. When she closed her mouth, her jaw had reshaped to fit those teeth, and Ari flipped over onto her hands and knees. Or rather, she flipped over onto her folded forelegs.

Just like that, it was over. Ari's ribs bellowed out with each breath as she turned her head and fixed now-golden eyes on her. She and the wolf stared at each other. Its eyes shined and reflected light Dale couldn't see. Its snout was brown and white and wide between the eyes like Ari's nose, but exaggerated to the current shape of her head. The muzzle led down to a shining black nose that twitched impatiently. Her skull was more pyramid-shaped now, with a flat mesa between the ears. Not technically human, she wasn't technically a wolf, either. She was canidae, a special creature that only a few knew existed. She was a myth, one of the most amazing creatures Dale had ever encountered, and against all odds, she was in love with Dale. Dale kissed her mythological girlfriend between the eyes and rubbed her neck.

"Be safe, Ariadne. I'll be waiting for you at home."

Ari licked Dale's face. Dale reached for the door and pulled the handle, pushing it open so the wolf could squirm out onto the pavement. She braced her legs and shook violently, flexing her muscles before she turned to look back at the car. Dale smiled and gave her a thumbs-up, and the wolf turned and began running.

Dale watched until Ari was out of sight before she reversed out of the parking spot. She thought her headlights caught a glimpse of brown fur through the trees, but she couldn't be certain. A part of her wanted to pace the drive home, an attempt to keep up with Ari on her journey through the city, but she knew it would be a fool's errand. Ari was quick and clever about the paths she took. She also didn't want the wolf to think she was spying or being overprotective.

She took the bridge home, parked next to Neka's car, and went downstairs to their apartment. She could have gone to bed, opened her book again, taken a shower, any number of things, but she thought about the night earlier in the year when she undressed and stood outside in the cold to see what it was like for Ari.

She left the apartment lights off, drew the curtains, and undressed. She stretched and then began to jog in place. After a few minutes she dropped down and did some pushups. She didn't count; it wasn't about an exercise regimen. She kept her breathing steady as she got up and started jogging again. She went around the coffee table, she did lunges, she held a plank position for almost a minute before her arms gave out. Sweat was shining on her forehead and trickling down her chest when she starting doing jumping jacks.

Her thighs burned. Her feet were sore. But she kept moving, going past the point when she wanted to stop. She was panting, shaky on her feet, sure that she would fall over if she stopped moving. At one point she leaned forward with her palms flat against the wall to catch her breath. She didn't look at the clock. She just kept moving. She did burpees. She did planks again. She did everything she could think of to keep her body moving.

Then at long last, she heard a scratch at the door. She was panting when she went to answer, legs rubbery and hands shaky as she twisted the knob and pushed it open. Ari brushed past her and the cool fur felt like magic against her calves. Dale closed and locked the door and watched as the miracle reversed itself and Ariadne Willow took the place of the wild creature in the middle of the living room. Ari stood up and popped her back, turned to look at Dale, and frowned. Ari was equally sweaty, just as breathless, and it took her a long moment before she could manage words.

"What...?"

Dale said, "I can't... run with you..." She blew out a lungful of air. "So I thought I'd... y'know... run... with you."

Ari's confusion cleared and she took a step forward. "Because you're my pack?"

"I'm your pack," Dale said. "I may not be a wolf, but maybe I'm a good substitute."

Ari said, "You're not a wolf." She reached up and twisted a sweat-darkened strand of Dale's hair around her finger. "With this red hair? You're definitely a fox."

Dale bit her bottom lip, eyes shining in the dark. Their bodies were both trembling from the adrenaline coursing through their bodies. Ari cupped Dale's face and kissed her. Dale whimpered and slipped her hands under Ari's arms. They clung to each other, the endorphins from their mutual exertion transforming into something else as they pressed against each other. Dale felt like her senses were on fire. She was incredibly aware of the natural odor of Ari's sweat, the dirt that had remained under her fingernails when she went back to human form, and the taste of Ari's tongue in her mouth.

"Let me take you to bed..."

Dale said, "No. Floor."

"Wall?"

Dale whimpered in response and dragged Ari across the room. When Ari hit the wall, Dale stepped back and let her hands skim over the smooth lines of Ari's body. Running five or ten or fifteen miles every few nights as the wolf kept Ari lean and fit, and Dale swept her fingers over the sweat that had beaded on her flat stomach. Her thumb pressed into the tight dip of Ari's navel before moving down to the hair that had remained between her legs when she resumed human form. Ari breathed in through her nose and let it out through her teeth. Her eyes were half-closed, but Dale could see them shining as they focused on her.

"Growl for me, puppy."

"You first, foxy lady."

Dale peeled her lips back and gave her best growl, flaring her nostrils and adding a quiet yip to the end. Ari shivered and tensed against the wall. She put her hands on Dale's shoulders and pushed her down, moving her feet apart. Dale wet her lips, angling her head so she wouldn't lose eye contact as she got onto her hands and knees. Ari pushed the lank hair away from Dale's face and looked down at her, smiling as Dale bent her neck and pressed her mouth against Ari's sex. Ari grunted at the first contact, her fingers tightening as Dale began to stroke with the flat of her tongue. She gasped in pleasure and urged Dale on, arching her back to press her hips forward.

"Good girl... good girl, Dale..."

Dale growled and moved her head, kissing Ari's thighs before she stood up and pressed tight against her. Ari bent her knee and guided Dale onto her thigh. She gripped Dale's ass with both hands as Dale put her hands in Ari's hair and pulled her in for another kiss. Ari moaned as their tongues met. She began guiding Dale's hips in a slow and steady rhythm, letting her ride her thigh. Dale's aches and pains from the workout had faded, although she was still dripping with sweat. Ari was in the same situation, beads of moisture dripping down the side of her face when she pulled back from the kiss and swept her tongue across Dale's lips.

Dale came with a quiet cry, her hand dropping to the back of Ari's neck and gripping it tight enough to hurt. Ari leaned forward and Dale let herself be carried down onto the floor. With Ari on top of her, Dale moved her hand down and worked it between Ari's legs. Ari sighed and repositioned her body, then gasped when Dale's fingers found her.

"You never growled for me," Dale reminded her. "Now. Do it now, puppy."

Ari moved her lips next to Dale's ear and growled low in her throat as she came. She moved her head down and pressed kisses against Dale's skin.

"That was damned amazing." She sank onto Dale, who took her weight without trouble.

Dale's face was covered by Ari's hair. "I can be a fox whenever you want me to be."

"As long as you're my Dale the rest of the time."

"Always," Dale said.

Ari lifted her head and kissed Dale's lips. "We should probably go to bed."

"In a few minutes. I seriously don't think I can move."

Ari laughed and kissed Dale's chin. "In a few minutes, then."

She put her head on Dale's shoulder and closed her eyes until they were able to relocate.

CHAPTER SEVENTEEN

THE NEXT morning, Ari called Diana to outline what she wanted to do. Diana got back to her after lunch and told her to be downtown at three o'clock. The DA was willing to cooperate if it did lead to a bigger fish. She couldn't promise a meeting with either of the Murphys, but she would see what she could do. Ari found Diana outside the common area where prisoners could meet with visitors or their attorneys. She was dressed in a Liz Claiborne pantsuit over a peach shirt, and Ari was again struck by how much better it looked on her than the formless uniform she'd been wearing when they met. It also made her feel self-conscious about her own blouse and slacks, even though she'd put a bit of effort into dressing professionally for the meeting.

"You clean up nice," Diana said, reading her mind when she saw Ari approaching.

"Any time I'm not wearing thrift show cast-offs."

Diana said, "That reminds me. You and Lucy are about the same size. If you ever need some clothes donated for your stashes, I can just tell her I dropped them at Goodwill."

"You'd lie to your wife?"

"I'm not lying. I'm just cutting out the middle man and saving you some cash. And I'm saving myself the trouble of explaining why you need it."

Ari said, "True. You could just tell her I don't make much as a private investigator. That's definitely not a lie."

"You don't mind if she thinks you're taking charity?"

"I mind it less than you lying to Lucy to cover up for me."

"I appreciate that."

A guard opened the door and waved them inside. Michael Murphy was just getting settled next to his lawyer, but he stood up again when he saw Ari.

"Forget it. I got nothing to say to this bitch."

Ari said, "That's hurtful language, Mike. After we got all dressed up and came down here just to talk with you."

Mike said, "She beat the crap out of me!"

"While you were in the process of trying to kidnap an innocent woman," Diana said as she took a seat. "Let's skip the part where you try to take the moral high ground and sit your ass down."

Murphy continued to glare as he sank back into the orange plastic seat. Ari sat down beside Diana and folded her arms in front of her.

"We're here to talk to you about a deal."

"You're not going to give me a deal."

Diana said, "Ordinarily you would be correct. You were caught in the act, and that's not even your biggest problem at the moment. We found steroids in your car. That's a Schedule III controlled substance, Mr. Murphy. You and your brother are looking at jail time for that alone. Add in what you were trying to do when Miss Willow stopped you, and I think we can say you're not going to walk out of here any time soon."

Murphy stared blankly at her. The lawyer said, "If you're just here to gloat, Detective Macallan, we're not interested."

"No, there's a purpose to this meeting. There's a chance we could make the kidnapping go away. Miss Willow here says that she has it on good authority that your intention was not to harm Tiffany Knight. You were just going to take her for a ride and have a conversation, then let her go on her merry way. It sounds like bullshit to me, but I trust Ariadne's word. If you help us, I might be willing to drop those charges."

"I'm not going to flip on any of my friends."

"We're not going to ask you to." Diana looked at Ari and motioned for her to go ahead.

Ari rested her elbows on the table. "I know you and your pals from the gym were following Clark Wilcox for three days before he died. You all had reason to want him out of the picture."

Murphy frowned. "Are you asking me to confess to murder to get out of a kidnapping charge? That's gotta be the stupidest plan I've ever heard of. Besides, none of us touched that guy."

"I know. The ME confirmed it was suicide. I'm trying to find the person who drove Wilcox to pulling the trigger. I don't think it was you or any of your bodybuilding pals. But if you were watching him for his final three days, you might have seen something that could lead us in the right direction. If you were to help us out, that could go a long way in getting that kidnapping charge dropped."

Murphy narrowed his eyes at her as if trying to feel the edges of what she'd said for a trap. The lawyer asked for a moment to confer with his client, so Ari and Diana stood and stepped out of the room. Ari had spoken with Tiffany on the phone to get her blessing for their plan. It wasn't ideal, but the fact was that the Creep Cousins never laid a hand on her and Ari believed they were smart enough to not try again. She felt confident Tiffany was safe, and getting the information was worth the price. She just had to hope Murphy agreed.

The lawyer came to the door and asked them back into the room. Murphy resumed glaring at Ari as soon as she came in.

She chose not to respond.

"I want the deal even if I can't be helpful."

Diana laughed. "That's not the way this goes, Mr. Murphy."

"No, I mean… I mean, I'll tell you what we saw. I'll tell you everything. But I don't know how useful it's going to be. I didn't see anyone walk up and put a gun in Wilcox's mouth. I never even saw him get roughed up. But I'm going to tell you as much as I can. I don't want my deal coincident with results."

"Coincident?" Diana said, looking at the lawyer.

"I think he meant contingent."

Diana said, "Ah." She looked at Ari, who shrugged and lifted her hand helplessly. She couldn't think of a better resource than Murphy's report. "I think the DA will agree to that."

Murphy shifted in his seat. "Well. Okay. We had three different cars and we took shifts so we could watch him 'round the clock. We were trying to figure out his schedule so we'd know the perfect time to…" His eyes darted from his lawyer to Diana. "To have a private conversation with him. It was usually me and Tommy, but sometimes Joel or Frank would take over if it looked like Wilcox was just going to be planted at his office for hours on end. They never reported much. He talked on the phone a lot. Spent most of the day on the computer. Around six o'clock he would go get something to eat and take it home to spend the rest of the night watching TV or whatever."

Ari said, "He never met with anybody during the three days you were watching him? Not a single client?"

"None I saw. Maybe when Joel was following him. He never really ventured outside his regular route. Apartment, office, back and forth. Sometimes he went out of his way to eat somewhere, but other than that…" He shrugged and then held one hand up. "Wait. He did go up into Fremont once. It was the Thursday night. You know, all those warehouses along the canal? Supply stores, garages, equipment rentals… just a bunch of big ugly buildings and chain link fences around them. No real reason to be up there after dark, know what I'm saying? He drove around up there for a while, then he got out and started walking. Joel said he couldn't follow without getting spotted, so he didn't know where he went. We all just assumed he'd gotten a whore, you know?"

Diana said, "Language."

"What is this, middle school?"

Diana aimed a finger at him and he rolled his eyes.

"Sorry. We assumed he'd paid a professional woman to do things to his pee-pee. Better, Detective?" He sighed and shook his head. "Anyways, he was up there for about ten minutes and then he came walking back out. Joel said he never saw who he met with, but another car pulled out behind him. Followed him across the bridge but turned off when they got back to downtown. Wilcox went back home and didn't leave until the next morning."

Ari said, "What did the other car look like?"

"It looked like a pair of headlights in the rearview mirror. We weren't doing a dossier on the guy, we just wanted to know what his schedule was like. We didn't care who he was meeting."

"You have no idea who he was meeting?" Murphy shook his head. "And forty-eight hours later, Wilcox was dead in his office."

Diana looked at Ari. "You think whoever he met up there put a scare into him?"

"Yeah." To Murphy, Ari said, "What was Wilcox like the day after?"

"He stayed in his office all day. That secretary of his was there all day, or else we would've taken the chance to have our talk with him." He made a fist with his left hand, closing his right around it to massage the knuckles. He looked at a point between Ari and Diana's heads. "I mean... looking back, knowing what I know now? Yeah. It looked like he was hiding.

But I don't see how that's going to help you find out who was scaring him."

Ari said, "Maybe not. But you did help. Thank you."

He grimaced and shifted his weight in his seat. "Yeah. Well. You're actually a pretty tough chick. I would've been impressed if I hadn't been on the receiving end of it."

Ari and Diana left Murphy with the guard and stepped out of the room. Diana said, "That actually helped? It seemed like a lot of vague nonsense to me."

"Maybe, maybe not. Now that I know there was a mysterious meeting by the canal, I can check Wilcox's memoir for any mention of it."

Diana said, "That clown has memoirs?"

"On his laptop. If he was hiding in his office all day after it happened, he might have tried to rewrite history. Make himself the dashing private investigator who saved the day instead of the hack who ran away and hid." She thought about the timeline. "The day he spent hiding in his office... he never went home. And that was the night he called and complimented me."

Diana said, "He must have been terrified."

Ari nodded and held out her hand. "Thank you, Diana. This was a big help. I owe you one."

"Pay me back by being safe, okay?"

"I'll try my best."

Diana smiled. "That's not as reassuring as you think it is. You're good at a lot of things, Ariadne, but watching your own back isn't really in your wheelhouse."

"That's why I have Dale."

"Ah. Then give her my best."

Ari promised she would and headed for the parking garage. She hoped Wilcox had written something about the mysterious meeting, otherwise she was back at square one with no other avenues to follow.

Ari had stretched out on the couch with Wilcox's memoirs.

Dale was at her desk in the outer office, singing softly under her breath. Ari hated the sound of people singing under ordinary circumstances. She couldn't even bear karaoke. She tapped her foot against the arm of the couch and offered harmony when whatever Dale was singing required it. They went through Brandi Carlile, to Adele, to Radiation Canary, back to Brandi as Ari skimmed through the writing. It was sad, when she thought about it. Wilcox, sitting in his office, writing about a dashing and heroic figure that he would never actually be.

She went to the end of the memoirs and looked for the start of the last entry. She finally found it and began reading. "I'd done this sort of thing a million times," he wrote, "and I still get the same thrill as I did the first time. I was told to meet the big man in a specific lot, an empty warehouse rising up like a broken tombstone in front of me. Gravel under my feet. I had my Glock under my jacket tucked into my belt. I could hear the water in the canal but it wasn't loud enough to drown out the sound of tires crushing the tiny stones on the ground under my feet."

Ari grimaced at his writing and reformed everything in what she felt was a more realistic light. Someone - the "big man" - had arranged a meeting in the middle of nowhere. Wilcox showed up and was scared enough that he'd brought a gun. It sounded like he was keyed up.

"Turns out," Wilcox continued, "the big man decided not to show up himself. I should've known. He sent a flunky. The moke's name--"

Ari said, "Dale, he used the word 'moke.'"

"Don't make fun of the dead."

Ari whimpered and continued reading.

"There was no reason to keep my ace in the hole, so I took out my gun and made sure he knew I had it. He didn't even slow down. 'There's no need for that, Mr. Wilcox. We're just here to hopefully come to an agreement. My employer doesn't appreciate messages like the one you left him. He doesn't like being threatened by people like you.'

'It's not a threat,' I told him. 'I'm just telling him how it will be. Do you know what's on that video? You know what he did, and you're still here defending him?'

'I'm here to do my job, Mr. Wilcox. My job is to protect my client at all costs.'

'You've said my name twice, but I don't know yours.'

'Let's skip names for right now. No names. You can just call me ombudsman. It's a nice word. It has gravitas.'

I didn't like the way he looked at me. Like he was better than me. Probably was, with his fancy-ass suit and his shellacked hairdo. I wanted to punch him on principal.'"

Ari put the iPad down and pinched the bridge of her nose. "Principle," she muttered too low for Dale to hear. After a few seconds to forget the misspelling she sighed and began reading again.

"'There isn't anything complicated about this, ombudsman,' I said. 'How much is he going to spend if this gets out? How much is he gonna lose? It's so much cheaper to just pay me and move on.'

'I have another option. You are going to be ruined, Mr. Wilcox. You are going to wish you never laid eyes on that video. The man you are threatening is not an enemy you want, but you've made him angry. He's read up on you and he doesn't like what he's found. You're the shit he scrapes off his shoe whenever he's forced to travel too close to Boeing Field. And you think you can extort money from him? You think you have some measure of power over a man like that?'

I was unshaken. 'Seems like your boss is the one hiding.'

He smiled. 'My employer doesn't want to waste his time out here with something like this. The only thing required from this meeting is to send a message, and that message is this: if you release that tape, we will make you regret it. If that video becomes common knowledge, my employer will suffer, and he will make sure that your suffering is ten times worse. He has friends. He has people who will make it their life's mission to destroy your world. People like me, Mr. Wilcox.'

He smiled then. He looked like a shark.

'We won't stop with you. We'll make Tiffany Knight's life hell, *too. We'll ruin her present and her future and we'll make certain she knows that all the pain is your fault. She will curse the day she ever met you. Can you live with that? Knowing you destroyed her life before it ever had a chance to start? You know what we're capable of, Mr. Wilcox. Think about whether you want to subject her to that.'*

He turned around to walk away, but I stopped him. I told him what I thought about his offer. I told him what would happen if he went after Tiffany and I wiped that smirk off his face. Then I walked back to my car and slipped behind the wheel. He was still staring slack-jawed after me as I pulled away. I reached down and felt the flash drive in my pocket and wished I could figure out what to do with it.'"

That was the last thing he'd written. The ending made Ari sad. Obviously Wilcox had been trying to rewrite history with the perfect comeback, the sort of rejoinder that would have put him back on top. And it was just as obvious that he hadn't come up with anything. So after meeting the ombudsman of whoever he was trying to blackmail, Wilcox had gone back home for the night. Then he went to the office and spent the entire day trying to think of a way out of his predicament. Almost twenty-four whole hours behind the locked door looking for an answer, finally finding it in his gun. He mentioned a flash drive in his pocket. There was no reason to change the iPad to a flash drive, so it had to be real. But she hadn't seen one in his office or his apartment.

"Dale."

"Mm-hmm?"

"Did you watch all the blackmail tapes?"

Dale said, "I think about eighty percent of them. Drugs and sex. Very little rock and roll."

"Anything world-ending? Anything big enough to threaten destroying the life of everyone who came into contact with it?"

Dale said, "Nothing that big. Why?"

"Because there's another video out there, on a flash drive. Wilcox must not have left a copy on the iPad. Whatever drove Wilcox to suicide has to be on that flash drive. It was sensitive enough for threats, so it must have been too sensitive to keep with all the others."

"So where's the drive?"

Ari closed her eyes and pictured the places Wilcox frequented. His home and his office. Somewhere between those two points was a flash drive with the answer to everything. She pictured his fancy new home appliances. She pictured his office with the splash of red behind his chair. The Creep Cousins ransacked the apartment. The police went over his office with a fine-toothed comb. But somewhere between his home and...

She rolled onto her side and sat up. She grabbed her jacket off the hook. "I'm going to go get it."

"But if it was in his office or his apartment, then the cops or the Creep Cousins or whoever this new supervillain is probably already found it."

"Not if Wilcox hid it where I think he did." She leaned across the desk and kissed Dale's lips. "I'll be back as soon as I can."

Dale said, "Where are you going?"

"Wilcox's apartment building. I'm guessing all the people who searched it in the past few weeks made the same mistake I did."

"And what's that?"

"We took the stairs."

Chapter Eighteen

The elevator doors were still propped open, and the same disgusting scent wafted out when Ari got close to it. She wondered if it was as potent to anyone without a *canidae* senses. She kept her breathing shallow as she stepped over the Wet Floor sign propping the doors open and stepped inside the car. The light was burnt out, but the lobby was bright enough that she could still see well enough. The button fixture was loose and canted to one side, revealing the innards of the device. She bent down to look inside but didn't see a flash drive.

"I wouldn't."

She looked out into the lobby and saw a man at the foot of the stairs, a shopping bag clutched to his chest. He gestured at the elevator and repeated his warning.

"I wouldn't. It might be a lot of stairs, but that thing is a hazard. Only people who use that are fellas trying to get their date caught between floors for a few hours. Don't risk it."

Ari said, "Thanks for the warning."

He shrugged, his civic duty complete, and Ari went back to

her search. The carpet was threadbare in the corners from years of people standing and pacing, but there were no telltale lumps revealing something hidden underneath. She thought about climbing onto the handrail to check the service hatch or the light fixture, but she realized that Wilcox would've had to do the same thing in order to hide it. If the handrail didn't look capable of holding her weight, it definitely wouldn't have held Wilcox. The hiding spot had to be somewhere within easy reach but not readily apparent.

Of course, she could also be completely wrong about where he'd hidden the flash drive. She stepped out of the elevator and avoided the Wet Floor sign again, but this time she noticed something she missed before; something was wrapped around one leg of the sign. It looked like just a piece of random trash tangled against an obstacle, but the closer she looked, the more unnatural it seemed. She crouched down and discovered it was the handle of a plastic bag, the rest of which had been pushed through the crack where the doors would ordinarily close. She fished it back up, twisting it a little to get the contents lined up right to come through the narrow opening. She held it up and saw the distinctive shape of a flash drive in the bottom of the bag.

"Okay," she whispered, "that was pretty clever, Wilcox. I'll give you this one."

She retrieved the drive and put it in her pocket as she stood up. It felt as if she'd been working on Wilcox's suicide for years, but now she was confident answers were at hand.

She tried not to think about what she would find as she drove back to the office. It could be another dead end, but she doubted it. Wilcox had been scared. Even in his ideal world, where he could muster up all the bravery and charm he required in any given situation, he'd come up empty. When he hid the drive, he was a man at the end of his hope. She knew that whatever was on the drive would be the key to knowing why he'd done something so drastic.

When she got back to the office, she held up the drive like a trophy. Dale quietly applauded her.

"So what's your bet?" Ari asked. "Sex or drugs?"

"Oh, sex. Without question. Drugs, you just do your time in rehab or you go to jail, like the Creep Cousins. This is something a lot bigger. Sex with a prostitute. A male prostitute. Underage."

Ari said, "I like your odds. I'll let you know what I find."

She went into her office and shut the door. She turned on the computer and plugged in the drive. The mechanisms hummed and growled, then a folder popped up on screen. There was only one file, and its thumbnail showed the wall of a hotel room. It was aimed at the nightstand between two beds, the center of the frame taken up by a light brown wall and a half-circle lamp. Ari clicked play and the video opened. Wilcox apparently used high-quality cameras, because the image was pristine and crystal-clear. The video ran for forty-seven minutes, so she was prepared to fast forward until something actually happened, but almost immediately she heard the sound of the door opening.

A woman laughed and crossed the room, passing in front of the camera. Ari caught a glimpse of a red dress and pale skin, but not much else. A man spoke from the doorway and turned on the light, but his voice was just a hollow grumble. The woman laughed again; she sounded drunk. The man appeared and moved to the foot of the bed, revealing a middle-aged man in a tuxedo. He tossed his jacket onto the bed and turned to look toward the woman, revealing his face for the first time.

"Oh, shit."

Ari leaned forward in her seat and paused the video so she could get a good look at the man's face. He had movie star good looks, with a rakish grin that accompanied every television ad and appearance on the local news. State Senator Michael Irwin was charming, liberal, and the man Ari planned to vote for in the next gubernatorial race. And now she had a video of him doing something in a hotel room that Wilcox had considered blackmail-worthy. Ari felt a tickle of dread as she hit play again. The woman moved into frame checking her phone. It was a hard angle to determine age, but she was definitely an adult.

"At least it's not someone underage," Ari muttered. The woman was probably someone's wife, or a member of his staff. That sort of scandal was survivable.

Irwin moved to stand in front of her, invading her personal space as he unfastened his cufflinks. "Are you sure you have to leave? The hotel gave me a ton of complimentary room service. I'll feel bad if it goes to waste."

"Thanks, but I better get going. I have a ton of calls to make after tonight."

"Speaking as your boss, I think I would understand if those waited until tomorrow."

She chuckled politely and started to step aside. "Really. It's late."

He put his hand on her arm. "Right. So why don't you just stay?"

Ari straightened in her seat and muttered, "Oh, no, no, no."

"Michael," the woman said, stepping back out of his reach. "I really need to go."

His grip tightened and he moved closer to her, crowding against her. He took the phone from her and tossed it onto one bed as he began roughly urging her toward the other. Her attempt to evade him became less polite, and his grip tightened on her arms.

"Michael... okay, Michael, stop."

Ari stood up quickly, hands tightening into fists at her sides. She wanted to yank the drive out to make it stop, but she knew she couldn't risk corrupting the file. She turned away from the screen and faced the large clock on the wall, staring at it as she tried to get her breathing under control. She could hear everything happening on the video; she didn't need to see it to comprehend those sounds. The woman made it crystal clear what was happening. Irwin's voice lost any trace of charm and became rough and cruel. Something ripped and Ari brought a hand up to cover her eyes as if she was still looking at the screen.

Eventually she bit back her nausea enough to return to the desk. She jabbed a finger at the keyboard until the sound went away. In the corner of her eye she could see movement, but she ignored it as she moved the tracking to the very end of the video. When she looked again, Irwin was sitting on the other bed. The woman was lying on the other bed with her back to him and to the camera. She was still mostly dressed, but she wasn't moving.

"Move," Ari whispered. "C'mon, honey, move..."

Irwin was in his underwear, and he stood up and leaned over the woman. She cringed away, but he still apparently managed to kiss her. Ari was too relieved that she was alive to be disgusted by the kiss. She turned the volume back up.

"~shower if you want. And the room service... like I said..."

"Just go."

He said, "Suit yourself," and disappeared out of frame. Ari heard the bathroom door close. A few seconds passed before the woman sat up and gathered her clothes. She picked up her shoes where they had fallen and carried them out of frame. The image froze as the video ended, and Ari shut the window. She wanted to scrub down her computer, but she settled for pulling the flash drive out and putting it on the very edge of her desk. She put her elbows on the desk and covered her face with both hands.

She didn't know how long she sat like that. It was more than a minute, less than five, before Dale knocked and stuck her head in. "Hey, is it ov~ hey!" She came into the room and knelt next to Ari's chair. She rubbed Ari's back. "What happened? How bad was it?"

"Bad."

Dale reached for the flash drive.

"No! Don't watch it. I don't want you to see that."

Dale withdrew her hand. "Who was in the video, puppy?"

Ari sat up and took a steadying breath. "Michael Irwin."

"The guy running for governor? Is he having an affair?"

"He's..." Ari closed her eyes. "He raped a woman in a hotel room."

Dale hissed and put her head on Ari's shoulder. "Oh, lord. I'm so sorry you had to see that. Are you okay?"

"I will be." She covered Dale's hand with hers. "Obviously whoever Wilcox met with at the canal worked for Irwin's campaign." She looked at the computer as if the video was still imprinted on the screen. She shivered. "I don't know who the woman was."

"Did you see her face?"

"Yeah."

Dale took the flash drive. "Let me see what I can find."

"Dale..."

"Let me see what I can find," she said again. She kissed Ari's forehead and temple. "Do you want me to call Diana?"

"I... don't know."

"What do you mean?"

Ari said, "I mean... I don't know what I want to do with the video."

Dale furrowed her brow. "There aren't a lot of options, Ari. The man is a rapist, and we have proof right here. Are you thinking of blackmailing him, too?"

"No, of course not. I'm just trying to think through all the consequences here. Irwin is running for governor. And he's... he's the good guy, Dale. Equal rights, living wage, climate, he's on the right side of every single issue. If he drops out of the race, then his opponent automatically wins. The guy who makes Arizona's immigration policy look moderate."

"But... okay, I don't care if Irwin says the right things when a microphone is shoved in his face. If he's this kind of monster in private, then I don't give a damn where he stands on the issues."

Ari said, "I agree with you. I do. But even if he's just going through the motions, he's making the right decisions..."

"He's a rapist, Ariadne."

"I'm not saying I like this, Dale. It's making me sick to my stomach just thinking this way. I don't want to believe I'm the kind of person who would just look the other way. But there aren't any good choices. Either we do nothing and someone we despise gets into office to do the right thing for the wrong reasons. Or we turn it in, and we have some hateful prick who wants to round up all the non-whites and gays and put them in a fenced-off area. In the grand scheme, as reprehensible as it is, what Irwin did is--"

Dale snapped, "Don't you *dare* call rape the lesser of two evils. Even if it was just this one instance, we can't just let it go. We can't just ignore what he did to this woman."

"I know. But we..." She ran her hand over her face. "When Irwin found out Wilcox had this video, he responded with violence and threats. He said that he'd reach out even from prison. If I turn it in, he'll come after us instead. You. Mom. Diana. You'd all be put at risk."

Dale said, "We have to do the right thing."

Ari took the flash drive from her and looked at it. "We have to do it the right way. With the least amount of risk to us."

"Right."

Ari handed the drive back. "Don't watch more than a few seconds. It's bad enough I had to see it. I don't want that in your head."

"Okay." Dale stood up and bent down to kiss the crown of Ari's head. "I love you, puppy."

"I love you, too."

Dale let her hand linger on Ari's shoulder before she finally took the drive out of the office. Ari opened her drawer, wishing she had the private eye trope of a liquor bottle in her desk drawer. She stood up and went back to the clock, then wandered over to the couch. She remembered the first day she'd awkwardly taken off her shirt so Dale could massage her shoulders after a transformation.

"Bra, too."

"I don't think that's~"

"C'mon, Ariadne. You want to feel better or do you want to be modest? I've seen bigger boobs than yours before."

Ari smiled. She'd never had to be fake with Dale, never once had to lie about who or what she was. Dale knew Ari was *canidae* from the moment they met. She went to the door and looked out at Dale, backlit by the window. Dale looked up when she realized she was under scrutiny.

"Someone shot you in the head once."

"Someone drugged you and tied you to a table. He was going to dissect you."

Ari said, "I got drugged and attacked you."

Dale nodded. "I remember."

"All that, and we're still here." She walked around Dale's desk and bent down to embrace her from behind. "We'll figure out how to do the right thing, and do it safely." She kissed the top of Dale's head, and Dale put her hands on Ari's arms where they crossed her chest. "Irwin said he was the woman's boss. Look at his campaign staff first. We're going to take this bastard down."

"Hell yeah, we are."

"Do you want me here when you watch it?"

Dale shook her head. "I think I would rather be alone for something this heinous. I'll need you later, though."

"I'll need you, too." She kissed Dale's head again and let her go. "I'm going to check out Irwin's campaign headquarters. It's somewhere downtown. Text me if you find anything."

"Will do. Good luck, puppy."

"You too."

CHAPTER NINETEEN

THE MICHAEL Irwin for Governor Campaign office was on the border of Capitol Hill and First Hill. It occupied a space surrounded by empty storefronts and buildings blocked from sight by a honeycomb of scaffolding. It reminded her of the Doozer constructions from Fraggle Rock, so she held onto that bit of childhood nostalgia to get her mind off what she had seen on the flash drive. The entrance to the building was plastered with campaign signs and a poster of the man from the video, and she grimaced as she went inside and found herself surrounded by even more representations of him.

The folding tables and temporary offices only took up a small fraction of the space. To the left and right were tables with T-shirts, buttons, lawn signs, and other swag with Irwin's name waited to be distributed throughout the city. A handful of volunteers occupied a phone bank that separated the front of the room from the private staff offices.

Dale had texted while she was parking. "The woman is named Kathleen Tully. Campaign fundraising dept." She included a picture from the website so Ari would be better able to identify her. She was looking at the picture when a volunteer with a large IRWIN button pinned to her blouse swooped in. The girl looked to be in high school, maybe college, on loan from a cheer or pep squad based on the size of her smile and the depth of her dimples.

"Hi there! Are you considering a vote for Michael Irwin as our next governor?"

Ari said, "Actually I'm here looking for someone. I think she works for the financial department. Kathleen Tully?"

"Kat? She's the head of fundraising." She turned and pointed toward the back of the room. "Straight back there, next-to-last room on the left. Have a button!"

She deftly removed a button from the pocket of her slacks and moved to pin it to Ari's blouse. Ari blocked the girl's hand before she could make contact, saving her the trouble of throwing out the shirt later. The girl looked surprised but didn't press the issue.

"Sorry."

"It's fine! Some people don't want the holes in their clothes. Do you want a bumper sticker?"

"No."

Ari walked past her and stepped around the phone bank. Six phones were in use, which meant six Seattle citizens currently being conned out of their money to help send a rapist to the governor's mansion. An hour ago, she might have been one of them. Ari tried to contain herself before she flipped over the table and scared off everyone wasting their time as volunteers for the monster.

Kathleen Tully's office was marked with "FUNDRAISING," and she was seated behind her desk. She had a cell phone in one hand while she wrote with the other. She looked up when Ari appeared in the doorway and, in a single gesture, managed to convey 'come in, sit down, just one moment' without missing a beat in the conversation she was having. Ari stepped inside and closed the door. Kathleen noted that, eyed Ari, but continued speaking. Ari took a seat across from her.

"Okay, I have to go. There's someone in my office. Okay. We'll talk more tomorrow." She hung up and smiled at Ari. "Hello! How can I help you?"

Ari said, "My name is Ariadne Willow. I'm a private investigator. I want to be as tactful as possible, but I know what happened between you and Michael Irwin."

Kathleen bit her bottom lip and turned her head to the side. "I'm not sure what you mean. We dated for a few months, but when the campaign started, we ended things."

"I'm not talking about that. I'm talking about the assault."

The shift in Kathleen's expression was subtle but noticeable. She sat up a bit straighter and placed her hands flat on the table.

"I think you should go."

"I don't–"

Kathleen stood up and moved around the desk. "I'd like you to leave. We don't have security, but I know one of our volunteers can escort you out."

Ari stood up. "If you think I'm here for blackmail or extortion, you're wrong. I just want to make sure he pays for what he did."

"He didn't do anything, Miss Willow. We used to date. And yes, maybe he got a bit... aggressive, but it was nothing we hadn't done in the past."

"You said no."

"How the hell do you know what I said?"

"There's a video."

Kathleen said, "You bugged my apartment?"

Ari said, "I didn't... wait, your apartment? A private investigator named Clark Wilcox hid a camera in a hotel room. That's the video I have. How many times has he forced himself on you?"

"I think you should go now before I call the police." She opened the door, put a hand on Ari's shoulder, and began guiding her out. "What happened in that hotel room is a private matter. I don't want you dragging my candidate's name through the mud just because it will make you feel better."

"Your apartment and the hotel room. How many other times were there? How long do you think it will be before he does it to someone else who works here, if he hasn't done it already?"

The same girl who had greeted Ari when she came in moved to intercept them. "Miss Tully? Is something wrong? Was I not supposed to let her in?"

"It's fine, Helen, it's..."

She had started to let her gaze slip over the girl, but something made her stop and stare. Ari watched Kathleen's face and saw the expression shift again. Her anger was still present, but her eyes softened as her thoughts turned to things she'd obviously tried to never think about. Helen kept a hopeful look, unsure if she was in trouble or not. Ari stepped closer to Kathleen and lowered her voice.

"If he gets away with it once, then he'll keep doing it. How many times do you think he's already gotten away with it? How many times are you going to let him get away with it?"

Helen now looked confused. "Miss Tully?"

"It's fine, Helen," Kathleen said again. "I just... there's actually something else Miss Willow and I need to discuss." She let go of Ari's elbow and stalked back toward her office. Ari followed.

Kathleen was holding the door and slammed it shut as soon as Ari was inside. "Damn you."

"I understand where you're coming from. Believe me, I do. Until this morning, I was planning to vote for the guy myself. But he can't just get away with something like this."

"Let's say we go to the police. I accuse him of forcing himself on me. It's a huge scandal, I become a punchline on the late night circuit, and in a few years Mike runs again anyway because people have short memories."

"Maybe if it was just your word against his. But this video doesn't leave much to the imagination. Believe me, no one will be making jokes about this."

Kathleen covered her eyes and then swept her hand over her face. "I just wanted it to go away. I don't want to keep reliving it in every deposition and talk show." She lowered her voice. "It just needed to be something that happened."

"And right now it might be happening to Helen. Or one of those other volunteers out there who don't feel like they can say no to someone like him."

"Why are you here and not this... the other guy, the one who planted the cameras?"

"He's dead."

Kathleen's face paled. "What? Was he..."

"No. He wasn't killed, not technically. He tried to blackmail Irwin, and someone threatened him. He was scared enough that he decided it was easier to kill himself."

"Threatened?" She looked toward the door and then rolled her head on her shoulders. "Jesus. It was Zahn."

"Who is that?"

Kathleen said, "Leonard Zahn. He's a fixer. Well, he's the director of fast-response. Usually that means he's the guy who keeps an eye out for potential controversy and squashes it before it can become an issue. But in his case, it's just an empty title. He takes care of problems and Mike keeps his hands clean. I thought it was just..." She sighed angrily. "Hell. I didn't want to think about what his job was. I didn't want to know."

Ari said, "I didn't come here to force you into anything. If you want me to drop it, if you don't want to be involved, I'll let it rest. But it should be your decision."

"Thank you. I appreciate that." She closed her eyes and bit her bottom lip, a wrinkle forming between her eyebrows. "I know it needs to come to light. I can't just ignore it and hope he never does it again. But... God. Everyone here has worked so hard on this campaign. I know it's only been a few months. But everybody put their hearts and souls into this. And now it's all going to be thrown away. I guess it's sort of a blessing that it's happening so early."

"A blessing?"

"We still have eleven months until the actual election. Someone else can declare. The primary is in a few months, and after that it'll be like he was never running." She sat on the edge of her desk.

Ari sighed, relieved. "I was worried. I thought taking down Irwin would mean his opponent would just walk right in."

"Eight months is a lifetime in politics," Kathleen said. "It's only been four months since Mike declared, and I feel like I'm losing my life's work. That's why I didn't say anything. Because this... all of this... and because I didn't want to admit it was... what it was."

"Human nature, I guess. Easier to just ignore it. But he can't be allowed to keep running. He can't be allowed to become governor."

Kathleen nodded.

"We still have to figure out what we're going to do. We can't just turn in the video to the police if this fixer guy... what was it?"

"Zahn. Leonard Zahn."

"Right. We don't know if he was operating on Irwin's orders, or if he was using his own prerogative. Either way, he's dangerous. I don't want you or anyone else coming forward until we know you'll be safe from retribution."

"How are we going to do that?"

Ari said, "We're not going to do anything. You're going to either keep working here like nothing has changed, or you're going to take a few sick days. I'm going to focus on Zahn and Irwin to see what I can find out. It's what I do. When Wilcox called me right before killing himself, I have to assume this is what he was hoping I would do."

"What if they do turn out to be dangerous?"

"Then they're going to find out I can be just as dangerous."

When Ari got back to the office, Dale was on the couch in her office. She had stretched out and covered herself with the blanket Ari used for naps, but she was awake and staring at the window behind Ari's desk. Ari crossed the room and knelt in front of her. She fished under the blanket until she found Dale's hands. Dale closed her eyes and burrowed against the pillow.

"I never want to see anything like that ever again," she whispered.

"Me neither." Ari leaned over Dale and kissed her cheek and temple. "C'mon. Get up. I want to take you somewhere."

Dale shook her head. "I don't want to go anywhere."

"Do you trust me?"

Dale lifted her head to look at Ari, then sat up and accepted her offer to help stand up. They locked up the office and Dale followed Ari to the car. The radio started with the engine, but Dale reached down and shut it off. Ari drove south in silence, hitting the edge of a rain wall and staying inside it until they turned west. After a while Dale seemed to realize they had a destination and weren't just driving randomly, so she sat up straighter and began paying attention.

Eventually Ari arrived at Alki Point beach. The rain had scared away most of the people who would have otherwise been sightseeing, and the strip of sand between land and water had transformed into a dark brown-gray quagmire. Ari twisted into the backseat to get their rain slickers. They squirmed into them, put up their hoods, and got out of the car. Dale came around the hood and held out her hand. Ari took it and guided Dale out onto the abandoned beach.

They sat together on the ground, not caring about their pants. Dale picked up Ari's arm and slung it over her shoulder, sagging heavily against her side.

"This is where you came when you ran away," Dale said. "When you were a teenager."

Ari nodded. "I thought that was the end of the world. I didn't think I'd survive." The rain drummed on the edge of her hood. "I wanted to take you somewhere pretty. I didn't think it would be raining."

"The rain is perfect. It's beautiful. I love this. I needed this." Dale lifted her head and looked at her. "Thank you, Ariadne."

"I needed it, too."

They kissed and then turned back to look at the water. Ari loved the way the Sound looked when it was raining. Dale was right; it was beautiful.

"Take him down, Ari."

"All the way," Ari promised.

After that they didn't speak; they just sat and watched the rain pelt the water for a while in silence, letting it wash away what they'd seen.

CHAPTER TWENTY

DALE FOUND a picture online for Leonard Zahn and printed it out so Ari could put it up on the wall, giving them a target. It was professionally posed, apparently part of a photoshoot he'd done for a magazine. He was completely forgettable, a face that would be rendered nearly invisible in a crowd. Brown hair, average appearance. There was a multitude of photos of him from his website, and Dale chose one where he was wearing a suit facing the camera with his arms crossed, an intimidating pose to match Ari's death stare.

It was even easier to find pictures of Irwin, but Ari asked her to look for one where he wasn't smiling or posing. She spent most of the day after meeting Kathleen sitting in her office and staring at the images. She only turned her attention away to do research on the candidate. She read about Michael Irwin's history of public service, his three years in the state Senate, and his campaign so far. Several articles mentioned that he was the front-runner for office even before he officially declared candidacy. He was well-liked and charming, and from Ari's point of view, he held the right position on every issue.

Dale, meanwhile, was working on Leonard Zahn. He was a professional fixer, with a beautifully polished website that used beautiful graphics to hide the fact he never actually said what his job was. He called himself a Crisis Management expert, specializing in "personal, political, and business" matters. He was single, never been arrested, and his photo gallery showed him shaking hands with the current governor, various political figures, and a slew of liberal celebrities. Dale wondered if any of the people in the pictures knew what kind of man they were dealing with.

Despite the appearance of being for-hire, Dale couldn't find a physical address for him. There was an email address and a phone number, but Zahn apparently didn't keep an office. Ari considered calling to set up an appointment, but she knew that would only alert him to her interest and blow her cover. At the moment he might not know she was investigating him. She wanted to keep the element of surprise for as long as possible.

Once again, Dale came to the rescue. She ran a background check on Zahn, just a quick scan of his credit card statements. They had the bare-bones results the next morning and discovered, amongst a truly startling amount of gas station receipts, there was a recurring charge at a particular bar on Capitol Hill. The charges at the bar were usually made during mid-afternoon. Ari waited until two-thirty, the earliest he'd ever used the card at the bar, and ended her staring contest with the board.

"Be safe," Dale said.

"Always."

The bar was abandoned when she arrived. Booths lined the wall to the left and right, with the bar set up directly ahead of the entrance. The man behind the bar looked up from a textbook and Ari waved a hand to keep him from moving to help her. She told him she would take a Redhook when he was at a stopping place. She took a seat in a two-top facing the door and took out her phone. The bartender brought over her bottle close to five minutes later after the second customer arrived to interrupt his studies. Ari considered asking if he knew Zahn, but the description would be far too vague to be helpful.

People arrived at the bar in groups or alone, some of them meeting others but a few drinking alone as Ari seemed to be. The majority were dressed in suits with loose ties, the jackets instantly draped over the back of a chair before they sat down. The women slipped out of their high heels under the table and settled in to relax. A female political advisor that Ari recognized from interviews on the news touched the hand of her female companion under the table, a brief and furtive moment of intimacy that almost distracted Ari from her task.

Zahn arrived just after four, dressed casually in a V-neck sweater and a leather jacket. He scanned the room from the doorway and went to the bar. Two drinks were delivered to him, and he took them to a man who had been sitting alone on the opposite end of the room. When he took a seat facing his companion, he dropped out of view. Ari finished off the drink she'd been nursing and moved to the bar. The bartender saw her coming and moved to intercept her.

"Another Redhook, when you have a minute."

He nodded and moved away. Ari rested her elbows on the bar and casually looked toward Zahn. He and the other man were deep in conversation. If she'd been in wolf form, she could have narrowed her focus and picked out their voices from the crowd. As it was, she had to rely on body language. The other man seemed agitated, but Zahn remained still and measured for their entire conversation. He cocked his head to the side, scanned the room, and kept his back straight against his chair. His legs were crossed with both fine-boned hands resting on his lap.

The bartender brought Ari another bottle and she thanked him. Zahn reached into his jacket and withdrew a manila envelope which had been folded lengthwise. He placed it on the table and made the other man lean forward to retrieve it. He opened it and peered inside.

Ari moved to the very end of the bar and looked at the posters framed on the wall. She was now close enough to overhear snippets of their conversation.

"~if you want. Can I tell my client you'll cooperate?"

The other man put the envelope down and covered it with his hand, as if he was afraid someone might try to snatch it. He kept his eyes averted as he nodded to the question.

"Excellent." Zahn pushed away from the table and stood up. "I trust my client won't have to worry about seeing you again. And then you won't have to worry about seeing me again." He smiled and turned, walking out of the bar. Ari took some cash from her wallet and settled with the bartender, then moved to take the seat Zahn had just vacated. His companion was startled by her sudden arrival but couldn't manage to articulate his surprise.

"Hi," Ari said. "Just wanted to get off my feet for a second. Hopefully you don't mind sharing your table with me."

"Uh..." He looked around as if expecting a punchline.

Ari took a deep breath of Zahn's scent. Lemon and sage over body wash, shampoo, and an underlying layer of body odor. She focused on his natural scent, the one thing he couldn't change. It only took a few seconds for her to be sure she could pull the same smell out of a crowd.

"Okay. It was nice meeting you."

He stared at her with utter confusion, which she ignored as she stood and walked out. Zahn had turned left out of the bar and was currently walking downhill on Olive. Ariadne gave him a head start before she followed. He turned on Howell, and disappeared after turning north again at the end of the street. He was well out of sight by the time Ari caught up with him, but his scent lingered long enough in the alley for Ari to know exactly where he had gone. She caught up with him at a parking lot, where he was leaning against the trunk of a car. At first she thought he was waiting for her, but he glanced up when she arrived and then went back to whatever he was doing on his phone. Ari continued on past him.

Before being bitten, she wouldn't even have considered what she was about to do. The pain wouldn't.have been worth the potential reward. She ducked into a wooded alley and jumped a gate, crouched behind a dumpster, and quickly stripped out of her clothes. With any luck, she would be back before anyone happened by, but she still made sure everything was well-hidden. She dropped down and transformed, the brief flash of pain followed by a surge of pleasure as she slipped into her four-legged frame. She opened her jaw and snapped it shut, then darted out of the alley to make her way back to the parking lot.

Zahn was still waiting by the car when she arrived. He paid more attention to the wolf than he had when she was a woman, tracking her as she moved along the edge of the lot. She paused to sniff the grass and followed the faint aroma of food, acting as an ordinary dog would. That behavior included keeping a wary eye on the human in the vicinity.

"Hey there, pup," Zahn said.

Ari looked at him, then continued her ruse of exploration.

Zahn lost interest in her when another car pulled up. He put his phone in his pocket and straightened his coat, his hands folded in front of him as the new arrival parked. A man in a suit stepped out and approached, but he stopped while he was still a few feet away from Zahn.

"Is it done?"

Zahn said, "I showed him the pictures. I told him what would happen if he kept bothering you. It's as done as it's going to be."

"What if he doesn't listen?"

Zahn shrugged. "Then we follow through with the ultimatum. Otherwise, what good is it?" He finally looked at the other man. "Threats only work if you mean them. If they're hollow, then they're just words. And in that case you might as well just say 'pretty please.' Threats are just language. They work if the recipient believes you intend to follow through. And I do."

"Nasty business, Mr. Zahn."

"So is what you're covering up."

The other man shifted uncomfortably, then reached into his jacket. He handed over an envelope, which Zahn deftly slipped into his own coat.

"Don't look so sour, Markus. Imagine what it would have cost you in legal fees. You're coming out miles ahead in the long run."

"Sure. I just hope I never see your face again."

Zahn grinned. The other man got into his car and pulled away. Zahn waited until he was gone before he pushed away from the car and walked to the driver's side. He unlocked the door and got inside, leaving the door open as he took out his phone and made a note. Ari creeped closer, head low to the pavement. Zahn glanced over when her movement caught his attention. They locked eyes and he frowned slightly, tilting his head to one side.

"Hey, pup..."

Ari backed away and left the parking lot. She watched him from out of sight, choosing a vantage where he couldn't see her in the mirrors. He kept one foot on the pavement as he used his phone. She thought about the meeting in Wilcox's report. Maybe the reason he didn't list an office was because he worked out of his car. It would also explain why he spent so much money on gas. She memorized the license plate number, hoping it wasn't a memory that would get lost when she shifted back.

"Mr. Lincoln," Zahn said into his phone. "I hope you've had the opportunity to think about what we discussed." He paused. "I'm sure you could get a fair amount more from the tabloids, but at what cost? You would have made an enemy for life. You will constantly be looking over your shoulder waiting for retribution. The stress alone would devastate you. What good is millions if you aren't alive to enjoy it? My client is willing to pay you a reasonable amount of money given what he's paying for is his own property. And, of course, your silence."

Ari wondered if the client was Irwin, if he had Zahn running all around Seattle quieting anyone who tried to report him as a rapist.

"If you agree, the money will be wired to your account within the hour." Another pause and then, exasperated, "Mr. Lincoln, you do realize we didn't have to make a monetary offer at all. There are other methods we could have taken to ensure your silence. My client won't allow your threat to linger indefinitely. When the time comes, this generous offer will be taken off the table and we will be forced to resort to other, less attractive solutions. Am I understood?"

Ari wondered why he'd gone directly to violence with Wilcox. If it was a blackmail attempt, money would have made it go away easy. Maybe Irwin hadn't been willing to pay. Maybe he thought Wilcox was beneath him, or too untrustworthy to enter into that sort of arrangement. Offering him a bribe to keep silent was just more ammunition of wrongdoing that Wilcox could use against him. Bank transfers would leave a paper trail. Someone running for office wouldn't want that. So it had to be a threat of physical violence.

"I'm glad we could come to an arrangement, Mr. Lincoln. I'll confirm when the money has been transferred."

He hung up and checked something on his phone. He made a note and put the phone down on the passenger seat. He looked around the parking lot again, and Ari got the distinct impression he was trying to spot her. She sank lower, her belly against the pavement, and wished the bush she was hiding behind was a bit fuller. Even as it was, he apparently didn't see her. He pulled his foot into the car and shut the door. When the engine started, Ari crawled backward into the alley so he wouldn't see her when he left the parking lot.

She waited five minutes before she left her hiding place and returned to the alley where she'd left her clothes. She transformed, grunting and gasping through the worst of the pain before she got dressed again. It was still thrilling to stand up straight after a transformation, to feel the burn but not suffer from it. She would have said she felt like a teenager again, but she hadn't been this pain-free even when she was a teenager.

She took out her phone and, her fingers still shaking from the change, saved a note with Zahn's license plate number. She didn't know if it was damning evidence in any way, but she knew that personal info was like ammunition for Dale. She wanted to make sure she had as full a clip as possible. She slipped the phone back into her pocket, checked to make sure no one witnessed her transformation, and started back to the office.

CHAPTER TWENTY-ONE

DIANA WAS already dressed for bed in a police department T-shirt and sweats when Ari showed up at the house. Ari tried to dismiss herself and put the meeting off until morning, but Diana insisted on hearing what she had to say. Lucy said goodnight on her way to bed as Diana escorted Ari into the living room. Diana sighed and looked warily at her guest as she settled on the couch.

"I get the feeling I'm not going to like what I hear. Visits from a private investigator at nine-thirty is never a good thing."

Ari took the chair across from Diana. "That's not super-late, though. What kind of person goes to bed before ten o'clock?"

"One with a four am shift."

"Oh. I really should go. This can wait."

Diana snapped her fingers and pointed at the seat. "No! Sit! Stay."

"Wow. How long have you been holding on to that?"

"Pretty much since I accepted the truth of what you told

me. What's going on?"

Ari sighed and rested her elbows on her knees. "I have a hypothetical for you."

"Fun."

"Yeah. Let's say that there's a video of someone in politics. It's a very bad video on which a horrible crime is being committed. The person in the video was approached by the person who filmed it in an attempt to blackmail them. Instead, the person in the video hired someone to threaten the blackmailer. Not only that, he threatened everyone the blackmailer cared about. He promised that the person in the video would be able to seek revenge even after being arrested. The blackmailer was scared enough of this threat that he~"

"He killed himself."

Ari said, "Good detectiving."

"So the blackmailer was Clark Wilcox. Who was on the video?"

Ari shook her head. "I won't say. The problem is, the video is now in the hands of another detective."

"You."

"A beautiful and brilliant detective who shall remain nameless."

Diana said, "You're worried that the same thing will happen to you. If you turn in the video, the criminal it takes down will focus on you and Dale."

Ari said, "Or if I turn it in to the police, he might take it out on the detective who makes the arrest and any loved ones she might have." She glanced toward the back of the house where Lucy had disappeared. "It's poison, Diana. Yes, it will take down a very bad man who deserves to go to prison, but it also puts whoever uses it in danger."

"Give me the video, Ari."

"No."

"Ariadne, this isn't a game. If a crime was committed..."

Ari said, "I have to make sure the damage is restricted to

the person who deserves it. I need you to help me do that."

Diana said, "Okay. Absolutely. Give me the video."

"I can't."

"You mean you won't. It's evidence in a crime. You have a duty to hand it over to the proper authorities. You didn't come here for advice. You came here because you knew it was the right thing to do. Give me the video and let me handle it. Then go home with Dale. Your name will stay out of it. Whoever you're scared of won't even know you were involved."

"I wish that was true, Diana, I really do. And if that's your advice, then I'm sorry I kept you away from bed for nothing." She stood up.

Diana stood as well. "I could take you into custody."

"For what? A hypothetical situation?"

"We both know damn well~"

Ari stopped her and put her hands on Diana's shoulders. "Do you trust me?"

Diana sighed. "I do."

"Then trust me when I say that the man we're talking about is powerful. He's dangerous. I'm protecting everyone by keeping the video right now. When I know how I can use it without hurting anyone I love, then I absolutely will."

"Protect and serve," Diana said. "It's right there in my job description."

"I know. And I'm helping you protect the one citizen of Seattle that counts. Go take care of her."

Diana said, "The second you need help~"

"You'll be the second call I make. After Dale."

"I guess that's fair. Be careful, Ariadne."

Ari nodded and let herself be escorted to the door.

On the porch, Diana said, "Can I at least ask who this big and powerful boogieman is?"

"Probably better if you don't know." She looked out over the neighborhood. "This is a great place you found for yourselves, Di. It's hard to believe you're that same beat cop who used to pick me up for trespassing and public nudity."

Diana grinned. "You could've just told me the truth."

"That I was half-naked because I'd just transformed back from being a wolf? How long would it have taken you to commit me for a psych evaluation?"

Diana laughed and rubbed her cheek with the back of her hand. "You have a point. I'm glad you told me, though. You've come a long way, too. Dale Frye is an excellent influence on you."

"Yeah. I think I'll keep her around."

"That's not how it works. You have to convince her to keep *you* around."

"Oh, is that the secret?"

"That's it." She bumped Ari's arm. "If you and Dale don't have plans for Christmas, we'd love to have you again."

Ari said, "Christmas. Right. That's coming up. Well, I'm Wiccan and Dale is Jewish--"

"Lucy is agnostic," Diana said. "It doesn't have to be about the birth of anyone. It can just be friends getting together and appreciating one another."

Ari chuckled. "I was going to say, we still do something every year. And I'm sure Dale would say we'd be happy to come, so... we'd be happy to come."

"It's good that she keeps you on a short leash."

"Oh, geez. How many more dog jokes will I have to deal with?"

Diana shrugged. "I don't know. Seven for every normal joke?"

Ari laughed. "Go get in bed with your wife, detective."

She left the townhouse, resisting the urge to look back at the domestic bliss as she returned to her car. She drove home and found Dale sitting at the dinner table with Wilcox's iPad. She had the cover folded so it was standing up in front of her, and she was frowning down at the screen.

"What are you doing?"

Dale said, "Just looking at this drug dealer guy. Didn't Murphy say that the drug dealer was the one who told them where to find Wilcox's secretary? So where does he fit in?"

Ari shook her head. "He doesn't. He's just an extra piece, someone who I guess gets a free pass from all of this." She moved behind Dale's seat and put an arm around her shoulder. "Come on. I want to take a shower and you're good at getting my hard-to-reach places."

"Okay." Dale shut off the tablet. "I was just thinking it would all tie neatly together, you know? Irwin's fixer was working with the Creep Cousins and taking one down meant we could take them all down."

Ari led Dale into the bedroom. "No, as far as I know, Zahn only met with Wilcox. He..." She stopped with her shirt half-unbuttoned. "He never went after Tiffany. And he never searched Wilcox's office for the iPad or the video."

Dale watched her. "What are you thinking?"

"I'm thinking something dangerous."

They took their shower and got into bed. Dale dozed off quickly, but Ari stayed awake thinking about the plan she'd come up with. It wasn't just dangerous, it was foolhardy and ran a big chance of failure. It also involved destroying evidence. But if no charges had been brought for the crimes she was destroying evidence of, then what did it matter? Was it really a crime if the destruction resulted in something good for everyone involved?

Dale stirred. "Are you still up? Do you need to run?"

"No. Stay." She guided Dale's head back to her chest and played with her hair until she fell back to sleep. She would work out the finer details of her plan in the morning, and she could decide then if the reward was worth the risk.

The next day was spent making a flurry of phone calls. Ari had decided on the plan, risk be damned, but now she had to get all the players to agree. She was going to paint a target on an innocent woman's back, and she wasn't going to get lazy on the prep work. She had to hope that she was right about Zahn. From what she'd overheard, he wasn't the sort of man to instantly resort to violence. If Wilcox's blackmail attempt had been refused, the threats had to come directly from Irwin. Zahn had to be working under orders. That meant there was a chance he could be reasoned with under the right circumstances. She just had to make sure those circumstances were safe.

Tiffany was the first call she made. Ari was hoping she was still in California, but she'd gotten back two days earlier. She sheepishly admitted that she had been too afraid to leave her apartment for fear of running into the men who had almost attacked her. When Ari explained her plan, Tiffany eagerly agreed to help out.

"I asked you to get justice for Clark. I want to be involved in taking down the bastard. And maybe this will help me get over the anxiety of almost getting kidnapped by those muscle heads. Whatever you need from me, I'll do it."

"I promise you'll be safe the entire time. I'm working on that part right now."

"Let me know when you're ready. I'll be there."

Ari's next call was to the Flex gym, where she asked to speak to any of the Creep Cousins who might be present. After a few minutes of searching, the receptionist came back to the phone with Frank Pearl. She identified herself, quickly insisted that he hear her out, and explained what she had in mind.

"Why would we help you?"

"Because if you agree, I'll delete every video I have of you and your pals buying drugs. There's no case against you because Wilcox was happy to keep it quiet as long as the payments kept coming in. I'm willing to forget they ever existed. Besides, you owe it to Tiffany for trying to abduct her. The Murphy brothers will still be on the hook for that. Nothing I can do there. But I can take some of the pressure off on the steroids."

Pearl thought for a long moment. "I have to talk to the

other fellas," he said finally, "but I think they would agree to that. And then we're done? No more blackmail?"

"I don't work that way," Ari promised. "I'll delete the videos in front of you if that's what you want. But after this is all said and done."

"Let me talk to the guys."

"Get back to me by this afternoon or the offer goes away."

He called back in twenty minutes. The rest of the Creep Cousins were in. Ari told them to clear their calendar for the next forty-eight hours, and she would be in touch with the rest of the details. Dale was watching from the door after patching the call through to Ari's phone. When she hung up, they looked at each other.

"So," Dale said. "We're working with a bunch of meathead assholes and using an innocent girl as bait for a guy who might be a killer."

"I don't like it any more than you do," Ari said. "Trust me, if I thought there was a better way..."

"There's not," Dale said. "Because I know you. I know if there was a better way, you'd find it. Just let me know what you need from me."

Ari said, "I will. Thank you."

Dale went back to her desk. Ari picked up the card that had been propped against her computer all morning, the final piece of her house of cards. She thumped it against her finger and then dialed the number underneath Leonard Zahn's name.

It only rang once before he answered with a terse, "Zahn."

When Ari spoke, she lowered her voice and added an inflection to every word. It wasn't meant to be a true accent, but rather an obvious attempt to disguise her voice. "Mr. Zahn. I have information that may be of interest to a client of yours. A video which has gone missing. A very incriminating video that could sway the results of an election. Do you know of what I speak?"

"I think I do."

She suddenly wished she had positioned herself as the target. It would've been just as easy, and it would have kept Tiffany at arm's length.

"The PI's secretary has it at her home. It's on a flash drive. She's talking about justice, making sure a bad man pays. I think you should hurry if you want to make sure the video never sees the light of day. Get the flash drive tonight or see your client's face on the news tomorrow."

"Who is this?"

Ari hung up. Dale had put a blocker on her phone that would hopefully keep Zahn from tracking it, but she was still uncertain about trusting it. Still, it was done. She made the same round of calls and got everyone in position. When she was finished, she turned off her computer and left her office. Dale was waiting with her coat.

"You ready?"

"As ready as I'll ever be." She kissed Dale, holding her tight and letting the kiss go on longer than necessary before letting her go. "And you know where you're supposed to be tonight."

"Spending the night with Diana and Lucy in their guest room."

"Good girl." She kissed Dale's forehead. "Wish me luck."

Dale said, "What do you need luck for? You're just taunting a known criminal who is willing to use violence to get what he wants and relying on a bunch of drug users who have also threatened you to serve as protection. But I know something they don't know."

"What's that?"

"They're going against Ariadne Willow. If anyone needs luck, it'll be them. And I refuse to waste my luck on those goons."

Ari smiled. "Atta girl."

She put on her jacket, checked to make sure she had everything, and then kissed Dale goodbye. When Ari was at the door, Dale said, "Hey."

"Yeah."
"Good luck. Just in case."
Ari smiled and winked as she left.

CHAPTER TWENTY-TWO

TIFFANY KNIGHT lived a few blocks away from the university in a house she shared with three other students. Two of them were already out of town for Christmas, while the other was convinced to stay at his boyfriend's house for the evening. There were three Creep Cousins helping her out with the plan. Tommy Carrow was watching Wilcox's office in case Zahn went there first. Kevin Forrester and Frank Pearl were inside the house with Tiffany. One was watching the backyard and would alert the others if he spotted anything unusual in the alley. Ari was parked at the end of her block where she could see the front porch. Ari thought they had every angle well-covered. She was proud of the set-up, and confident that no matter what Zahn did, they would be prepared.

She was understandable miffed when, twenty minutes after everyone was in position, Zahn arrived and parked two spaces ahead of her.

It wasn't yet dark, so she was concerned he might notice someone else staking out the same piece of property. She got out of the car and walked around the block out of sight. The homes on this block had concrete retaining walls around the front yards, most of them defaced with graffiti, and she sat down on one to group-text everyone the new development. "LZ outside house now. Stakeout." Once the message was sent, she stood and moved to where she could see Zahn.

The first reply was from Dale: "He might have realized it was a trap."

From Carrow: "Should I relocate?"

Ari responded to Carrow that he should move closer, just in case they needed backup, but she didn't want Zahn to witness any musclebound bodyguards going into the house. She texted Tiffany that she should go out and check the mail if she felt comfortable doing so. "I just want to make sure he knows you're home. If he makes a move to grab you, I'll be there."

Tiffany responded, "My guardian angle." She then sent "Angel*" and Ari smiled. A few minutes later Tiffany came outside and walked to the curb. She opened the mailbox, peered inside, and looked down the street as if searching for the mailman. She looked away from where Zahn was waiting, but he still had to have gotten a good look at her face. He stayed where he was, head slowly turning as he scanned up and down the street. He was using his mirrors to examine the cars behind him. She felt confident Dale's theory was correct; he smelled a trap and was making certain before he made a move.

"Everyone stay put," she texted. "Guys in the house, stay out of sight."

Night came slowly, with subtle shifts in the color of the sky, and then all at once. When the shadows spread across the sidewalk, Ari felt comfortable inching closer to Zahn's car. The flow of traffic on the interstate just outside the neighborhood provided a constant hum of white noise. There were enough trees and overgrown bushes to keep her out of sight if she moved carefully. She could still see him behind the wheel, but now his attention seemed completely focused on Tiffany's house. One of the second story windows had a light on, but the house was otherwise dark. Ari held her phone against her chest to block the light and sent another group text.

"Tiffany: turn off lights and take cover. KF & FP, front and back doors."

The light went off a few seconds later. Zahn remained where he was. Ari knew she would have to be patient, but it was killing her to just sit and wait for him to make a move. How cautious could he be? Finally, after twenty minutes, he opened his door and stepped out of the car. He had disabled the overhead light so it wouldn't automatically snap on. Ari lowered the brightness on her phone as Zahn started across the street. When he was on the front steps leading to the porch, she dialed 911. She gave the address as soon as the operator answered.

"I'm watching a guy break into the house right now. He's on the porch checking the windows. Hurry, I think there's a girl staying alone in there."

She hung up as the operator was asking her for a name. Zahn had moved in front of the door by that point, knowing that the quickest way to avoid suspicion was to look like he belonged. No sneaking around the back, just a brazen approach and a quick-as-you-can picking of the locks. Ari texted "Front door" without looking and hurried across the street. Zahn got the door open. She cut over the lawn as she heard the first blows landing, a grapple in the dark between Zahn and whichever Creep Cousin was watching the front door.

"Son of a bitch!" Zahn grunted. The front door, still standing open, was illuminated by the flash of a gun going off. Someone cried out as Ari leapt to the porch. Zahn rushed out the door so fast he didn't see Ari. They collided hard enough that they both came to a complete stop, but then Zahn's superior weight and speed threw Ari backward. She grabbed his shirt and pulled him down with her, not counting on the fact he would crush the air out of her when they landed hard on the front walk.

The only bright side was that Zahn had dropped his gun in the fall and didn't seem eager to find it. He sat up and punched Ari hard in the face. She'd been in fights before, she'd even been hit before, but she was still unprepared for how much it hurt. Her head was knocked to the side and, when it swung back forward, Zahn punched her again with equal force. Her mind was rattled as her brain flooded with pain alarms. Her back ached, her jaw was sore, and even as she was cataloguing all the ways she was hurt, he punched her again.

She could feel herself starting to black out. Another punch would likely shut her down. So instead of accepting her defeat, she surrendered her consciousness and brought the wolf to the forefront of her mind. Suddenly she was a wild animal, a fighter that had been pinned by someone trying to show dominance. The wolf would not abide that.

Ari's eyes flashed up and she brought up both arms. She crossed them at the wrist and shoved them up into Zahn's throat hard enough to make him choke. If she'd been in wolf form, it would have been a bite and he wouldn't have gotten up from it. As it was, he gagged and stopped himself mid-punch to grab his throat. His weight shifted and Ari let out a roar as she flipped him off of her. She rolled on top of him, put her forearm on his neck, and bore down with as much weight as she could.

"What the hell are you doing?" One of the Creep Cousins grabbed Ari under the arms and physically lifted her off Zahn. She snarled and kicked her legs as she was roughly dumped onto the grass, still itching for a fight. The Cousin crouched down next to Zahn and hit him square in the jaw. Zahn's body went limp. He stood up and went to Ari. "You said we needed him alive."

She wasn't sure if her ears were ringing or if the police had just pulled onto the block. She turned and saw the strobing lights of a squad car approaching.

"I got a little out of control."

He cupped her face and forced her to look at him. "No concussion, I think. You might need a doctor. Your eyes look... weird."

She swatted his hands away. She'd partially transformed, let the wolf in without actually changing shape, so there might have been some residual gold in her irises. She would play it off as a trick of the light if anyone asked.

"I'm fine. What happened in there? Who got shot?"

"Frank got grazed. He was the one by the front door."

Ari said, "That makes you..."

"Kevin."

"Right. Kevin. I know. I just... it's not a concussion, it's just hard to keep track of all your names." The police had gotten out of their car, and Ari held her hands out. "I'm Ariadne Willow. I'm a private investigator. I'm the one who called you." The nearest officer asked for some identification. She handed it over. "The man on the ground is Leonard Zahn. My friends Kevin Forrester and Frank Pearl were inside, and they chased him back out. That's where he literally ran into me and assaulted me."

The other officer aimed his flashlight at the fallen man. "That *is* Zahn. This is going to be a fun night of paperwork."

Ari said, "Could you do me a favor and let him stew until morning? There's one more person I want to bring in, and I should probably wait until a reasonable hour to call."

"He'll be pissed."

"We're going to want him pissed. Trust me."

She let the cops deal with their unconscious prisoner and went into the house. Frank was sitting in the front hallway with his back to the wall, legs splayed out in a V in front of him. His left sleeve was cut open and Tiffany was using a first-aid kit on what looked to be a very minor scrape.

"Everyone okay in here?"

"I got shot!" Frank howled.

Tiffany said, "Frank. Stop it."

"Well, I did."

She glared at him. "You got shot protecting me. And I'm very grateful, but that doesn't mean I want to hear you whining about it. It looks so much more macho if you just suck it up."

He grimaced and rested his head against the wall.

"You were extremely brave," Tiffany said as she bandaged the wound. "I don't know what I would've done if you weren't here to protect me. You were my hero tonight, Frank Pearl."

Frank mumbled something and looked everywhere but at her. Ari was stunned to realize they were flirting and, unsure of what to make of that, decided to ignore it completely.

"So, uh. The police are here. They're probably going to want your statements. You both know what to say." They both nodded. "I need some ice. Can I get some ice?"

"Of course. The kitchen is through there."

Ari thanked her and went to retrieve it. She filled a dishtowel with cubes and pressed it gently against her jaw. Hopefully she could control the swelling. She leaned against the counter and took out her phone to text Dale. She thought about lying, but Dale would see the bruise and-or black eye soon enough, so there really was no point.

"It's done. A little roughed up, but nothing I couldn't handle."

Dale responded, "TLC, coming right up."

Ari smiled and hissed at the pain in her cheek. She decided she might need more than ice and went to ask Tiffany if she had any aspirin.

By morning, Ari was sporting a beautiful black eye, a bruise that made her look as if she was wearing half a raccoon mask. Dale had applied makeup to help minimize its appearance, but they eventually decided she was just going to have to wear it as a badge of honor for the fight she'd won. For her part, Dale had taken news of the attack well. She gave Ari an in-depth massage to help soothe the pain in her back from falling onto the concrete. And if she happened to hold her a little tighter when they finally went to bed, Ari wasn't about to complain. She had to wake up early, when the sun was still below the horizon, and she slipped out from under Dale's arm without waking her.

Once she was dressed, she bent over the bed and whispered Dale's name against the shell of her ear. Dale whimpered and rolled over, reaching up blindly to touch Ari's cheek.

"Puppy?"

"I'm heading out. I didn't want you to worry if you woke up without me."

"Okay. Run?"

Ari said, "No, I have to meet..."

"Oh. Right. Okay." She sat up and kissed Ari's lips. "Good luck, puppy."

"Thanks. Go back to sleep."

She tucked Dale in and left the house. She shouldn't have been surprised when she discovered Cecily Parrish lived on Mercer Island, but it seemed ridiculously affluent even for a lawyer of Parrish's apparent heights. Ari crossed the bridge from normal rich to celebrity rich, passing the homes of Seahawks and computer geniuses in search of the address she gotten from the internet. She found the house at the end of a long dead-end drive that plummeted down toward the shore. It was mostly invisible from the road, as it was meant to be seen from the water, but she eventually found the right number and parked behind a BMW.

She saw three other luxury cars parked in front of the house in a lot the size of a tennis court. Either Parrish was a collector, or she had guests. Either way, Ari couldn't waste time. She rang the doorbell and looked out over the water that made up Parrish's side lawn. The sun had started to rise, and Lake Washington was tinted a beautifully rich yellow. Or maybe the water was always colored gold when viewed from Mercer Island. It was hard to say.

The door opened and, instead of Cecily Parrish, Ari found herself facing a blonde with tousled hair, wearing a sloppily-buttoned dress shirt with apparently nothing underneath. She leaned against the doorframe and smiled.

"Hi."

"Uh. Hello. Is this Cecily Parrish's residence?"

"Mm-hmm." She stepped back and opened the door wider. "C'mon in, beauty."

Ari entered with some trepidation. The entrance led to a kitchen, where the remnants of a catered party remained in a cluster of empty packaging and rows of empty or half-empty bottles. The living room spread out to her right, a massive space with a wall of windows that looked out over the lake. One naked couple, gender undetermined, was lying together on the couch, and a woman who had been covered by a sparkling silver dress was curled up on the floor in front of the fireplace. The blonde who answered the door moved with the heavy-footed clumsiness of someone who was half-awake and still a little drunk from the night before.

"What's your name?" the girl asked.

"Ariadne."

"Wow." She blinked slowly. "That's an awesome name. I'm Rebecca." She pressed her lips together and swayed a little. "Wanna party?"

Ari said, "I think I'll just see Cecily."

"Okay," Rebecca said, sounding a bit sad. "I'll go get her."

Rebecca turned and weaved to the stairs. Ari remained where she was, nearer the kitchen than the slumbering threesome in the other room. The house smelled of sex, much more sex than the five people she knew were in the house could've achieved on their own. It must have been one hell of a party. One of the sleeping people on the couch woke up and looked at her.

"Oh. Hey. Ariadne, right?"

It took her a moment to recognize the man she'd briefly

met in the GG&M break room. "Oh. Yeah. Denver. How's... it going?"

"Pretty good."

"I can see that."

He grinned. "Are you here to~"

"No. No, no, no. Just dropping by."

"Cool."

"I thought you said you were asexual."

His grin was lopsided. "Yeah. I'm not sure what happened."

"Okay then."

"Yeah. Well. Nice to see you again." He put his head down and continued snuggling with the other person, whose gender was still unknown.

Rebecca returned in less than five minutes, followed by Cecily Parrish. She was wearing a short salmon-colored robe that left nothing to the imagination. The puffiness of her eyes indicated she had just woken up, but she moved with the same poise and self-assuredness that she'd had in her office. Ari noticed that, barefoot, Parrish was a few inches shorter than she was. Rebecca let her gaze linger on Ari before she went back into the living room and curled up next to the woman on the floor.

"Miss Willow. I don't remember issuing you an invitation to my home."

"You didn't. And I didn't, ah..." She gestured vaguely toward the living room. "I didn't know I would be interrupting... um..."

Parrish smiled at the people in the living room. "It was a bit of an unintentional bacchanal. I won a case. I was feeling celebratory." She reached up and touched her own eye to indicate Ari's shiner. "You seem to have had an interesting couple of days."

"You could say that."

"Are you here to accept my offer of employment?"

"No. I'm willing to work with you on a case-by-case basis. But I keep Bitches, I keep working my own cases, and I keep Dale. The only difference is that every now and then I'll take a job from you."

Parrish said, "That is nowhere near what I offered. Why would I agree to that?"

"Because I'm about to hand you the case of the year."

"It's December."

"I meant next year."

Parrish crossed her arms and lifted her chin slightly. "I'm listening."

"Michael Irwin is a rapist. I have videotaped evidence proving it, I have the victim, and, with your help, I'll have someone who works for him ready to corroborate everything."

"The state senator," Parrish clarified.

Ari nodded. "The very same."

"It's cut-and-dry rape?"

"The tape makes it abundantly clear. The woman in question works for his campaign. I've already spoken with her, and she's willing to take this as far as it has to go. Irwin threatened a private investigator named Clark Wilcox and scared him enough that he committed suicide. I don't know how far he would go to keep this quiet. That's why I didn't just mail the flash drive to the first news station I could think of. I have the guy who does his dirty work dead to rights on breaking and entering and assault. I want you to make a deal in exchange for Irwin."

"You must have great confidence in my abilities."

"You made me look like a fool. So…"

Parrish smiled. She drummed her fingers on her biceps and then turned toward the living room. "My apologies, lovely people. Mommy has to work, so I'll have to ask you all to get dressed and go back to your own homes."

The four people moaned and groaned in what Ari assumed was an echo of the night before.

"Yes, yes, I know, but my infamous Christmas party looms. Thank you for everything. You were all wonderful." She turned her attention back to Ari. "Today will be a dry run. We'll see how we like working together. If it works out, I'll entertain your counteroffer. Deal?"

Ari nodded. "Sounds good to me."

"Excellent. Let me get rid of my guests and we can begin."

"I thought..." She gestured at the people currently getting dressed in the living room.

Parrish winked at her. "My favorite guests are upstairs." She started for the stairs and then stopped, turning with her hand on the bannister. "Oh, and if you do enter into my firm's employ, you and Miss Frye are both invited to the Christmas party."

Ari coughed nervously, looked into the living room, and went to wait in the kitchen. She hoped there weren't any naked people in it.

Chapter Twenty-Three

ARI DIDN'T expect the reproachful look from Diana when she arrived at the police station, and she expected even less how ashamed she would feel. It was like she had disappointed her mother when Diana stepped forward and silently examined the bruise around her eye.

"It looks worse than it felt."

"According to your statement, he threw you down and hit you three times in the face."

Ari said, "Well."

"Are you okay?"

If she had sounded pissed off, Ari would have responded with an off-hand joke or some casual comment about being a badass. But the concern threw her a little.

"I'm fine," she said. "Dale took care of me."

"She's a saint, that woman. Lucy absolutely adores her. If things ever go south between the two of you, Lucy and I are taking her side."

Ari laughed. "That's probably going to be the right side to

be on."

Diana motioned for Ari to follow her. "We've got Zahn waiting in interrogation. He's been asking for a lawyer since we brought him in last night."

"He can have one. I brought my own."

"I heard. Cecily Parrish? She's a shark." She looked down at Zahn's file. "Insanely hot, though."

Ari said, "That's what everyone seems to think..."

"We're going to need a shark against the monster Zahn has. He's been brought in multiple times, but nothing has ever stuck to him."

"Now we have him on breaking and entering, we have him on assault..."

"And from what Dale explained, you're planning to let him walk on all of that."

"Bigger fish, Detective Macallan."

Diana sighed and shrugged. "If you say so."

She led Ari into the interrogation room where Zahn was waiting with his head down. He sat up when the door opened, glancing at Diana before he locked onto Ari.

"Are you the girl I beat up last night?"

Diana took a seat. "Well, there's the confession business out of the way. Thank you, Leonard."

Ari said, "How's your throat? Your voice is sounding a little rougher than the last time I heard it. You okay? You need a lozenge or some water?"

He smirked.

Diana's phone buzzed, and she looked at the screen. She typed out a response as she spoke. "You're a frequent guest of this establishment, Mr. Zahn."

"Yeah. You pick me up and bring me here, then let me go home. You're like an Uber that shows up at random intervals and never takes me where I want to go."

"This time I think you'll be missing the second part of your round trip. Breaking and entering. Assault. You still haven't produced a permit for that weapon we found on you."

"And you still haven't produced my lawyer."

Diana said, "His offices weren't open when you decided to break the law. We had to wait for business hours. But we do have a lawyer present."

The door opened and Cecily Parrish stepped in. The robe was gone, Ari was sad to see, and was replaced by a dark red suit over a white surplice blouse.

Ari said, "Wow, nice timing on that."

"I got a text saying she was here. I told them to send her on back."

Cecily stood at the head of the table between Diana and Zahn. "I'll be frank, Mr. Zahn, you're barely worth my time. The charges they're holding you on are penny-ante. If they held you for a few hours, the further offenses I'm certain they'd certainly find would also be of little interest to me. I don't want you. But I am more than willing to fight and get the maximum sentence on each and every charge they pin on you unless you cooperate."

Zahn wet his lips and repositioned his hands on the table in front of him.

Diana said, "We want Michael Irwin. We want you to testify against him about hiring you, about the video, about the threats he made toward the people who had the video. The way we see it, Irwin just told you to make the threats. Actually following through on them would've been your job. Your contacts. So if you're the one making the story public... well, I doubt you would sic those dogs on yourself. So in exchange for the video, we can make sure your record stays as squeaky clean as it was before all this unpleasantness."

Zahn said, "The only problem with that is, I don't actually have the damn video."

Ari took a flash drive out of her pocket and placed it on the table. Zahn stared at it.

"So," Cecily said, "you can either go to prison and I can start gathering evidence of every law you've bent or broken in the service of your clients, or you can give me something juicier. You can give me Michael Irwin and I'll forget I ever heard your name. You can go back to sweeping messes of the rich and famous under their Persian rugs."

The door opened and a man in the most expensive suit Ari had ever seen entered. He looked annoyed and rushed, resting his weight on the ball of his foot as if he was just ducking in before sweeping back out of the room in a single motion.

"Leonard, stand up and come with me, please. Detective, I hope you miss the uniform, because I'll have you back in it so fast~"

"Hello, Joseph."

The man lost all momentum when Parrish spoke those two words. He looked away from his client and focused on her, straightening his posture and staring at her. She smiled coolly at him, one hip cocked. Her arms were still crossed. Ari found herself unbelievably aroused and, judging from the way Diana shifted in her seat, she was feeling something as well. Ari was perturbed; she had to find out what this woman's deal was.

"Miss Parrish."

"Sit down. Your client was just about to accept a deal."

Joseph moved around the table and pulled out the chair across from Ari. He sat down, all of his bluster fading. Parrish looked at Zahn.

"I'm waiting for your answer, Mr. Zahn. I'm not a patient woman. This is a very generous offer, and it will go away faster than you would believe. Shall I begin a countdown?"

Zahn looked at his lawyer and exhaled sharply. "No need for that. I know when I'm beaten. More importantly, I know what I was protecting Irwin from. Fuck him." He reached out and put his hand on top of the flash drive. He pushed it from the position in front of Ari to a spot in front of Diana. "I officially hand this over to the Seattle Police Department as part of my deal."

Ari said, "Oh. That's not the actual flash drive. I wouldn't be stupid enough to bring the real drive in here and just leave it on the table."

Parrish said, "The symbolic part of the deal is made. For now, if Miss Willow would kindly give me her seat, we can hammer out the actual details. Ariadne?"

Ari stood up and let Parrish take the chair. "If you guys don't need me for anything else, I'll just step out."

Zahn said, "It was nice running into you, gorgeous."

Ari turned and winked at him. "Just remember who had to be pulled off whom. I'll see you around town, sweetheart."

Ari waited at Diana's desk until she and Parrish reappeared. Zahn and his lawyer made a hasty retreat, neither of them looking very happy with whatever had transpired. Parrish, however, looked like a lion who was walking away from a pile of bloody bones. Ari stood up as they approached, and Parrish smiled at her in a way that was only a little disconcerting.

"The deal is complete. Zahn will testify to every conversation he had with Irwin. Combined with the video you handed over this morning, Michael Irwin's campaign is about to crater in a big way."

Diana said, "I wish I could say that was good news, but damn it, I liked the guy. He's a monster. I know he's a monster, and I can't wait to see him rot in jail for what he's done. But that doesn't change the fact that until this morning, I wanted him to win."

Parrish shrugged. "It's still very early in the campaign. The same people who put Irwin on top will just find another candidate to take his place. The only thing you've really done is give the pundits two big stories to talk about: the fall of one politician and the rise of another. It should keep them busy until January, at least." She looked at Ari. "Walk me out, Miss Willow. We have much to discuss."

Diana waved her off. "Go on. We can catch up later. Be

warned, I plan to scold the hell out of you for some of the stunts you pulled during this case."

"I'd expect nothing less, Detective Macallan. I'll see you for Christmas."

She followed Parrish out of the station. There was an open area in front of the building, larger than a sidewalk and smaller than a plaza, and Parrish waited until they reached it before she spoke.

"*Canidae.*"

Ari tried to keep her reaction neutral. "Can a dee what?"

Parrish said, "I've been doing some research since our last encounter. There are only a handful of creatures in this world who are affected by me the way you were. It took me some time to separate fact from fiction and determine which of them actually existed. Once I had that list, it seemed painfully obvious. The dog collar, Bitches Investigations. You are a *canidae*, crudely called a werewolf."

"And what would that make you?"

"Succubus."

Ari raised an eyebrow. "Really."

Parrish smiled. "You may have noticed an unexpectedly elevated sense of arousal around me."

"I noticed your parties seem a lot more fun than most lawyer parties I've heard about."

"Hm. Yes, it was a wonderful night." Her mind wandered, but she snapped her attention back to Ari. "You were in my office. You saw the red picture in the frame. That was what affected you."

"What was that?"

"It was a focus. I had a very acrimonious meeting that afternoon. I wanted my appeal to be as strong as possible. An ordinary person wouldn't have been affected any more than they would by a paint swatch. But *canidae*... there's a bit of a bleed-through with your kind. Don't be concerned about consent or anything like that. I assure you that my abilities only heighten latent feelings."

Ari said, "So you're like a few shots of whisky. Just enough to get past the hang-ups, not enough to regret it in the morning."

"A few shots of whisky...? You must be a fun date."

"No complaints yet."

Parrish tugged her suit jacket into place and smoothed out the wrinkles. "Arresting Michael Irwin will be a very big deal for the firm. The publicity alone will be astronomical. That's enough to earn you a probationary period. You'll keep your agency. You'll keep Miss Frye. Occasionally we will come to you with a case that you can accept or refuse. But if you accept a case from us, it will be your top priority. You will work on it and nothing else. For this, you will be handsomely compensated. Say, twice your standard rate."

Ari said, "That sounds reasonable." She held out her hand. "I look forward to doing business with you, Miss Parrish."

Parrish took Ari's hand. Instead of shaking, she brought it to her lips and kissed the knuckles. She looked up at Ari through her lashes as she did it. Ari had to admit she felt another surge of arousal, and Parrish smiled knowingly as she released Ari's hand.

"Go use that on your girlfriend, Miss Willow. We'll be seeing each other again soon."

When Ari got back to the office, she told Dale about their new arrangement with GG&M, then revealed the secret to Cecily Parrish's appeal. Dale took the information in stride, simply considering it for a moment before she nodded her head and went back to typing.

"That's it? That's your whole reaction?"

Dale said, "This summer, a woman transformed into a mermaid right in front of me. I'm not going to be surprised by anything we run into."

Ari chuckled lightly, the most she could do without hurting

her face, and got the ice pack Dale had made out of the freezer. She stretched out on the couch and placed the ice on her black eye. She turned the TV on a game show and muted it. She watched as group of people from carefully-chosen demographics played games of luck to win fantastic prizes. A woman in a garish outfit started jumping up and down as the host revealed a car, but before she could see if the woman won it, the image was replaced by a flashy Breaking News graphic. Ari fumbled for the remote and jabbed the volume button.

"Dale, I think it happened."

Dale came in with a warm compress. She took the ice off Ari's eye and replaced it, then sat on the arm of the couch to watch as Sofia Kennedy appeared on-screen.

"We apologize for interrupting regular programming, but we have some breaking news happening right now. Our crews have just arrived at State Senator Michael Irwin's office where it has been revealed the senator and gubernatorial candidate is being taken into custody by the Seattle Police. Details are sketchy at this time, but we have been told that he is being arrested on multiple charges, including conspiracy and sexual assault."

The image cut to Irwin's office, where he was being led into a corridor by uniformed officers clamped on to either arm. The hall was flooded with photographers and reporters shouting questions, all of which were ignored by the politician and his escorts. He wasn't as handsome or charming when he was scowling, Ari discovered.

"We're still getting information now, but we're being told that Cecily Parrish from the law firm Gilles Girard & Moreau is bringing the charges against the senator. She will be holding a press conference in just a few minutes to hopefully clarify some of the facts in this case for us. Senator Irwin, you'll remember is currently running for~"

Ari muted the television. "Looks like that's that."

Dale gripped Ari's hand, squeezing it hard. "You got him,

puppy. I'm proud of you."

"I just hope and pray whoever they get to replace him is half as good as this jackass looked on paper."

"They'll be better. Maybe it will be a woman."

Ari said, "Oh, that would be good. Be nice to have a woman in charge."

"I've always been a fan of it."

Ari chuckled and rolled onto her side. "What do you say I take you out for a great big dinner to celebrate everything? Irwin's arrest, our new arrangement with Parrish, all the hard work you did to keep this place up and running while I was away... and in honor of Clark Wilcox."

"Ew."

"Hey, come on. He was an asshole, and he was a criminal, but there was a glimmer of goodness in him. He had a line he wouldn't cross and he gave his life for this case. We should show him a little respect."

"I suppose you're right." She nodded at the TV. "None of this would've happened without him. I just wish he'd actually asked you for help instead of taking such a drastic step. It would have saved so much time. And his life." She put her head down on Ari's shoulder. "Okay. We can celebrate in his honor along with everything else. It's a little early for dinner, though."

"I'll need five or six hours just to cover this black eye."

Dale gently kissed Ari's cheek. "I like it. It's a badge of honor. But I'll help you with the makeup if you insist on it."

"Oh, will you?"

"Mm-hmm. C'mon."

Ari let Dale help her up and followed her into the bathroom.

Epilogue

On Christmas Eve, Dale and Ari brought a turkey and a pecan pie to the Macallan home. They started the evening by watching non-traditional Christmas fare (Dale chose a Claymation episode of *Community* while Lucy's suggestion of *A Nightmare Before Christmas* spawned debate about whether or not it was actually a Halloween movie) before opening presents. Lucy, by virtue of wearing the elf hat, declared it her job to hand out the gifts.

She grabbed the final package was Dale was in the kitchen getting a refill of eggnog. She turned it over in her hands looking for a tag before she finally gave up. She showed it to Ari. "Who was this one for?"

"I don't know. Are you sure it's one from us?"

Lucy said, "Not our paper." Dale had returned so Lucy held it up. "Who was this one for?"

Dale said, "Oh, that one. Um..." She stepped around the couch and knelt in front of Ari. "Ari, I know you spent years without really celebrating Christmas because you didn't have anyone to spend it with after you ran away. But there was someone else who lost the holiday when you left. And she's still spending it by herself. So I got that gift because I think we should take it to your mother's house after we're done here. I let you talk me out of Thanksgiving, and I understand why now, but this is Christmas. And it's your mother. I'm not ready to completely forgive what she said, and I know you're not, either. But you know her true feelings about me. You know how she feels in her heart. If we skip this, you'll risk falling back to the way things were. You don't want that."

Lucy quietly cleared her throat. "My parents weren't the most open-minded of people. When I brought home a girl for the first time, they insisted on hearing 'girlfriend' as two words. She never accepted who I was or the women I loved. She never got a chance to meet Diana." She reached out and touched Diana's ear, pinching the lobe in an affectionate way. "I would do everything over if I had a chance. And since time travel is impossible, all I can do is make sure you don't make the same mistake."

Ari said, "Thank you, Lucy. And you..." She cupped Dale's cheeks and leaned forward to kiss her. "Thank you. We'll head over there as soon as we're done here."

Diana said, "Why wait? I don't want to intrude, but if you need the moral support, Lucy and I would love to meet your mother."

"You wouldn't be intruding. It would actually be really helpful to have you there."

"Then what are we waiting for?"

Diana got up and began gathering the remnants of their desserts, while Lucy retrieved a bag for them to carry the presents in. Ari put on her jacket at the door and waited for Dale to get her scarf on before she pulled her close.

"Thank you."

"I feel the same way Lucy does. I lost my mom. I don't want to see you throw away your chance to have a real relationship with her."

Diana had found a Santa coat and hat, smiling as she brought the presents into the hall. "Are we all ready to go?"

They piled into Ari's car and she drove along the lakeshore so they could see all the boats bedecked in their holiday finest. When Ari pulled onto her mother's block, she first realized that maybe her mother wasn't alone. Maybe she'd made plans with friends or had a date. But she remembered their time at the cabin, their conversations about how Gwen had isolated herself during the war with the hunters and still didn't quite understand how to be social.

The lights were on when they pulled up in front of the house. Gwen had kept the decorations limited to a single strand of white lights strung along the eaves and a plastic top-hatted snowman on the porch steps. Ari took a breath in front of the door, looked at Dale, and rapped her knuckles against the wood. She took a step back so they could all be seen through the peephole. A moment later, Gwen answered. She was dressed in a red sweater and black leggings, and she eyed the group on her porch with a confused but sincere smile.

"Hello, Ari. Dale."

"Hi, Mom. This is Diana and Lucy Macallan. They're friends of ours. We thought... well, Dale thought... Dale thought and I agreed..."

Dale clutched Ari's upper arm to shut her up. "We thought it wouldn't be Christmas if you were celebrating alone, so we thought we would come over. We brought pie and cookies and presents... It's okay if you didn't get anything for us..."

Gwen said, "No, I did. I bought presents for you and Ariadne both."

Ari said, "You did?"

Gwen looked at her daughter and smiled. "Every year, Ariadne."

Dale said, "So is that a yes? Can we come in, Mom?"

Gwen turned to Dale, her smile fading as she was

overcome. It returned almost immediately a few degrees brighter.

"Of course, Dale. Please, come in. There should be enough to drink, but we may need to start some coffee."

"I can take care of that." Ari hugged her mother and whispered, "Diana knows. Lucy doesn't."

"Noted." She turned and hugged Dale extra tight. "You look gorgeous, Dale."

"You too."

She introduced herself to Lucy and Diana. "I didn't know you were coming, but I'm sure Ariadne would be willing to sacrifice a few of her accumulated presents from the last decade or so."

"No, she's not," Ari called back over her shoulder.

Gwen said, "Christmas spirit, Ariadne."

"Fine. But if there's a train set, I've been asking for that since I was *five*. So dibs." She joined Dale in the kitchen. "I'll make some tea for you."

"Thank you, puppy."

She hugged Dale from behind and buried her face in her hair. Dale pressed back against her. They held the position as they listened to Gwen and the Macallans getting acquainted in the other room.

"This was a pretty great present, Dale."

"You're welcome."

Ari held her a moment longer and then got to work on their drinks. It had been a hell of a year, starting with wolf manoth and ending with Wilcox's suicide, but she and Dale had made it through together. The coming year was destined to be interesting. She still wasn't quite sure what to expect from her work with GG&M, and Irwin's trial was going to be a madhouse, but she was sure that she could weather any storm with Dale by her side.

She finished the tea and kissed Dale before dragging her out into the living room so they wouldn't miss the gifts being opened.

ABOUT THE AUTHOR

Geonn Cannon is the author of over sixty novels, including the Riley Parra series which was adapted into an Emmy-nominated webseries by Tello Films. His novel *Can You Hear Me* was adapted into *Static Space*, an award-winning short film. He's also written two tie-in novels for the television series *Stargate SG-1*. He was the first male author to win a Golden Crown Literary Society Award for his novel *Gemini*, and he won a second for *Dogs of War*.